"Cian MacFarlane is one of the most complex and fascinating characters I've ever read in a book. This book has it all—turn the page suspense, a story of the bond between brothers, betrayals, secrets, and romance. BREATH of DECEIT is Selena Laurence at her finest." - *Sandra Owens, author of the best-selling K2 Team and Aces & Eights series.*

"Laurence's tightly woven story is a superb mix of sexual and political tension that's certain to please fans of both." — *Publisher's Weekly review of The Kingmaker*

"Selena Laurence has the ability to bring to life complex characters you instantly start rooting for from page one." — *Ilsa Madden-Mills, Wall Street Journal Bestselling Author on Buried*

Also by Selena Laurence

The Powerplay Series
Prince of the Press
The Kingmaker
POTUS
SCOTUS
The Darkhorse

The Hidden Series (Coming 2018)
Camouflaged
Concealed
Disguised
Buried

BREATH OF DECEIT

Dublin Devils 1

SELENA LAURENCE

everafter ROMANCE

Copyright © 2018 by Selena Laurence

All rights reserved.

ISBN 978-1635764789

"And in the end you're completely alone with it all."
Tony Soprano

Chapter One

Cian turned the corner and glanced behind him, making sure no one was on his tail as he started down the darkened alleyway. One small light shone over the dirty metal door at the back of Banshee, the nightclub he and his brother Connor owned. He passed under the illumination quickly, his shoulders tense beneath the supple leather of his expensive jacket. Five steps farther, he was enveloped in darkness again when a small flame flashed three feet in front of him.

"Fuck," he hissed as he ground to a halt, the odor of garbage shifting in the air around him. "A little warning next time if you don't mind."

The lighter flickered to life again as a sharp-featured face interrupted by shadows peered back at him.

"Lucky I'm not one of the Vasquez boys," the owner of the face said with a sneer in his voice. "You might be facedown in all this muck by now."

"If you were one of the Vasquez boys," Cian snapped back, "*you'd* be the one facedown in the muck right now. With a bullet in your head."

The man's eyes went cold, disdain slithering over his features. Cian was used to it, the fear mixed with disgust that people turned on him if they knew who he was. Unlike his brother Liam, Cian could move around in the outside world without being pegged for what he was, but it didn't really matter because sooner or later everyone found out his name, and then he might as well have been sporting a shaved head with tattoos on his scalp and an orange jumpsuit. No one normal and decent wanted to know Cian MacFarlane.

"Just get to it, MacFarlane." The man leaned back against the brick wall and flicked the lighter again as he lit a cigarette and blew the smoke out in a whoosh, mere inches from Cian's face.

"Where's Don?" Cian asked, refusing to be rushed even though he was risking his own life standing around in the filthy alley with this guy.

"He has other things to work on. You have something for me or not?"

Cian reached out, snatching the cigarette from the man's fingertips and flicking it onto the ground. "That shit'll kill you," he said as the man shoved off the wall and snarled at him.

Holding up both hands in a "no harm done" gesture, Cian grinned at his nemesis. "Just trying to help you live a long life."

The man's eyes narrowed. "Thanks for your concern. Now, I have places to be. You got something for me or not?"

Cian's grin fell away as he turned the last twelve hours over in his mind. Did he have something for

Bruce Adams, federal agent? Yeah, he damn well did. But he never enjoyed giving it up.

A hot wind shot through the alley, and both men immediately fell silent, turning to look through the gloom toward the entrance to the narrow walkway. Once they were satisfied they were still alone, Cian began to speak.

"Vasquez is pushing back against the Juarez cartel. He wants to cut a new deal with a bigger percentage for him."

Bruce spat on the asphalt next to Cian's feet, and Cian had to count to ten to keep from smashing the man's head into the brick wall behind him.

"And what's the cartel's response to that?" Bruce asked, his expression making it clear he already knew the answer.

"They're less than interested in the proposal, seeing as it gains them nothing."

"And is a war imminent?"

Cian's gaze checked to the end of the alley as a group of drunk twenty-somethings stumped past.

"I don't think so, but Vasquez is on a bender, pushing boundaries in all directions. It's bound to cause fractures within his own house. He's getting greedy and sloppy in the process."

"I want a play-by-play of what he communicates to the cartel," Bruce demanded.

"You'll get what I give you." Cian's voice was cold as an arctic night.

"Do you want to keep your brothers out of lock-up or not?" Bruce asked, that lip curling once again.

Cian moved fast, his arm pinning the fed against the wall by the throat. He nudged his knee between

Bruce's legs, the threat to cock and balls clear as the guy gasped for air from his rapidly bruising trachea.

"Do you want to keep your life?" Cian growled. "You'll get what I give you. And not one iota more. You make it work or don't, that's not my problem, but either way, my brothers aren't part of the discussion. Are we clear?"

Bruce squirmed, but Cian could tell it was an attempt at a nod of affirmation. Cian slowly released him, waiting for the agent to draw down, but his hands went straight to the collar of his button-up shirt, loosening his tie as he coughed and struggled to catch the breath Cian had just squeezed out of him.

"You won't fucking get away with this, MacFarlane," he croaked.

Cian brushed off the front of his five-hundred-dollar dress shirt. "Watch me," he said before flashing a smile and silently making his way back up the alley.

**

Lila Rodriguez wondered if her new job was going to be more trouble than the six-figure salary was worth. As the new systems coordinator for Rogue, she knew she'd be expected to find ways—mostly illegal—to advertise and sell items on the dark web. She'd been doing that for years and had no problem with it, but now her boss had gone and begun discussions with Chicago's notorious Dublin Devils, otherwise known as the Irish mob in the Upper Midwest. Of all the things she'd figured out how to sell on the internet, drugs had never been one of them, save the occasional ounce or two of weed. But the MacFarlanes, the family who ran the Devils, were proposing Rogue sell large quantities of opioids and heroin—online, shipped via United States Postal Service. It was like the whole damn world had lost its mind.

"Vacuum packed and submersed in lavender bath salts," her boss, Xavier Rossi, said as his eyes darted between her and his computer screen.

"You really think that's going to be enough? You do realize drug dogs smell in parts per million?"

Xavier shifted in his big office chair. He wasn't terrible looking but was dripping with awkward boy-nerd-computer-genius vibes—nervous, uncomfortable, and taciturn. The only good thing was he rarely approached her because he hated talking to anyone. Unless business required, he left her well enough alone, and she was fine with that.

"Actually it's per *billion*," he corrected. She rolled her eyes internally. "The vacuum packing alone is probably enough, but the oil is another blocker, and the lavender odor won't hurt either. They only bring in the dogs if the inspectors suspect something. MacFarlane's people have researched it. They'll pack it up nice and tight. It'll look like any other shipment of bath shit. Lavender Love is the name of the company. It'll wash our money at the same time. A win-win."

Lila shifted from one leg to the other, the back of her neck tingling with a warning that this was a very bad idea. Lila was a risk-taker, but a thoughtful one. She liked a challenge, but not being stupid. She was a lot like her father that way.

"I still don't like it. That's major prison time. One postal machine breaks open a box and USPS is looking through it, and then we're screwed."

"Again," Xavier said, impatience winding its way through his voice, "all they'll see is the bath shit."

"Okay, if you say so. I'll start setting it up. I'll have to put a system on that verifies their IP before it allows them onto the page."

"I want a basic-level background check on any customers too," Xavier said. "If they don't want to provide it, then we won't sell to them."

She nodded. "On it, then."

His gaze went back to his screen. "I'm figuring out the final agreement with MacFarlane, but you need to be point on the project. You'll be working with Finn MacFarlane on the technical details, but the head of the family, Cian, wants to meet with you too." He clicked something on his keyboard. "I just sent you his info. He's expecting to hear from you this afternoon."

Shit. Was he serious? The guy was a mobster. She'd always worked with shady people, she was a hacker at the core after all, but it had always been online. And shady computer geeks were a far cry from an honest-to-God mobster.

"Uh, what do you mean, be point?"

"Sit down with him, hammer out all the details about the ordering, shipping, packaging, payments, offshore accounts. Make sure the entire process is foolproof. Then you can present it to the rest of us."

Lila swallowed. "I'm not sure if I'm the best—"

Xavier waved his hand dismissively. "I hired you because you're the best. You'll figure it out, and the MacFarlanes are pros. Between you and them, it'll all be fine."

Fuckity fuck fuck, she thought as she nodded tightly and slouched out of his office. "Jesus," she muttered to herself. Six figures definitely wasn't enough for this. But she couldn't resign now. It would look like she was a security risk at best, and an undercover fed at worst. The idea of being hunted down by the MacFarlanes didn't really work with her long-range plan to live to the age of ninety-eight. Her hand shook as she picked up her phone off her desk and looked at the text Xavier had just sent.

You really screwed yourself this time, Lila, that little voice inside her head said. Yeah, her penchant for flipping off the law, even if somewhat thoughtfully, might have finally gotten her in too deep. Her chest burned a little with anxiety as she tapped the number and pulled up a message box.

This is Lila from Rogue. I've been told to contact you.

The answer came almost immediately, and Lila couldn't help the sinking feeling that cascaded through her as she held the phone and read the screen.

Hi, Lila from Rogue. Let's meet asap. What's your schedule this afternoon?

Shit. Xavier wasn't kidding. They wanted to get this rolling immediately.

I can be somewhere in an hour.

Good. Meet me at this address…

She read the address, then quickly clicked on it to bring up Google Maps. Her breath rushed out in relief as she saw it was a very innocuous Starbucks in the trendy Wicker Park neighborhood.

Ok. See you at two.

She locked the phone and put it away, wondering what kind of a mobster met business associates at the local Starbucks. And also what kind of a twenty-seven-year-old woman spent her days helping sell illegal items on the dark web and her nights worrying that she'd never balance the bad karma from her days.

**

Connor MacFarlane jabbed and struck gold, his opponent's face mask giving way, jaw snapping left as Connor brought his arm back to repeat the motion before his brother Liam could return the favor.

"Dammit," Liam groused as he took a quick step to one side to avoid the second jab. "What the hell's gotten into you today?"

Connor bounced lightly on the balls of his feet, grinning at his bigger, burlier, and meaner older brother. "Nothin's different with me, sunshine. You're just hungover and slow as hell. Maybe you should give the whiskey a rest before you come out to spar."

Liam pulled off one glove, signaling the practice session was over, and Connor sighed, wishing his brother Cian had come along so there'd be someone else to work out with. He was strangely wired and needed to blow off some steam.

"Whiskey's never stopped me from landing a solid punch. You're like the fuckin' Energizer Bunny. You hitting the product?"

Connor snorted in disgust. "Please. I might be younger, but I'm not dumber."

Liam grunted, whether in agreement or disagreement Connor couldn't tell and didn't really care, because at that moment, all the air went out of his lungs as the door to the gym swung open and Jessica O'Neil walked in, her long dark hair swinging out behind her and her fine ass squeezed into a pair of exceptionally tight faded jeans, complete with holes that gave glimpses of her silky skin. The holes weren't the kind that came with the jeans, but the kind that had worn naturally over time, caused by many washings, and Connor was pleased to recall, his fingers trying to get to certain places under the jeans. In fact, he distinctly remembered causing that hole right beneath Jess's left ass cheek.

"Oh hell," Liam muttered. "Don't do it," he warned.

"Don't do what?" Connor asked, already pulling off his gloves and face mask, tossing them over the ropes of the sparring ring.

"Seriously?" Liam asked, spitting water into a bucket on the floor as he leaned over the ropes.

Of course, Connor knew exactly what Liam meant. He didn't *care*, but he *knew*. His brothers saw Jessica was his weakness, something none of them could afford. Weakness was what got you killed, what had gotten countless friends and employees killed, what had landed Liam and their father in prison three years ago. But luckily, a procedural error had developed out of nowhere, and the MacFarlane patriarch and head enforcer were still free, walking the streets of Chicago, running a crime syndicate that held most of the Midwest drug trade in its palm.

But when it came to Jess, Connor didn't care if it made him weak. She'd been his girl for five years until he'd messed up, and he wasn't about to give up on getting her back.

He winked at his brother—who rolled his eyes— and climbed through the ropes to hop down from the practice ring before sauntering toward the office at the back of the gym where Jess's father, Sean O'Neil, kept shop.

He stepped into the doorway of the office and leaned a big shoulder against the frame, watching as

Jess hammered away at the keyboard of her dad's old desktop computer.

"Lookin' good, Jess," he murmured. She didn't bother to turn around, but he saw the way her back stiffened and her typing slowed.

"What do you want?" she asked in a tone that implied she really didn't care.

"You know what I want," he answered, low and rough.

"Go away."

He bit the edge of his lip. She didn't tell him to piss off. That was an improvement over the last three months. Maybe he was softening her up.

"Come on, babe, you know that's not what you want."

She slowly turned in the revolving office chair, standing as soon as she faced him. Her eyes shot daggers, but he saw the flash of pain that skated across her face before the mask of anger took over. That flash was what kept him coming back, even when she refused to give him the time of day. He knew she still cared, and until she didn't, he was going to keep trying. Because Jessica O'Neil was his, and MacFarlanes didn't give up what was theirs—ever.

"Connor," she said, wearily. "Give it a rest, will you? I don't have time for this crap today."

He cocked his head, watching her carefully. Something was off about her. Her face was pale, her hair mussed not in a sexy bedhead way, but a she-was-too-tired-to-brush-it way.

"What's wrong?" he asked, ready to go into fixer mode. It was, after all, what he craved to do with her, for her.

She sighed, focused on the desk beneath her hands as she leaned on it, elbows locked.

"Nothing you can help with."

He took a step deeper into the office, his gaze raking over her again, taking in every little detail that might give him a clue as to what was haunting her.

"Come on, babe. Whatever it is, you know I can make it better. Let me help."

She snorted in a very unladylike fashion, and it made his heart flutter in response. Such a tough girl. He loved that about her—not as much as he loved her ass, but it was a close second.

"And what's the price of your help? A blow job? A quickie in the locker room? The key to my new place?"

He narrowed his eyes, his lungs tightening in anger. "Come on, I know I was an asshole, but when have I ever put conditions on my help?" He stepped closer again, sitting one ass cheek on the surface of the desk and reaching out to run a finger down her cheek. To her credit, she hardly moved as he did it.

"You're the love of my life, Jess," he told her softly.

"You have a funny way of showing it," she answered, all quiet strength and that stubbornness he was beginning to resent.

He sighed. "How can I help? No strings. What's got you upset?"

She lifted her head, gave her hair a toss, and pasted on the phoniest smile he'd ever seen. "It's business. Da's business, so I have no place to discuss it with anyone, especially you."

Connor's brow furrowed, and he watched as she straightened some papers on the desk. He stood, her renewed silence like a wall of ice between them. "Does he need an extension on some of his insurance payments? I'll get Cian to approve it. As long as you need."

Like pretty much everyone in the area for the last three decades, Sean paid the MacFarlanes insurance money every month. It insured the MacFarlanes themselves didn't come after you, as well as buying their protection from other forces that might be even worse.

Jessica shook her head. "What difference would it make? He'd just owe more in a few months."

"It'll buy him time to get some new clients in—"

She put a hand out. "Don't, Connor, please." She shook her head slowly. "I appreciate the offer, but it's not the solution we need, and there's nothing you can do, so if you'll excuse me, I need to get back to this." She gestured to the computer.

His lips sealed tightly, frustration rolling in his gut, he gave her a curt nod. "That's fine, Jess, you keep it to yourself, but I will find out what's going on, and I'll fix it. If I have to spend the rest of my life fixing things for the smartest, best woman I've ever known, I'm happy to do it."

She looked up in surprise.

He leaned forward, bringing his forehead to hers—she didn't pull away. "You don't believe it, but I love you, and I may not be perfect, but I'll never make a mistake like last summer again. Someday, you'll see that. Until then, I'm going to do everything I can to take that look off your beautiful face. Don't underestimate me, babe."

He took one deep breath, reveling in the scent of lemon that was so familiar and noticing the small sound that escaped her lips. Then he stepped away, giving her a nod before he turned and strode out the door.

Chapter Two

Cian's gaze slipped to his watch, the sweeping second hand rounding to twelve just as he looked. Two p.m., on the dot. He sincerely hoped the Rogue girl—Lila—would be on time. He needed to get to Banshee and talk to Connor as soon as feasible. There'd been a surprise liquor license inspection, and Connor had barely managed to keep the inspector from finding the product he'd apparently stashed in the DJ booth. Cian was beyond pissed. He had one rule for the MacFarlanes' legitimate businesses, and that was that they stayed legit. No mixing the two ends of the family's enterprises. It was just plain stupid and made it nearly impossible for them to launder the money that poured into the family coffers monthly.

But his younger brother always had a hard time following instructions and had apparently been using the club as a transfer point for their distributors in that part of the city. It was just the sort of foolish risk-taking that Cian had come to expect from Connor. The youngest of the four MacFarlane boys, Connor was an odd combination of reckless and organized. He played the role of the distribution manager in the family, supervising the men who put the product out on the streets, but then turning around and doing something like he had last summer—cheating on his longtime girlfriend with the sister of Alejandro Vasquez, a rival boss. Connor had not only lost a good woman, he'd brought the wrath of Vasquez down on them and created an ongoing headache for Cian.

Cian saw his guy stationed near the door to the coffee shop glance his way with a slight nod, and then knew to watch the brunette who'd just walked in. She was petite, her hair long, cascading from a high ponytail. Her facial features gave her away as mixed race, Asian and something else, and fit with her slight frame.

Her eyes were big and such a dark brown, they were almost black. Fine, arched brows sat like wings against her ivory skin, and Cian couldn't help but think the whole effect was somewhat like cookies-and-cream ice cream. She wore skintight jeans and a plain white T-shirt with a V-neck. Her arms were adorned with a stack of silver bracelets as well as a variety of tattoos, all in black ink. But in the midst of the almost severe nature of her appearance was one slash of color—bright, shiny, and utterly beguiling. Lila from Rogue wore apricot lipstick on her full, decadent mouth, and as she walked up to his table while he stood to greet her, all he could think was how much he wanted to lick that shit off and see if it tasted even half as amazing as it looked.

"Mr. MacFarlane?" she asked as he looked down at her.

"In the flesh," he murmured, putting out his hand. She stiffly shook with him, and he marveled at how tiny the bones of her hand were. He could crush them in a heartbeat. It made him feel strangely powerful and also concerned at the same time. How did a woman like this keep from being bruised by the mere weight and size of most other people?

"You Googled my picture, I assume?" he asked, watching her.

Her gaze snapped to his. "I'm a professional computer security specialist," she huffed. "You don't think I'd go to meet a new associate without finding out what he looked like, do you?"

"Of course not," he answered, gesturing for her to sit down as he did the same. "Which is why my man sitting in the corner by the door has your entire dossier on his phone right now."

She nodded as if to say "touché" and sat across from him.

"Can I have Danny get you anything?" he asked, fascinated by the precise and compact way she sat, taking up very little space, blending into her surroundings so well, except for those lips.

She turned and peered at Danny for a moment. "So he fetches coffee too?"

Cian didn't take the bait even though he fought the urge to smirk. "He does what most employees do—whatever their boss asks them to."

She gave him a look that spoke volumes. "My guess is his boss is somewhat like mine, meaning Danny gets asked to do a hell of a lot more than the average employee."

He tilted his head in acknowledgment. "Be that as it may, he'll get you a latte if you'd like."

"I'm fine, thank you."

Cian watched her for a moment. He wasn't sure why it bothered him, but he wanted her to take his offer of a cup of coffee. The fact was he chose coffee shops for meetings like this for more than one reason. They were out in the open, making it next to impossible for anyone to threaten him. Conversely, they made him appear less intimidating to those he was meeting with. There were times he wanted to be scary, but there were plenty of times he didn't. With a girl named Lila who worked on computers all day, he didn't need to be the big, scary mob boss.

And finally, meeting in a coffee shop made Cian feel a little more normal. He liked to at least pretend he was an average businessman. Meeting someone at one of the family's many rental properties, which were generally filled with their mules and dealers, or one of their bars, which were filled with the regulars you'd find at any liquor establishment, only furthered the image he secretly loathed—that of a criminal.

He tried not to let it show that her rejection of a cup of coffee was the cause of his existential angst. He needed to get his head examined, for fuck's sake. *It's coffee,* he reminded himself, *and you are a criminal whether she drinks it or not.*

"So, I assume your boss has gotten you up to speed with the plans thus far," he said, turning away from his errant thoughts and on to the business at hand.

She sat up straighter, reaching down to the slouchy leather bag she'd carried in and removing a tablet. She touched the screen, bringing it to life, and pulled out a stylus. "He told me the plan was to ship the bath oils via United States postal." She looked up at him, skepticism everywhere in her expression, "I can't help but question the wisdom of that."

He smiled slowly, watching the way a strand of hair that had fallen from her ponytail moved alongside her face as she talked. Her hair was shiny and thick like silk yarn, and when he looked closer, he saw that among the dark mass, there were stripes of red and purple. Subtle, but there, another chink in her armor of black and white.

"You wouldn't be the first one to question our shipping choice, but I'm confident it will work," he said, leaning back casually, one arm slung over the rigid back of the empty chair next to him. He noticed her track his movement, and he wondered what she thought of him. Cian generally dressed in expensive but not flashy clothes. He avoided the clichéd mobster-in-a-suit look, as well as anything that spoke of flash, trash, or, as Connor would put it, "something one of the Sopranos would wear."

Today he was wearing a knit collared shirt, flat-front black pants, and a pair of lace-up boots that his cousin Maggie swore were the height of fashion. He didn't really care, so long as they were comfortable, and they were. His sleeves were pushed up to his elbows, and while his left forearm sported a TAG Heuer watch, his right was covered in a depiction of the Battle of Clontarf.

"I take it you don't agree," he said, one eyebrow raised.

Lila's gaze shot back up to his, those beautiful, plush lips rolling together for a moment as she considered her response. Watching the movement made certain body parts spring to life in a very inopportune fashion.

"I think it's a serious risk. One package breaks open and those bath oils will be all over the place," she said. "Then postal inspectors get involved…" She let her sentence trail off at that point as she leaned forward slightly.

"These are bath *salts* actually," he said, reaching for his cup of coffee. "It's oil and salt all mixed together. Sloppy stuff in a very thick glass container."

"Expensive to ship," she interjected.

"Trust me," he murmured. "We've run the numbers. The profit is substantial."

"And if the container gets broken?"

"If it did, the salts would get everywhere."

She looked at him, eyebrows raised as if to say, *And?*

He smiled, sipped his coffee, and finally leaned forward, his voice low and rough. "The items you're worried about will be vacuum sealed and attached to the bottom of the glass container. If it gets broken, that will look like part of the packaging. It's not going to be obvious," he assured her. She didn't look convinced.

"And dogs?" she asked quietly.

"They'll always be a risk, but the oils and vacuum sealing should minimize it. If a package were to get broken open while a dog was right there, maybe, but beyond that, I don't see anything to worry about."

"How much money are we talking here?" she asked, writing something on her tablet.

"One hundred fifty a package, with costs of about fifty per package. That's a hundred in profit. Multiply that by a few thousand orders a month, and you begin to see why this is a good idea."

She sighed. "Okay, then. I guess we need to discuss the logistics."

He nodded, taking one last look of longing at those lips. Yes, logistics. He was here for that. Not apricot lips or cups of coffee. Because at the end of the day, all the coffee shops in the world couldn't change the fact that Cian MacFarlane was a mobster, and he would be for life.

**

Lila watched the man in front of her as he described what safeguards they'd need in place to protect their internet drug trade from the prying eyes of the feds. He wasn't a tech guy, so he didn't know *how* to do it, only what needed to be done. Her job was the how. She was simply a tool in his arsenal.

Lila had been ten years old when she'd realized she was also simply a tool in her father's arsenal. She had a knack for numbers—and odds and fast calculations—and once he'd realized what she could do, he became her biggest fan, taking her to the track, making her sit next to him while he played online blackjack, trying to find unique ways to use her abilities to give him an advantage. And Lila had been so desperate for his approval and his love that she'd learned how to hack, breaking into online gambling sites to cheat the system so her gambling-addicted father could finally win more often than he lost.

She pushed away her inclination to compare her current situation to her childhood. They weren't alike at all, she reminded herself. After all, her father had never paid her a dime for everything she did for him—not in cash, and sure as hell not in love.

She refocused on the man in front of her. She had to admit she'd expected Cian to be a lot more threatening. She'd dealt with criminals her entire life—hell, if she was being brutally honest, *she* was a criminal—but they were gamblers, addicts, tech nerds, hackers, former hackers, wannabe hackers. The people she normally dealt with got revenge by draining someone's bank account, not hanging them from a hook in a meat locker and letting them bleed to death.

So, Lila had come to the Starbucks in Wicker Park—one of the newest, trendiest Starbucks in the city, teeming with hipsters and people who worked on laptops in coffee shops all day—expecting Cian MacFarlane to be…well…*scary*. And he was, but not in the way she'd expected. No, Cian MacFarlane felt mostly like a threat to her libido.

He was tall, dark, and hot, and she was disgusted with herself for being distracted by it—really for even noticing it. *Thou shalt not lust after mob bosses.* If that wasn't in the Bible somewhere, it should be. Right along with *thou shalt not take a job with an insane genius no matter how many zeroes are in the salary.*

She sighed as Cian drew with his finger on the table, explaining that all customers would need to pay through a third-party vendor to put further distance between the money and the MacFarlane family.

"You could use cryptocurrency," she said, interrupting him. He looked at her with blue eyes like cut glass.

"Bitcoins?" he asked.

"Yes, but a different brand. They're untraceable. Easy for the customers to buy, and Rogue's system is already set up for them."

"But they're hard to convert." He looked at her again, and his gaze made her heart take a small skip.

"They are," she admitted. "But there are ways."

"Ways for six or seven figures? Month after month?"

She moved her head from side to side. "What about a certain percentage in crypto? Ten or twenty percent? We can adjust as necessary. I'd set up the whole system to monitor itself and adjust every forty-eight hours. So, if the percentage of crypto purchases fell below our benchmark, it would increase the number of crypto-only product listings. If it was higher than we designated, it would add other pay methods to more listings. Make sense?"

He nodded. "Perfect. Then we'd just need to convert the crypto each month?"

She liked that he was facile, quick to understand, and sparing in his questions.

"You might want to have it ongoing. Do smaller amounts every week or even every day. It won't raise any red flags, and the income will be relatively consistent for that portion of the sales."

He leaned back in his chair, crossing those nicely muscular arms across his broad chest. She couldn't help but glance at the tattoos running up his right arm. Some sort of battle scene, it was chaos, all dark lines with bright splashes of color.

"It's the Battle of Clontarf," he said, smirking at her.

She snapped her gaze to his. "I wasn't—I mean—"

"It was done by an old friend of mine. He owns a shop on Washington." He looked down at his arm and used the opposite hand to point. "This is Cian mac Máelmuaid," he said, sounding incredibly Irish as he pointed to the central figure who wore armor and a metal helmet while brandishing a large sword with two hands. "He and his father-in-law, the High King of Ireland, won the battle, freeing Ireland from the Vikings, but they perished in it as well."

"That's very sad," she said, feeling oddly disturbed by the idea.

His voice was deeper and quieter as he answered. "Sometimes you have to lose something that matters in order to win something even greater."

"So you were named for him?" she asked, reaching across the table before she'd even realized it to touch the warrior's face on his forearm.

He made a small hiss as her skin touched his, and she moved to pull away, but he was faster, grabbing her fingers with his own, tracing over the lines of ink as he spoke softly.

"I was born on April twenty-third, the same day as the Battle of Clontarf. My mother saw that as a sign. Luckily, she chose Cian as the warrior to name me after and not Murchad or Toirdelbach."

He chuckled, and she couldn't help but join him. But as their gazes met, the laughter died out and all that was left was his hand on hers as they both touched his arm. Heat sizzled in his eyes, and warning sirens screamed in her head.

She snatched her hand away as if she'd been burned. Leaning back, her heart racing like a rabbit caught in a snare, Lila clicked off her tablet and hurriedly grabbed her bag off the floor, swinging it over her shoulder in one rushed motion.

"I think I understand all the security protocol we'll need for this project," she said, her voice tight, words clipped. "I'll have Xavier get in touch as soon as I have it ready."

He watched her warily, as if she were a wounded animal, prepared to strike should anyone get too close.

She opened her mouth to speak again, but no words came out. She was so disturbed by the feeling of his skin on hers, it had rendered her speechless, like some sort of high school girl when the quarterback speaks to her in the hallway. Finally, she simply muttered, "Okay, then…" and turned to go.

"Lila from Rogue," he said, not loudly, but commanding all the same. She managed a quarter turn, looking at him over her shoulder, her breath frozen in her lungs. "Next time, you'll take a cup of coffee."

It wasn't a question and not quite an order. Simply a statement of fact, a reminder that she could run, but she couldn't hide. From him. From his family. From whatever the hell had just happened. All Lila could do was walk away, something inside her flaring with the realization she'd finally crossed a line she couldn't come back from.

Chapter Three

Connor lounged on the leather sofa in the back office of Banshee. Cian was lecturing, and Connor had heard it all before. He understood it was Cian's job to make sure nothing ever raised a red flag that would get unwanted attention, but good God, did he need to lecture as if Connor was a child?

"…And before you say Pop used to do it, I'll remind you what nearly happened to Pop and Liam three years ago," Cian said, jabbing a finger at Connor. Connor considered snapping his brother's finger off, but decided it was more trouble than he wanted to go to.

"They didn't get hauled in because they mixed the legit with the not so legit," Connor muttered.

"You have no idea what triggered the investigation, and we're on the feds' radar worse than normal ever since. Did you notice the sedan parked around the corner by the bakery this morning?" Cian shot back.

Connor's heart skipped a beat. "What?"

"Right." Cian's expression could only be described as smug. Fucker.

"Sons of bitches," Connor snarled. "They can sit out there for the next year and they'll never get a warrant to search. They're like neutered dogs. They can hump all day long and not do a damn bit of damage."

Cian's brows drew down. "What's it going to take to get through to you?" he asked in exasperation. "This isn't the good old days when Pop was running things and we had our people doing pickups and drop-offs from his pub all damn day. We have to keep the money separate, we have to keep the dealers away from us. We can't keep the product in central locations. There's no room for sloppiness here. I don't care how many judges and cops Pop's got on the payroll, you can't know what the feds might have on us at any given point in time."

Connor closed his eyes as he laid his head back on the sofa. Damn. He'd messed up. He could admit it to himself, but he really didn't want to admit it to Cian.

Cian looked at him, and suddenly, he didn't seem angry anymore, only tired. Connor felt the wind leave his sails. His brother loved him, he knew that. Never doubted it for one moment. If only he'd give him a little rope.

"I need you to stop taking these kinds of risks," Cian said softly as he leaned back against the desk. "When Liam was inside, I thought I might lose my mind. I need you three out here where I can keep you safe. Please don't take these risks. Stop for me if you won't stop for you. You're young, I get you feel invincible, but I'm telling you, you're not."

Connor sighed but nodded his assent. "Fine. I'll follow the rules. No product at the legit businesses, everything spread out, nothing central. But the guys are going to bitch."

Cian's expression hardened. "And if they do, you make sure they remember who's in charge here. They work for *us*, not the other way around. Anyone gives you blowback, you tell them they can talk to me about it."

Connor had to smirk. He'd never seen his brother do serious harm to anyone, but his reputation was that of a total badass, and for whatever reason, the men had a healthy fear of him. Connor wished he was able to get Cian to discuss it. He suspected Liam knew what had gone down, but neither older brother would give up the goods. Connor had a vague memory of Cian's eighteenth birthday, he and Liam coming home with their father late one night. There was shouting, their mother crying. Cian's eyes the next morning were dead and flat. At ten years Cian's junior, Connor had been too young to understand it all, and Finn had only been twelve.

Whatever had happened, the reputation had stuck.

Cian walked toward the door and opened it. "Now, don't you have things to do?" He raised an eyebrow.

Right. Get the product out of the back room. Because he'd been an idiot to think he could take the easy way out by keeping it here.

"Aye aye, Captain," he muttered with a little salute to his brother.

As he passed by Cian in the doorway, his brother's big hand clamped down on his shoulder. "I love you, you little bastard," Cian said, his voice rough with emotion. "Everything I do is to protect you."

Connor felt his throat tighten as he nodded. "I know. I'm sorry."

Cian squeezed his shoulder, then gave him a gentle shove. "Go fix it, then we can have some dinner at the pub. I'll text Finn and Liam."

**

Connor went about the business of getting his men over to the club to move the product, small batches of it going to each of about a half-dozen locations the MacFarlanes kept within a rotating batch of nearly thirty. Connor had been drilled on the rules since he was eighteen and started working in the family business. Each year, the family bought and sold several run-down office and industrial properties, using them for storage and distribution of the drugs that were the mainstay of their empire.

It was a complex system, the purpose of which was obvious—never let anyone know where the drugs might be stored. The distributors would be told an address one hour before they were scheduled to pick up product, and it would be a different address each week. They hated the system and complained about it endlessly. They couldn't plan ahead and often had to arrange transportation at the last minute. Chicago's traffic made it hell to get anywhere quickly. When they complained to Connor, who was in charge of local distribution, he often gave in to them. The fact was, he'd brought all the product to one location several times before for weeks on end. Cian simply hadn't known.

Once the onerous task of moving the week's shipment was handled and Connor had put Cian's main man, Danny, in charge of the particulars, he walked outside to the back parking lot, swinging one leg over the seat of his Ducati. He revved the engine, fishtailing as he peeled out of the parking lot and turned toward Halstead, where his brother had seen the feds parked earlier. Sure enough, when he got to the corner, there sat a late-model dark American sedan. He shook his head in disgust. Didn't they ever learn? The damn car was like a neon sign flashing *cop*, especially in a neighborhood like this one.

As he slowed his roll around the corner heading the opposite direction the car was parked, he saw the agent in the driver's seat turn his head to watch. Okay, so maybe they weren't trying to be incognito. The agent lowered his sunglasses so he could peer at Connor over the top and grinned. Connor flipped him off, hitting the gas hard as he popped a wheelie and flew down the street. Motherfuckers. He tried to make the rapid rhythm of his heart be about the speed of his bike and not the insidious fear that worked its way through him when he saw the confidence the agent displayed, sitting in broad daylight, watching everyone who came and went from Banshee and baiting them. Connor had never realized just how serious his family's business was until Liam and their father had been arrested. Now he lived in constant fear of ending up in prison.

He'd gone only a few blocks when a familiar set of legs and an ass that was the stuff dreams were made of caught his attention on the sidewalk. What the hell was she doing here? This part of town wasn't the best, and after dark, it became downright sketchy, nothing like the solidly working-class neighborhood both their families had historically lived in. He pulled over, cutting in front of a cabbie who flipped him off and yelled at him in Arabic.

Jess glanced over her shoulder to see what the commotion was about, and he watched her face go through about a dozen different emotions when she saw him.

He switched off the engine, jammed down the stand with his booted heel, and dismounted, reaching Jessica in ten seconds flat.

She looked up at him, her face weary but not angry for once.

"What do you want now, Connor? And are you stalking me?" she asked.

He ran a hand through his hair that was wild from the wind.

"What are you doing here?" he asked, taking her by the elbow and scanning the area around them before he led her to a small niche in front of a pawn shop. He took comfort in the feeling of his gun holstered under his left arm.

She breathed deeply and rolled her shoulders like she was about to go into a center-ring brawl. "Just some business for my dad," she answered.

"Yeah? He know you're doing it?" Connor kept his hand on her elbow in spite of her scowl, and she didn't pull away.

"What does it matter? I'm a grown woman. I don't have to get my dad's permission to walk around town."

He let go of her and put a hand to his forehead for just a moment. "No, you don't, but Jess, you know as well as I do, it's not safe for you down here, especially as my girlfriend. Vasquez's territory is only a few blocks to the south. He hangs in Pilsen all the time."

"I'm not your girlfriend," she said brusquely, as if that settled the issue.

He sighed. The woman was killing him with this shit. "Anyone who's paid any attention knows how I feel about you, Jess. Through you is the easiest way to get at me."

He saw her obstinance waver for a split second.

"Well, maybe you should quit hanging around everywhere I am, then. It's putting me at more risk."

"The only thing that's putting you at risk is refusing to get back together with me so I can take care of you."

He looked at her hard, his jaw flexing in frustration. Her face softened incrementally until finally she reached out and touched his arm with the tips of her fingers. "Connor," she said softly. "Even if you hadn't done what you did..." She paused, swallowing as a cloud passed over her eyes. "I wouldn't want you to take care of me like that. Things have changed—I've changed. And isn't that why you did it in the first place? Because you could feel what was coming?"

Connor's throat ached, and he ground his teeth, watching her as she gazed at him in sympathy. Yeah, he'd felt it. The shift when she'd started avoiding his family functions, didn't want to tell people his last name when they were introduced, started complaining when he had to work late with his brothers. Jess had wanted to live together, go out with friends, do the things other couples their age did. So yes, Connor had definitely felt the change, the transition from her loving him no matter what to her loving only the parts of him that weren't tied to MacFarlane business.

"I'm not the same girl you met all those years ago. I've grown up, and I can't go back to that—to her."

He leaned against the wall next to them, looking down at their hands that had somehow become linked, her fingers wound through his the way they used to, no thought, just instinct.

"So, I'll change too," he whispered. "I'll do whatever you want, be whatever you need."

She shook her head sadly. "No, you won't." She paused, and it was significant, the space filled not with what she *did* say, but what she *didn't*. Until finally, "You can't."

Connor swallowed, the backs of his eyes burning like he was a fucking pussy. If Liam could see him now, he'd have a fit. "Anything but that, Jess. I'll do anything for you but that."

A tear rolled slowly down her smooth cheek, and Connor's chest squeezed. "I know. It's why I've never asked, but it's the only thing that would change this."

"They're my family," he whispered.

She caressed his cheek with the back of her fingers before going up on tiptoe to kiss his lips chastely. His insides twisted in panic.

"I know. And I can't have them be *my* family. I want more—I want things you can't give me."

"Shit," he gritted, his voice so rough, the word was almost unintelligible.

She stepped away and gave him a sad smile before she resumed her walk down the dirty pavement. Connor breathed deep, releasing the pain on an exhale before he walked to the curb, mounted his bike, and pulled into traffic, following Jessica's lead for the next ten blocks until she turned into familiar territory and the safety of a popular business district.

Then Connor gunned his bike, weaving in and out between gridlocked cars until everything around him was a blur and the racing of his heart was truly about speed and not his wrecked life.

Chapter Four

Xavier stared at the screen of his computer as it showed Cian MacFarlane buckling his belt. The man was an early riser, like Xavier himself, and that got him a few points of respect. On screen, Cian sat in an armchair in his very modern high-rise apartment and laced up an expensive black leather boot. Xavier wondered where Cian had bought the boots, and if maybe he should try a similar pair. It seemed like the mobster had a handle on the whole dressing-for-success thing, unlike his three younger brothers, who looked like varying degrees of rich, spoiled hoodlum.

As Cian grabbed a wallet and keys from the dresser, Xavier's heart beat a tad faster—*don't close it, don't close it*, the mantra played on a loop in his head. When MacFarlane then walked out of the room, and Xavier's line of sight, he breathed a sigh of relief. He pressed some buttons on his keyboard, and the image of the room zoomed in. Xavier looked carefully at the various pieces of furniture in the image—a nightstand, the armchair, a lamp, the bed, and there—at the far left of the screen, on the floor in the corner was a large potted plant, undoubtedly put there by an interior designer or an ex-girlfriend to soften up the cold space. It was on a stand, a strange thing made of what looked to be white Lucite. But it had curves, and the plant was lush and full. It would work.

Xavier picked up the phone and pressed two numbers.

"Yeah, he's out. There's a plant stand in the corner of the master bedroom. Last night, I was able to see the home office, and there's a trophy in there, a large cup on the shelf behind the desk."

He paused as he clicked off the image on the screen. "You'll have to wing it in the living room."

After he hung up the phone, Xavier muttered to himself. How most of the supposedly intelligent people in the world could refuse to admit the fact that their laptops provided cameras available to anyone with even rudimentary hacking skills was perplexing to him.

**

The text came at six a.m. on a Tuesday, and all Lila could think was that Cian MacFarlane must be nothing like Tony Soprano, because she knew for a fact Tony stayed up all night snorting coke and screwing hookers and wouldn't have been caught dead texting people at six a.m.

We need to meet. Eight a.m. at Starbucks?

Lila squinted at the phone, because, unlike her mobster associate, she was not normally awake at six a.m.—business in the world of the dark web started

sometime around ten—and had been sleeping sound-
ly before his texts started chiming in her ear.

Now the only question was what the hell did the
man want at such an ungodly hour?

*Why are you texting me at six a.m.? Normal business
hours don't start until 8. Mine don't start until 10.*

She waited for a response, her tension ratcheting
up as the little dots danced on the screen while he
typed. Her judgment at six a.m. wasn't the best. Maybe she shouldn't have mouthed off to the mobster.

But when the answer finally came, it took her
breath away, and not out of fear. No, it was breath
stealing for an entirely different reason.

*I was thinking about you all night, so it seemed only natu-
ral to contact you first thing this morning. Will nine work?*

Just like that. No warning. No explanation. Simply "I was thinking about you all night." Did that mean
about her in her capacity as a *her*? Or her because she
was part of the *project* he was thinking about all night?

Lila stared down at the phone, a slight tremor
passing through her body.

I'm not sure what to make of that, she typed out.

I'm not either, he replied quickly. *But regardless, we
need to discuss the project.*

She agreed to the nine a.m. meeting and spent
ninety minutes lying in bed, trying desperately to go
back to sleep. When it became apparent that she was
wasting her time, she climbed off the nine-thousand-
dollar mattress she'd splurged on with her ill-gotten
gains and went to the shower, trying not to think
about the scary guy she had to go meet with.

It didn't make a lot of sense to be so nervous
about him. She'd probably met mobsters dozens of
times when she was younger—her father's bookies,

the guys he made debt payments to, the guys who set up the backroom poker games he attended. There was rarely a car ride with her dad that didn't include a stop involving his "job," as he'd called it. There had to have been mobsters around in all that. But not a one of them had made her feel like Cian MacFarlane did. The man scared the crap out of her. But she didn't want to examine why too closely.

At nine oh five, Lila walked into what seemed to now be "their" Starbucks. She stifled the urge to slap the inner her who would think of hot mobster Cian MacFarlane in any context that resulted in "we."

"Good morning," he said as she arrived at the table he'd staked out in a back corner away from the front windows and all the activity of the fancy reserve coffee bar. She wondered if he always sat away from glass in case of drive-bys. While she had to worry about getting caught up in an investigation of dark web activity and finding the FBI on her doorstep someday, she'd never had to fear for her safety walking around in the world. She was hidden behind some of the thickest virtual walls ever erected. Almost no one knew who she was, what her real name was, or how she earned her living. She couldn't help but wonder what it was like to be a moving target every time you set foot outside your armored car.

Lila gave Cian a small nod in acknowledgment before sitting in the chair he'd pulled out for her in a gesture that was oddly gentlemanlike.

"What can I get you for breakfast?" he asked.

Lila peered at him, her brain still somewhat foggy from lack of sleep. "How do you know I haven't eaten already?"

"Because I woke you up far too early, and you spent the next two hours trying desperately to go back to sleep before you finally had to crawl out of bed and rush to get here five minutes late."

She stared at him, disgusted by how accurate his assessment was.

"It was only an hour and a half," she muttered.

"What will you be eating?" he asked again, a placid smile on his face.

She huffed out a breath before giving him her order, which he texted to Danny.

"Now," he said, a satisfied smirk in place as she tucked into the breakfast sandwich and chai Danny delivered to their table, "I have more questions about the security."

Thirty minutes later, Lila had explained the entire setup of Rogue, with technical details she knew damn well Cian didn't understand. But for some reason, he seemed to want to keep talking to her, asking question after question, ordering his henchman to refill her chai, and nodding thoughtfully as if he understood half of what she was saying.

"And that access code is switched out every thirty days?" he asked.

"Yes. We have a randomizer that pulls a new one at an exact time each month, then automatically sends it to Xavier and me. We then distribute it to two other staff members—different ones each month—so they can do certain types of work within the system."

"And how do I know those other staff members are trustworthy?" he asked, looking at her from under his brows as he idly stirred his third cappuccino.

"How do any of us know anyone is trustworthy?" she answered, tiring of the inquisition. "Xavier pays well. The entire business is black market. There's no reason to think our staff will suddenly go to the cops over your part as opposed to any other."

Cian gave her a wry smile. "Lila from Rogue," he said in that deep tone he had that set something in her stomach swaying. "You have no idea the types of enemies my family has. They would think nothing of bribing or threatening one of your staff members to jeopardize my business. They would love nothing more than to see my brothers and me in federal lock-up."

She felt her cheeks burn with the recognition he was right. This wasn't like their ordinary business. Rogue had never been associated with anyone like the MacFarlanes.

As if he sensed she was fresh out of snappy comebacks, he continued. "I want all MacFarlane business separated from the rest of Rogue. And I want no one but you and Xavier involved. You will do all the work on this. You will be assigned to our account full time. And if Xavier balks at this, remind him how much his cut will be."

Lila sat back in her chair, arms crossed, huffing out a breath as she did. "I wasn't aware Xavier had made you co-owner of the company."

Cian gave her a slow, dark smile, like the richest chocolate dripping from a spoon. "Do we need to go there?" he asked, leaving the unsaid…well, unsaid. *Yes*, his eyes communicated, *I can insist on whatever I want because I'm bigger, richer, and meaner than Xavier Rossi will ever be, and he knows it.*

His words were like a slap in the face, and she realized she'd been getting…comfortable…with him. She'd forgotten for a moment he wasn't only mysterious, charming, and very sexy, but also dangerous, unpredictable, and very powerful.

"No. I apologize," she amended quickly. "I'll let Xavier know how you'd like it arranged." She stood abruptly, something she seemed to do a lot around this man. Her hands shook slightly as she snatched her tablet off the table and lifted her messenger bag from the chair back. "I really need to get in to work now. I have a lot to do."

Cian looked at her with those ice-blue eyes, then gave a small nod. He stood as well. "I'll walk you out," he said.

"It's really not necessary—"

He suddenly stepped around the table, taking her elbow gently in his hand. Warmth rushed through her at the same time a strange chill did.

"I don't—" He paused, his gaze fixed on something over her head before he looked down, straight into her eyes, penetrating and so intense. "I don't hurt civilians." His voice was quiet, his lips only inches from hers. "I'm not a monster, Lila. Just a businessman. You don't need to be afraid of me."

She swallowed hard as she looked up at him. A wry smile caused his lips to turn up ever so slightly at the corners. "You'll get these things set up as I've asked?"

She nodded again, unable to speak for reasons that went far beyond fear.

"Good. Let me know when you're done."

His hand left her elbow, and before she realized it, he was walking away, his long legs eating up the space between her and the door. Danny was on his feet and at his boss's side before she could blink. The two men strode into the weak sunshine and disappeared into the back of a dark SUV that mysteriously appeared at the front curb.

Lila realized she'd stopped breathing minutes ago and took a bracing breath, her heart racing, her elbow still tingling where he'd touched, held her captive, if only for a moment.

Times like these, Lila truly regretted the world her father had raised her in. Because no matter how scared she was by Cian MacFarlane, she was also drawn to him, like a piece of iron to a magnet. And *that* was the worst idea Lila had had in years.

Chapter Five

Connor slipped in the back door of his parents' house, nodding to the man who stood guard outside before he shut the glass-paned door that had somehow survived the comings and goings of him and his brothers for thirty-plus years.

He stood still for a moment, his eyes fixed on the small light over the kitchen stove, the only thing illuminating the room, and listened, wondering if his parents had already gone to bed.

A gruff voice came out of the darkness in the corner where the kitchen table sat. "You get that shipment squared away at the docks like I said."

Connor's heart did a flip but he knew better than to let his surprise show. Like his brothers, he'd been trained to keep a poker face no matter what. If you didn't, your face would meet the back of the old man's hand. He took a deep breath and sauntered over to the table where his father sat in the dark, sipping a tumbler of whiskey.

"Hey, Pop," he said, reaching for the bottle that sat in front of his father.

"Get a glass, or I'll wipe those lips off your face," the old man muttered. Connor couldn't help but smirk that his father knew him so well. He walked across the kitchen and opened the cabinet to extract another tumbler.

As he returned to the table and sat, he poured a healthy serving and took a long swallow, the top-shelf whiskey burning its way down his throat, helping sharpen his senses, something that was always needed if you were going to have a conversation with Robbie MacFarlane.

A flame hissed to life across the table as his dad lit up a cigar. The orange flame illuminated the old man's craggy features, his thick shock of white hair standing at odd angles that told Connor he'd come to the kitchen from bed. Probably unable to sleep.

Robbie MacFarlane had immigrated to the US from Ireland at the age of twenty, entering the country on a work visa with an Irish manufacturing company. The manufacturing company was, of course, a front for the Dublin Devils, Irish organized crime, and Robbie and the other young men who'd come in on visas spent more time running backroom gambling operations and dealing drugs than they ever had working the line at the factory.

Over the next two decades, the Devils changed. Robbie worked his way up, and eventually, when the leaders in Dublin decided to scale back and liberate the American arm of the organization, they handed Robbie the reins—for a significant sum of cash, of course—and suddenly, Robbie was forty and in charge of an organized crime network with ties to Ireland and a legion of soldiers at his beck and call.

He'd married the much younger Angela Milligan, daughter of one of Chicago's old political families, a year later, and she'd borne him four strong boys to carry on the family legacy. Connor, as the youngest, had gotten the least of his father's expectations and pressure, but he'd felt the force of Robbie's hand enough times to realize when the old man told you to do something, you did it.

"Yeah, Pop, of course. The shipment's all stowed, and the guys will send it out to Wisconsin tomorrow."

"Good. You tell your brother I want that product on the street within ten days? We're holding on to the damn stuff too long. The longer it's in our hands, the more time the feds have to track it to us. He oughta know that by now. Some days, I wonder if I'm gonna have to come back and run shit. He's too fuckin' soft."

"Yeah, I told him. He'll work on it." Connor felt a prick of unease as he always did when his father talked about Cian. He'd never known the old man to give Cian any praise. Cian never worked fast enough, never worked hard enough. Yet the men respected him deeply and would die for him if they were asked to, and so would Connor, Finn, and Liam. Robbie had enforced his rule with an iron fist. Cian had earned his authority.

"You know, Pop, it wouldn't hurt to have a little confidence in Cian once in a while. He's doing a good job."

His father scoffed quietly before pulling the bottle back toward him and pouring a few fingers into his own glass.

"Cian noticed some feds at the bar this week. You seen any of 'em hanging out around the house here?" Connor asked, trying to move the conversation away from his brother's perceived faults.

Robbie looked at him from under his bushy white brows. "Bloody bastards have been parked at the bottom of the drive every day for the last two weeks."

"Dammit," Connor spat as he banged a fist on the tabletop. "Can't we do anything about it? It's harassment. Why aren't the lawyers filing some kind of restraining orders?"

Robbie stood, throwing back his whiskey in one go. "Nothing the lawyers can do. Feds have us like a bunch of rats in a hole, and that's why we can't afford any screwups."

Connor nodded before his dad said good night and took off to the upper floor of the house. He sat in the silence of his parents' kitchen and drank the rest of his whiskey, thoughts circling his mind. It was three years ago that Liam and Robbie had been picked up in a raid on one of the MacFarlane distribution warehouses. The place had been full of product, and Robbie and Liam had been in the midst of selling wholesale to a trusted associate from Springfield who, unbeknownst to them, had become an undercover rat, when the DEA had descended, pulling in everyone in the place in the wide net they'd thrown.

Liam and Robbie had been caught red-handed, their sales discussion on tape, the product sitting in plain sight. The entire event was shocking and sloppy, something Robbie never was. Cian, Connor, and Finn had been frantic, desperately afraid they'd be next, and also terrified they'd never get their father and Liam out.

But then, in the midst of a storm of constant media attention, pressure to give each other up to the FBI, and every business associate for five hundred miles cutting off the MacFarlanes like bad karma, the feds had suddenly, with no warning, released both Liam and Robbie.

The lawyers were told an obscure rule regarding chain of possession in the evidence process had been broken, nullifying the entire case. But no one in the MacFarlane family believed that. They feared someone in the organization had turned against them, promising to be an informant from the inside. It would be too tempting for the feds to have the possibility of getting not only Robbie and Liam but all four brothers plus associates. However, nearly three years later, no internal search Cian had done had yielded any results.

In the meantime, Robbie's heart had nearly given out, and he'd had to hand the business over to Cian to manage. He might not give his oldest son much credit, but Cian had kept things running smoothly with no more arrests, and income was at an all-time high.

But the feds hadn't faded back into the woodwork. They were like little dogs nipping at the MacFarlanes' ankles, showing up here, then there, taunting, harassing. So Connor and his family operated as if there was a gun at their heads all the time. And now the feds were poking around yet again. Connor knew it wasn't a good sign. And damn, he didn't want to go to prison.

His phone buzzed from the table where he'd laid it. When he picked it up to see the screen, his brother Finn's name flashed, and Connor couldn't help but smile. Finn was two years older than him and the real middle son of the four MacFarlane boys. In a family of alpha men boxing, wrestling, and shooting guns, Finn kept up fine with the pack but had little interest in the things that had occupied his brothers growing up. Finn was the genius in the family, the closest to their mother, the technology whiz and family fixer.

Where are you? the text read.

Connor's thumbs flew across the screen. *Pop's house. You?*

Club Destiny. Jess is here. So is Vasquez. You may want to come down.

Connor tipped the chair over in his haste to get out the door. His heart raced as he lunged outside, the door slamming behind him.

"I need men," he snapped at the guy stationed outside. "Three. One of them needs to be Ricky. Meet me at the car."

The guard nodded, speaking into his earpiece before Connor could even stride through the cobblestoned courtyard. He swung open the iron gate that led to the driveway, and by the time he reached his Range Rover, there were three of his father's best men jogging to catch up.

"You're shotgun," Ricky said as Connor moved toward the driver's side. He nodded and backtracked to the passenger side while the other two henchmen piled in the backseat.

"Where're we going, and what's happened?" Ricky asked as he started the car and backed out of the driveway, crusher fines flying beneath the big tires.

"Club Destiny," Connor answered, his heart racing. "Vasquez is there, and so is Jess."

Ricky just nodded, moving a hand to his inside breast pocket in reflex. Connor knew a Glock rested there, as did one in the waistband of his own jeans. He hoped they wouldn't need to use them, but when it came to Jess's safety, he wouldn't pause to think about it. He'd never killed, but he would in a hot second for the only woman he'd ever loved.

Chapter Six

Connor strode to the back door of the nightclub and pounded on the heavy metal door. It was opened by a large bouncer, gun drawn.

"Oh, sorry, Mr. MacFarlane," the man said, lowering the weapon immediately.

"Full house tonight?" Connor asked as he moved past the man, his three henchmen following in his wake.

"Yes, sir."

"You know Alejandro Vasquez?" Connor asked.

The bouncer rubbed a hand across his short, rough hair. "Yes, sir."

"He tries to leave this way, you stop him, got it?"

The man looked profoundly uncomfortable, and Connor stifled the urge to toss him against the wall of the dark hallway they were crammed in.

"I really need to talk to the boss, Mr. MacFarlane. We don't have any problems with Vasquez. I'm not sure he wants to invite it now."

Connor said to hell with restraint and pinned the guy against the wall, forearm across his windpipe. The bouncer didn't even fight back, his eyes wide in his round face.

"This club isn't in Vasquez territory, is it?" Connor hissed in the man's face.

"No, sir," the bouncer choked out.

"Then it's not Vasquez you need to be making nice with. You got that?"

The guy nodded as well as he could with half his air being cut off.

Connor released him and shook out his arm. "Now do as you're damn well told and not a word to anyone that I'm here."

The bouncer nodded again, taking up his spot next to the back door as Connor and his men moved away down the hall.

As he walked, Connor texted Finn. *I'm coming in the back. Where is Vasquez?*

Finn replied in seconds. *Main level, east side of dance floor. Still chatting up her friend Carmen. Jess is in the bathroom.*

WTF?! Connor typed as his blood pressure ratcheted up another notch. Anyone could get her back there.

As the dots on the screen indicated Finn was responding, Connor and his men reached the club, entering through a small door behind the coatroom.

"You two," Connor commanded, "east side of the dance floor. Vasquez is there talking to a girl. Send her away, get him and his guys out of here." He turned to Ricky. "Jess is in the bathroom. You're with me."

Ricky nodded as the other two men moved away, shuffling clubgoers aside the way only large, armed men can.

Connor and Ricky crossed the coatroom and entered another hall with glow-in-the-dark art on the walls and a line of women and the occasional man leaning against the walls vaping, talking, and drinking.

When he reached the door to the women's room, Connor muttered, "Excuse me," to a couple of girls blocking the door.

One of them smirked as she eyed him up and down. "Um, that's the ladies', hottie."

"Yeah, I left something inside," he replied before he swung open the door.

A couple of girls yelped when he and Ricky strode into the lounge that preceded the actual bathroom stalls. One of the girls had a small mirror on her lap as she snorted lines. "Oh shit!" she screeched. "Cops!"

"Get out," Connor said, giving her a harsh look. She and her two friends jumped and ran, leaving the coke and paraphernalia behind. Another couple of girls scurried past him and out the door. Connor marched into the adjacent bathroom, where he was confronted with a curvy brunette applying lipstick at the mirror.

"Got her," he said to Ricky over his shoulder.

Ricky nodded. "I'll be outside," he answered before turning and exiting the restroom.

Connor leaned a shoulder against the doorframe between the lounge and bathroom. "You knew I was coming."

Jess looked at him, her beautiful lips shiny and dark red. She turned back to the mirror, rubbed her lips together a couple of times, then put the lipstick back in her purse, moving as if she had all the time in the world.

"Once Finn told me who Vasquez was, I figured you'd be here soon." She turned back and rested her butt against the granite countertop, glaring at him with her vivid blue eyes.

Connor's arms were crossed, and his lungs were tight with fury. He knew this wasn't her fault, knew if he were only normal, she'd never have to go through this, but her defiance was enough to make him crazy.

"And so you figured until I got here, it'd be a good time to go to the one place Finn couldn't keep you safe?"

Her mask of defiance slipped for a split second, but then it was back in place, her eyes blazing, jaw stubborn and set.

"It's a public place. No one's going to gun me down in the middle of a night club."

"No," he answered, his own expression rigid and determined. "They'll just corner you in the bathroom here, shoot you full of sedatives, and drag you out the front door looking like any other club girl who OD'd on a Friday night."

Her skin paled in the fluorescent lighting of the bathroom.

"You're an asshole," she hissed, pushing off the counter, her arms wrapped even tighter around her middle.

He took a step toward her, making it clear she'd have to get around him to leave. "No, I'm truthful." His voice softened a touch. "Vasquez came clear down into MacFarlane territory to go to a club that's not special in any way on the very night the woman I love is here for her best friend's birthday party. That's too much coincidence for me, Jess."

Her breath shuddered as she released it, her eyes still hard and angry.

He stepped closer again. "These guys…" He ran a hand through his hair, wishing he could soft-pedal it to her, but knowing he couldn't. "They won't hesitate. They won't go easy on you. They don't care who you are or what you are. It doesn't matter to them that your old man depends on you, or you have friends who need you. To get back at me, they will follow you, they will take you, they will torture you, and they will kill you."

They stood there, eyes locked, the faucet on one of the nearby sinks dripping as the bass from the club music boomed softly in the distance. He saw when it happened—when she broke—and it tore his heart apart. But there wasn't an option. He'd rather her hate him forever than end up in pieces in Lake Michigan.

"Damn you," she whispered.

"I know," he answered, because he was starting to realize it himself. Beginning to understand how messed up *his* world had made *her* world.

"I'm not even your girlfriend," she muttered, holding a hand to her forehead.

"They don't care."

She cleared her throat, hopelessness written in the way her shoulders slumped and her gaze dropped to the floor. "What am I supposed to do now?"

"I will fix this," he said, finally stepping close enough to pull her into his arms. He softly kissed the top of her head. "But I need to talk to Cian and figure out how. In the meantime, you're going to have to let me assign one of the guys to you. I can't have stuff like this going on. It'll kill me, Jess."

She nodded into his chest.

"You know Ricky," he said, setting her away from him so he could look her in the eye. "Let him shadow you for the next few days, and Cian and I will come up with a plan. I don't want to go to war with Vasquez, but it's pretty clear he's not over what happened with his sister."

A wry smile twisted Jess's beautiful mouth. "That makes two of us," she said softly.

Connor just pulled her into his arms again and held her in silence. He'd made a mess, and now he was going to have to fix it. But more importantly, he felt like something was going to have to change, because he was only twenty-four years old, and already, he felt like an old man.

**

"What do you mean you have a bodyguard?" Carmen shouted into the phone as Jess pulled groceries out of the bag and put things away in the cabinets at her dad's house. The phone lay on the counter on speaker, and Jess was relieved she didn't have it pressed to her ear when Carmen went to decibels best heard by dogs.

"That was Alejandro Vasquez and his guys at the club last night. And he wasn't there to find a hookup."

Carmen made a disgusted sound. "As if cheating on you wasn't bad enough, he had to pick Vasquez's sister. I swear, Jess, I don't know how you can stand to be in the same room with him much less accept one of his men as a bodyguard."

Jess sighed as she put a can of soup away. "Look, I know what he did was horrible. Trust me. And it still hurts, but in a way, I think it was what needed to happen. You know I was unhappy, and I don't think I'd have been able to break it off with him otherwise." She paused, looking out the window at the kids playing soccer in the street outside her dad's row house. "I think deep down, he knew what I needed and that I couldn't do it myself. He made himself the bad guy so I wouldn't feel guilty. He made it easy for me. He sort of did me a favor."

"God, Jess, that's the most convoluted way of explaining a guy being a cheating dick I've ever heard."

Jess smiled to herself. She knew it sounded nuts to anyone else, but in her heart, she knew even if Connor wasn't conscious of what he was doing, in his own twisted, bizarre way, he'd been trying to give her what she needed—freedom.

"Well, I admit, he could have chosen his floozy better. But the fact is, until he and Cian bring Vasquez to heel, I'm not going to turn down the security detail."

Carmen snorted. "As if he gave you a choice."

"And there's that." Jess laughed.

The front door slammed, and Jess heard her father's heavy footsteps as he made his way toward the kitchen in the back of the house.

"Hey, I gotta go," she told Carmen. "I'll text you later and maybe we can grab some breakfast before work tomorrow."

As she disconnected the call, Sean walked into the room. He was dressed in his usual track pants and hooded sweatshirt, his frame still wide and imposing even though his bald head and sagging cheeks showed his age to be on the far end of his middle years. Jess had been a late event in Sean's life, and one her mother hadn't stuck around for after the first couple of years.

"What the hell's one of Robbie's guys doing hanging out on my steps?" Sean demanded as he scowled, hands on his hips.

Jessica folded up the empty grocery bag and bussed the old man on the cheek as she walked by him to slide the bag in the gap between the fridge and wall with others.

"He's hanging out with me for a few days," she said.

Sean stood in the middle of the worn vinyl kitchen floor and rotated to follow her as she busied herself cleaning up dishes from the drying rack and pulled out the ingredients for biscuits from the pantry.

"You dating him?" Sean asked.

"No! Of course not. You think Connor would let one of his guys date me?"

Sean threw his hands up in the air. "I don't know much, do I? I don't know why there's one of Robbie's men on my front stoop. I don't know why you and Connor MacFarlane broke up. I don't know where you got the money to pay the utilities at the gym the other day. I feel like a fucking visitor in my own life."

Jess sighed and rubbed her forehead where a headache threatened.

"Dad, don't you trust me?"

He stepped closer, his big hand closing around her upper arm. His fingers were knobby from the many times he'd jammed and broken the knuckles, and the pinky on his left hand wouldn't bend at all.

"Little girl, you know I trust you with my life, but you need to trust me too. I may be old, but I'm not dead. You don't need to do everything yourself. Haven't I taken good care of you for twenty-four years? Do you think I can't anymore?"

She stepped close and put her arms around his waist. "Of course you can take care of me, Dad. I just thought maybe it would be good if I took care of you for a while."

He rested his chin on the top of her head. "Oh, Jessie girl," he said softly. "I worry about you so much. I thought maybe the MacFarlane boy would be the one to marry you and take care of you after I'm gone. Why'd you break up with him? Hmm? Can't you at least tell me that much?"

She pulled back and looked in his faded blue eyes. "He cheated on me. But you had to have known that. Everyone in the whole neighborhood knows it."

He stroked a hand down her hair. "I don't listen to gossip. You know that." His eyes were sad, and she watched his Adam's apple move as he swallowed. "He still loves you, though, don't he?"

"Yeah, but it doesn't matter. I can't live that life."

"So, why's Ricky O'Malley on my stoop?"

Jess pulled away, walking back to the mixing bowl and measuring out flour and baking powder from memory as she talked. "Alejandro Vasquez is pissed at Connor, and he was in the club where we had Carmen's birthday last night. Connor freaked out and told me I'm stuck with Ricky for a few days."

Sean's hands flexed into fists as he began to pace the small kitchen. "That fecker approach you?" he asked as his normally mild Irish accent grew heavier.

"No," Jess answered as she turned to face him. "But he and his guys were hitting on Carmen and some of the other girls."

"Maybe I need to take some of the guys from the gym and pay the motherfecker a visit."

Jessica rolled her eyes. "Dad. It's not that big a deal. Honest. Just let Connor and his brothers deal with it. Ricky will watch my back, and it'll all be fine."

He looked at her from under his heavy brows, then pointed a finger at her emphatically. "You tell me if you see Vasquez or any of his men again, you hear me?"

"Yes, Dad." She refrained from more eye rolling. God help her, how she dealt with all these Irish men and their testosterone, she'd never know. "But he won't. It's not a problem."

"Maybe I need to talk to Robbie about this. The boys may not have told him." Sean had started his life in the US working for Robbie long before Jess was born, but when his fists had been more useful in an amateur ring than as an enforcer, Robbie had been good enough to release him from his duties, and Sean had gone on to open the gym.

"Shit, no, Dad. Don't get in the middle of their family crap." As if Robbie gave a damn what happened to her anyway. Jess knew Sean thought of Robbie as an old friend, but the Robbie she'd come to know while she was Connor's girlfriend wouldn't lift a finger to help her unless there was something in it for him. Robbie could barely manage to care about his own sons, much less someone else's daughter.

"Fine, I won't say nothing right now, but I better not hear about Vasquez hanging out in this neighborhood."

"Okay, okay," Jess answered impatiently, desperate to change the subject. "Do you want gravy with your biscuits? I thought I'd make you some for dinner since I'm here. And maybe we can invite Ricky in to have a bite with us?"

Sean muttered something under his breath but then started toward the front door. "Fine. We'll invite him to eat. I guess it's the least I can do since he's looking after you."

Jessica pulled the flour back out to double the recipe. Some days, she thought no matter what she did, she'd be spending the rest of her life cooking for one Irish man or another. If she was being honest, she understood why her mom had left. She just wished her mom had cared enough to take her along.

**

Cian paced alongside the loading dock of the empty warehouse, his expensive shoes making a slight thumping noise as they hit the concrete. He'd come from mass with his parents, and that always meant button-up shirts and dress shoes, just like when they were little boys. He checked the time on his watch and saw his meeting was now six minutes late. One more minute, he told himself, then he would go. But of course, at that very moment, headlights came weaving through the empty parking lot, a late-model American sedan bouncing over the myriad potholes and cracks in the surface of the pavement.

When the car finally pulled to a stop, headlights pinning Cian to the wall he'd leaned against, he'd pulled his gun from the discreet shoulder holster he kept it in and let it dangle casually at his side, behind the edge of his pants.

The car doors opened, and dark figures emerged from the driver's and passenger's sides.

"You want to turn off the lights, or did you intend to send out engraved invitations to this?" Cian asked.

The driver swore but opened the car door and doused the headlights, allowing Cian's eyes to adjust to the new darkness as the men once again walked toward him.

He deftly tucked the gun into the back waistband of his pants, slid his hands into his front pockets, and waited quietly.

"Make this quick, MacFarlane. We have better things to do with our time," the passenger of the car said.

"Just relax, Bruce," Cian answered, not moving from where he lounged against the bricks. No matter what he might feel on the inside, he looked like he had ice water in his veins. The only time Cian had come close to losing it was long ago and far away, in another warehouse with his father in his face and a trusted employee bound to a chair.

The federal agent flipped him off.

Cian shook his head slightly to clear the memory. "You guys have a big date planned or something? Don going to take you out dining and dancing in your new pink cocktail dress?"

Bruce did what Bruce always did and lunged at Cian. Don did what he always did and stopped him.

"Will you quit taunting him, MacFarlane? Surely you have worthier prey to play with."

Cian nodded his agreement. "True. He's not worth the trouble."

"You called this shindig," Bruce spat as he pulled a pack of cigarettes out of the breast pocket of his jacket. "What do you have for us?"

Cian strode a few steps away from the men. "I want to know why you've got guys sitting outside my place of business twenty-four seven. The whole point of what I'm doing here—risking my life, I might add—is so my family doesn't have you assholes breathing down our necks all the time."

He heard Bruce snort, and Don chuckled in response.

"No, MacFarlane, the reason you do this is so your old man and Liam don't spend the rest of their lives in federal lockup getting it up the ass twice a day."

Cian's pulse flared and his stomach turned as he spun on the men. He had Don's tie in his fist so fast, all Bruce could do was stumble back before Cian's elbow landed in his eye.

"Listen to me," Cian growled in the shorter man's face. "I could make you disappear into thin air. They'd never find a trace of you, and your wife would have nothing to bury. That sweet daughter of yours would never know what it was like to have Daddy walk her down the aisle, and your fucking golden doodle wouldn't have anyone to go to the park down the block with anymore. You think because I cooperate with you that means you own me? Think again."

He shoved Don away, ignoring the coughing and wheezing that followed. Bruce stood a few feet away, gun drawn, ready to shoot if Cian took things too far, but in spite of what the agents might think, Cian would never take it too far. He was always in control. Did it make him sick when they talked about his brother in prison? Yes. Did it make him lose control? No. But he had to flex his muscle, make some threats, play the game the way they expected if he wanted to survive this and keep his brothers safe.

He turned to face Bruce, holding his hands out from his sides. "You going to do anything with that or just pretend you're an actual cop?"

Bruce slowly uncocked the weapon, lowering it when Don muttered he was fine.

"Is someone going to answer me about the surveillance on my place?" Cian asked. "I need to get back to work so my men don't wonder where I am."

He saw the two agents glance at each other and knew then he wasn't going to like what came next.

Bruce leaned down and picked up his unlit cigarette from the asphalt where he'd dropped it during the scuffle. He put it between his lips and pulled out a lighter. After he'd taken a long drag and blown the smoke to one side, he spoke, eyes glittery in the dim light from an adjacent light pole.

"We made a deal you'd gather information for us, and we'd let your old man and Liam off the hook. We never said we wouldn't continue to investigate MacFarlane activities."

Cian took a deep breath, because now he did feel like losing it.

"You understand if you're on me all the time, you'll make it so I can't get you information on anyone? No one will be doing business with me if I have a tail twenty-four seven. You wanted me to inform on associates and the Vasquez family. I've been doing that, but I can't do it with feds glued to my ass."

Don cleared his throat, but his voice was still rough. "What you've been giving us isn't enough."

Shit. Cian had been waiting for this day. Sharing information that couldn't be traced back to him or implicate his family wasn't easy. He walked a fine line between giving the feds enough info to keep them engaged while not giving them anything of real value. He'd obviously erred on the side of too much caution, something that wouldn't have surprised his old man a bit.

"I can't make information appear out of thin air—unless you want me to start planting things, which, considering it's the Vasquez family we're talking about, wouldn't bother me in the slightest."

"Look, we know there are limits on what you're going to be able to get on the Vasquez operation. Unless you have someone on the inside, you can't get the kinds of details we need to make significant charges stick."

He folded his arms, feeling the heightened pulse pounding there under his wrists.

"Start small. Isn't that what you guys do? Bring them in on whatever you have so you can get search warrants and subpoenas? I've given you things that would get the ball rolling. Even without a fancy law degree, I know that."

"The bureau's sick of the resources it takes to make convictions that don't slow you scumbags down," Don said with surprisingly little animosity. "They want bigger convictions, bigger fish. They want to show a real impact. We've got the Senate Judiciary pushing hard for progress on organized crime and the opioid crisis."

Cian frowned.

"Sorry." Don shrugged.

"What's it going to take to get your men off my back?" Cian asked, suddenly so tired, he felt as though he could go to sleep and never wake up.

Don shot a look at Bruce, who quietly turned and walked back to the car, where he pulled out his phone and began a conversation of some sort.

Don stepped closer to Cian as though he had things to say he didn't want Bruce to hear, but Cian knew it was all a ploy to seem as if they had a level of intimacy they didn't. The feds and their constant head games. Sometimes he really believed they thought he was stupid.

"Look, I personally don't have a problem with the info you've been giving us. It's all panned out. You haven't screwed us over once, which is pretty rare for informants at your level."

"But?"

"But like I said, it's not enough, and no matter what you do, you can't get us what we need on the Vasquez organization."

That was when Cian finally got it. "You've found someone inside to flip on Vasquez."

Don just looked at him.

Cian's chest squeezed, and sweat broke out along his hairline. He knew what came next.

"And what do you want from *me* now?" he asked, only because he needed it said out loud before he told them to screw themselves.

"MacFarlane info," Don said blandly, as if he wasn't asking Cian to betray his own flesh and blood.

Cian swore under his breath before he leaned in and spat in Don's face, "Fuck. You."

"I'm sure the girls think you're very pretty, but I prefer tits."

Cian growled before he began to pace in a tight line up and down in front of Don. Out of the corner of his eye, he could see Bruce watching him from where he leaned back against the car, probably ready to shoot him in the head if the mood struck right.

"We're done here, then," Cian said, stopping to pull his car keys out of his pocket.

"That's fine," Don said before turning to look behind him. "Hey!" he called to Bruce. "Was it Finn or Connor we caught on camera making that big buy last month?"

"I don't know, man, which one has his cute girl-friend's initials tattooed on his forearm?"

Cian's heart sank to somewhere south of his knees. *Connor.*

"Yeah, that's right," Don said snapping his fin-gers. "Connor. The baby, right?" he asked Cian.

"No," Cian snarled. "You will not get anywhere near Connor." He'd given up trying to be cool. His self-control had officially snapped.

"I'm sorry, but we have him taking a shipment from the Martinezes down in Albuquerque. On cam-era. Cash passed. The whole nine yards. It's like a dream come true."

"You son of a bitch," Cian whispered, not even looking at the agent.

"So, ball's in your court. Here's the offer. Immun-ity for you and Connor. Everyone else is fair game, and you'll give us what we need to put Liam, Robbie, and your lieutenants in prison for life. We want the Devils shut down or at least crippled to the point it's down for years, not months."

Nausea rolled through Cian, his hands tingling as he flexed them over and over again. This wasn't how it was supposed to go down. He needed to keep them *all* safe. Let his father take the fall and rot in prison until he died alone, Cian couldn't care less about what happened to Robbie. But how was he supposed to choose one brother over the others? No. He simply couldn't. He had to get all three of them out, no matter what.

"What about Finn?" he asked, voice rough with resignation.

Don shrugged. "No one cares much what happens to him. If he gets caught in the net, fine. If not, it's no deal breaker. We know he doesn't have what it takes to run the show. If the other players are out, Finn's rendered irrelevant."

Jesus. His tenderhearted, talented, brilliant brother reduced to "irrelevant." It was shocking, even to someone as jaded as him.

"Immunity won't be of much use to us when everyone finds out I've cut a deal for me and Connor. If you think my old man can't or won't get to us from a prison cell, you don't know him as well as you think you do."

"Oh, did I forget the other part? Witness protection," Don said, a smug smile on his shiny face.

Cian sighed as he quickly shuffled through the options. If he could get witness protection, Connor would be out for good. Then he'd have to figure out what to do about Liam and Finn. But maybe one less brother to worry about was the best choice under the circumstances. Lighten the load for a bit. Give him some breathing space to calculate the next move. It wasn't as if he had a choice anyway.

"Fine," he finally told Don. "Witness protection for Connor…" He thought for a moment. "And his girlfriend, Jessica O'Neil."

"Thought they split up," Don said, demonstrating once again his vast knowledge of all things MacFarlane. It would be a little creepy if Cian didn't know the man was paid to keep track.

"It's complicated," Cian said. "But in case, I want her included in his package."

"Fine. New identity for the old boxer's daughter too."

"It's going to take me a while to get you what you need—financials, emails, that kind of thing."

Don nodded. "I want the overview of the activities first, then I'll tell you what evidence is useful and what isn't."

"And in the meantime? The surveillance?"

"I think we'll keep it right where it is," Don said. "It's proven to be useful for all sorts of reasons."

Cian swallowed the bile and nodded sharply. Then, without another word, he walked to his car and started it up. Five miles away, on a quiet street a few blocks from Union Park he pulled the car over to the curb, turned off the engine, and leaned his head against the steering wheel as a single tear rolled down his cheek.

Chapter Seven

"Where the hell have you been?" Connor griped as Cian strolled into the private balcony at Banshee at midnight.

"Nice to see you too," Cian muttered as he slid into the booth where his three brothers sat, and sank back into the cushions, exhausted.

"You look like shit," Liam noted as he held his empty tumbler aloft and gestured for one of the waitresses to get him another.

"Thanks, nice to see you too," Cian answered.

"Sharla!" Liam called out after the girl who was on her way to get his drink. "Grab the whole bottle and an extra glass for Cian." She nodded and went on to the bar.

"We've been waiting for forty-five minutes," Connor continued. "You left without taking anyone with you. What the hell is up?"

Cian sighed, rubbing a hand across his eyes for a moment. "Nothing. There was a little dustup at one of the dispensaries—the one on Lake Street, an easy walk right here in the neighborhood. I thought it'd be nice to get a break, go outside. And yeah, get away from the guys for a few minutes—so sue me."

Liam scowled. "I told you owning those medical MJ shops was going to be more headache than it was worth."

"Sixty-seven million dollars," Finn interjected. "Since the authorization passed the legislature, legal cannabis in Illinois has grossed sixty-seven million dollars. Those three little shops of ours made a three-hundred percent profit in the last eighteen months. It's worth it."

Liam flipped his younger brother off, and Finn just smirked and shook his head. The brawn and the brain of the family often tussled in wars of words, and Finn invariably won. Luckily, Liam might be rough, but he wasn't cruel, and he loved Finn as much as he did Cian or Connor. Cian sometimes thought Liam said the things he did in part to give Finn the platform for demonstrating his intellect. Finn didn't get a lot of attention from their father, nor was he particularly popular with the men. When Liam set him up to shine, Cian doubted it was by accident.

The waitress placed a large bottle of Connemara whiskey down on the table and handed Cian an empty tumbler with a look of sympathy. Sharla had been at the club long enough to know when Cian was having a rough night.

"So what's the big emergency?" Cian asked as Liam poured him a generous amount of whiskey and pressed the bottle into his free hand.

Connor's brow pulled down over his eyes, and Cian couldn't help but remember that same look on his face when he was a tiny boy, running to get Cian's help when Finn or Liam had teased him to the point he'd snapped. The ten years between them made Cian feel more like Connor's father than his brother sometimes. He remembered every moment of the kid's life—the good, the not so good, the completely ridiculous. Something in his chest lightened a touch when he thought about Connor and Jess somewhere far, far away—safe, happy, in love.

"Jess and her friends were at Club Destiny celebrating a birthday when Alejandro Vasquez showed up."

Cian sat up straighter. "What?" he ground out.

Liam nodded. "I vote we head out there tonight when they aren't expecting it, take four or five of the boys, and slam some heads together. Even if we don't get to Vasquez himself, we'll make an impression, show him he can't come onto our turf and mess with our women without consequences." As the family's head enforcer, Liam enjoyed a good rousting whenever he could work one in.

Cian's mind started turning, as it always did. "Did Vasquez touch her?"

Connor shook his head. "No. Finn was there and watched her until I came with Ricky and a couple of the other guys. They escorted Vasquez off the premises, and I made it clear to Jimmy McGuire that he's not to let Vasquez in the door next time."

"So Jess is okay?" Cian asked, taking a long swallow of his whiskey and relishing the way it burned all the way to his empty gut.

"For now," Connor answered. "I left Ricky with her, and he's sticking until we figure this out."

"So you think Vasquez was just playing games?" Cian looked at Finn.

"Hard to say," Finn answered. "He definitely knew who she was, didn't approach her directly but made a point of chatting up some of her friends. He had a couple of his guys with him, and they kept a close watch on Jess and her party, but once they saw me, they stepped it back."

"We have to do something," Connor announced, looking each of his brothers in the eye one by one. "He's gunning for me, and he's going to use Jess to do it."

"Exactly," Liam agreed, nodding enthusiastically. "That's why we need to head out there tonight. Make a clear statement we won't put up with this."

"I'm not going to war with the Vasquez family over this," Cian announced. "We have more than enough on our plates right now with these new web sales. We don't need to be in a street fight on top of it all."

"I don't care about whether we go to war or not," Connor interjected, "but I won't have Jess harmed. Not when it's my fault we're here at all."

Cian looked at Connor, one eyebrow raised. "It wasn't your finest moment."

Connor hung his head. "I know."

"Hope Vasquez's sister was a good lay, that's all I can say," Liam muttered.

Cian tipped his chin up at Finn across the table. "What do you think?" he asked. Cian had never felt the need for a consiglieri to consult with. His father still had his eye on the business, and with three younger brothers, Cian was always being scrutinized.

But when he did want someone else to chime in, it was Finn he went to.

Finn MacFarlane was soft-spoken, thoughtful, sensitive, even in the midst of a brawling, testosterone-fueled pack of Irishmen. If analysis needed to be done, it was Finn who would do it. If a creative solution was sought, it was Finn who would provide it. And if anyone had a chance at making something of themselves outside the violent, gritty world the MacFarlane boys had grown up in, Finn was the one who did.

Finn cocked his head at Connor the way he always did when thinking about something, mulling it over in his oversized brain. "Why don't you negotiate?" he asked.

"Negotiate what?" Connor asked. "We going to offer up Jess if he'll stay out of our territory?" He scoffed in disgust.

Cian held up a hand to quiet Connor, his gaze never leaving Finn's. "Continue."

Finn gave him a small smile. "If we knew something that was useful to Vasquez, we could use it as a peace offering. Trade it for his promise that he'll forgive Connor's indiscretion. He's been insulted, and he needs to have his pride assuaged. Once that happens, he'll get over it and move on."

"Ass-wayjed?" Liam snorted. "What does that even mean?"

"He needs to feel like he's had a win after Connor embarrassed him," Cian clarified.

"That's all fine and good," Connor added, "but we don't have anything to trade."

A smile spread across Cian's face. "Actually, we do."

"What's that?" Even as he asked the question, Liam's attention diverted to a waitress walking by whose short, tight skirt revealed the lacy tops of thigh-high stockings. His lips turned up in delight.

"Word is there's a rat inside Vasquez's organization, and the feds are going to nail Vasquez with the rat's help."

"How do you know these things?" Connor asked, shaking his head.

Cian shrugged. "Pop has a lot of contacts, even some inside the FBI." Luckily for Cian, it was true, and he frequently had information that seemed to come out of thin air, so this tidbit fit right in with his typical patterns.

"Then go to Vasquez with it," Finn said. "Suggest a deal. Make him promise he'll let Connor off the hook."

Cian mulled it over for a moment. He'd have to meet with Vasquez without the feds finding out. Not a simple task, but certainly not impossible. If it would get Vasquez off his brother's ass and protect Jess, it was definitely worth it. In addition, if it queered the deal between the Vasquez rat and the feds, it might make Cian valuable to the FBI again, give him some more leverage than he currently had—which was next to none.

"Okay. But we need the meet-up to be absolutely confidential."

"And how do we know one of the men he brings with him isn't the FBI informant?" Connor asked.

Liam reached out and snagged the hand of the waitress he'd been eyeing, his attention lost once the details of a plan didn't involve brawling or women.

Cian shrugged. "Only one way—neither one of us brings men."

That got Liam's attention, and he slapped the waitress on the ass to send her on her way.

"Abso-fucking-lutely not," he growled.

"Hear me out," Cian said, one eyebrow raised at his brute of a younger brother.

"I don't need to," Liam said. "There is no way you're going into a meeting with Vasquez without guards. He won't agree to it anyway, so it's pointless to talk about." He put his tumbler down with a little more force than was strictly necessary, looking pleased that he'd wrapped up the issue.

"He will agree," Cian said simply. "He wants respect after Connor disrespected him so badly, but he doesn't want a war any more than I do. Everyone knows the feds have been amping things up the last two years. No one wants to draw attention to things right now. A war would do just that. Vasquez is an asshole, but he's not an idiot."

Liam scowled and shook his head. "I can't let you meet without backup. I *won't* let you meet without backup."

Cian's eyes narrowed, and his voice grew soft but cold. "You think I can't handle myself? As if you haven't seen me do what's necessary before? I'm in charge of this family. It's my job to make sure the rest of you are taken care of. This will get Connor in the clear again, protect Jess, let the two of them finally relax. If you think I'm somehow not capable of doing my job here, you'd better say so now."

Liam's gaze on Cian was sharp, knowing. "I never said that. I know you can handle yourself."

"Good, then it's settled." Cian looked at Finn. "You set up the meeting. Explain we want to make things right after what Connor did. And make sure there's no way the feds can trace either of us when it happens."

Finn nodded. "Consider it done."

Connor let out a long, slow breath. "You sure about this?

"Yeah. It has to be him and me, one on one. He'll appreciate the fact that I'm the head of the family. It shows him more respect." Cian put a hand on Connor's shoulder, noticing the look of worry on his handsome face. "I wouldn't do this if I didn't think it was safe. Finn's instincts are right, Vasquez needs to feel like he got his due somehow. I doubt he cares a lot which way he gets it."

At least that was what Cian hoped. Otherwise, he wouldn't be around to get his brothers out of the family business, and that would be Cian's greatest failure.

**

Lila nervously swiped at the screen of her tablet, as she sat alone at the long wood table. The back room of the old pub Robbie MacFarlane owned smelled of stale beer and peanuts, and she could hear the voices of the bartender and the waitress on the other side of the door. The pub itself was nearly empty. A few older Irishmen had been playing dominoes when she'd walked in, and what looked to be a commodities broker of some sort was drowning his sorrows in the corner.

Most of the coordination for the Rogue-MacFarlane project had been done by her and Finn, so she'd only met with Cian a total of three times, and she hoped she'd answered or anticipated all his concerns. He made her uncomfortable—in good and bad ways. He was dangerous, she knew—she'd asked around. But he was also smart, straightforward, and seemingly a very savvy businessman. While part of her was afraid of what he'd do if she failed in her assignment, another part didn't want to disappoint him. It was a confusing mixture of feelings and one Lila was unused to.

The door to the room swung open, and in strode the man himself. He wore his usual dark colors, but dressier than the last few times she'd seen him—his suit was obviously custom cut, and his high-thread-count dress shirt was snowy white. As he entered, he shot his cuffs, rolling his powerful shoulders and giving her a glimpse of polished platinum cuff links. As she stood to greet him in her black wool jumper dress, black wool knee-high stockings, and red-and-black Mary Janes, Lila felt like a little girl in comparison.

"Lila from Rogue," Cian said, his voice like velvet, sending shivers down her spine. "You're early." He grinned, and her heart raced.

She narrowed her eyes, pressing her lips together, hoping he couldn't tell how discombobulated he made her feel.

"I take my work very seriously, Mr. MacFarlane," she answered.

"I've never doubted it," he said, also serious. He gestured for her to retake her seat, then chose the one next to her, rotating his chair so he could look at her full on. She fussed with her tablet screen, unable to meet his gaze.

"You don't need to be nervous," he told her softly. "My father only cares that the job gets done. He'll not understand any of the details, and my brother Finn says you've done an excellent job preparing the systems."

She nodded, finally looking at him, but then away again just as quickly.

"I'm not nervous," she lied.

He rested one arm on the table, leaning into her space, his head tipping toward her in an intimate gesture.

"I've missed our coffee dates," he said, his voice gravelly and deep. Lila felt everything inside her become heated and pliable.

"They were business meetings, not dates," she corrected primly.

"Call them what you will, I enjoyed them. Much more than any other business meeting I've had."

She couldn't help the smile that snuck across her face then, along with the blush she felt heat her cheeks. Cian chuckled softly but pulled back, turning his chair to the table as the door opened and several other men entered.

Lila looked up to see an older man with white hair followed by two younger men and Xavier. She could have picked out the MacFarlane patriarch in a crowded room. He was somewhat rough, but wore authority like a second skin, every mannerism dripping with the assumption that his orders would be followed. He was shorter than Cian, but she could see the resemblance immediately. Robbie MacFarlane still cut a powerful figure, his physique solid, his blue eyes sharp, his clothing casual but immaculate.

Behind him was a much younger man, very like Cian in appearance, but with darker eyes and a certain lightness to his demeanor that Lila doubted Cian had ever worn. The final MacFarlane brother, Finn, was thinner than Cian and an inch or two shorter as well. His hair was in need of a trim, but beneath the floppy bangs were eyes the most beautiful shade of green Lila had ever seen.

Cian stood as the men worked their way into the room and selected seats at the table. Only when his father had sat did Cian sit back down as well.

"Pop," he began. "I'd like to introduce you to the Rogue staff member who will be presenting the system to us. This is Lila Rodriguez. Lila, this is my father"—he gestured toward the silver fox—"and my brother Connor"—the one with darker eyes. "You know Finn, of course."

Lila smiled and nodded to the head of the table on her left. "It's a pleasure to meet you, Mr. MacFarlane."

He gave her a charming smile and an extra dose of Irish brogue. "They make computer geeks much prettier than they did in my day," he joked, but his blue eyes were cold, and a frisson of discomfort crawled down her spine as he reached out and patted her hand where it lay on the table.

She heard Cian clear his throat on her other side, and then Connor was leaning over the table from where he sat on his father's other side. He extended his hand. "It's nice to meet you, Lila," he said. She shook his hand while Finn gave her a sweet smile and a nod of his head.

"So," Robbie said, turning his attention to his eldest son. "Let's see how you're going to earn the family more money."

Lila felt Cian stiffen beside her, but she kept her gaze forward. She'd dealt with enough alpha businessmen in her line of work to understand Robbie was going to be a jerk now. From what Xavier had told her, Robbie had a heart condition that had necessitated his retirement. Cian was officially in charge of the family business, but Robbie was the man behind the curtain, keeping tabs, manipulating events, and still very much the source of approval that any new undertaking would require.

But it wasn't Cian who answered Robbie. It was Finn.

"I can tell you how it's all going to work, Pop," he said, leaning into the table.

Robbie raised a brow, his head swiveling slowly toward Finn's side of the table.

"Finn has managed all this," Cian said quickly. "He developed the shipping methods, and he's met several times with Lila and Xavier about technical details I don't understand."

Finn continued to look at their father, his face calm and determined. Lila could feel the tension in the room, and watched as Robbie leaned back in his chair, his barrel chest expanding as he took a long, slow breath.

Across from her, Connor's gaze was pinned to the tabletop. At the opposite end from Robbie, Xavier was otherwise engaged with his phone, obviously leaving Lila to dangle along with Finn.

"So, let's hear it," Robbie finally said, and the room gave a collective sigh of relief.

Finn launched into an explanation of the internet sales, with asides from Lila regarding technical security measures. Cian and Connor chimed in with details about the packaging and distribution.

When they were done, Robbie looked at Cian. "You really think this'll work?"

Cian nodded slowly. "I trust Finn's judgment."

"That's not what I asked," Robbie fired back.

Cian's gaze checked left to Lila, and she gave him a sympathetic smile. His father's disdain for Finn was obvious.

"It'll work," Cian answered evenly. "And it'll earn. A lot."

Xavier finally piped up from the far end of the table. "We sell body parts on the internet," he said. "This is simple by comparison. As long as your people handle the packaging right, this will work."

"It's certainly in your best interest that it does," Robbie shot back. "You're getting a hell of a cut."

Xavier leaned forward, his eyes pinned to the older mobster. "If you're not earning six figures a month in the first three months, I'll cut my percentage in half. How's that?"

Robbie smirked. "Big words from a small man."

Xavier gave him a cold smile. "I know my business, Mr. MacFarlane. This will work, and it will earn. We'll both get very rich from the arrangement."

Robbie gave one sharp nod, then stood abruptly. "All right, then. Do it. Cian, you watch this one personally. I come to you with questions, I want *you* to have the answers." Then he turned to Finn. "This goes south, it's on you, understand? And I can tell you right now, they'd have you for lunch at Menard."

He chuckled darkly, the mention of the state's largest maximum-security prison turning Lila's gut cold.

"I'll handle it all, Pop," Cian interjected before his eyes met Finn's across the table. "I'll be happy to tell you anything you want to know about it."

Finn didn't respond, leaning back in his seat and seeming to shut down after having presented the entire project in great detail.

Before he turned to leave the room, Robbie gave Lila another of his charming smiles and lifted her hand as though he was going to kiss it. "Lovely meeting you," he said. "You make sure to let me know if my boys don't treat you right." Her skin crawled, but she gave him a weak smile in response, and then he was gone, the door shutting behind him.

"Holy shit," Connor breathed as he laid his head down on the table.

Finn smiled. "It wasn't so bad. He didn't throw anything."

"Or punch anyone," Cian added darkly.

"I have to be somewhere," Xavier said, as though no one else in the room had spoken. "Lila, after you wrap this up, can you check on the backup servers? I don't have time today."

"Sure thing," she answered.

Xavier left, his head down, still frantically tapping at his screen. Even for him, he'd been weird and rude, and Lila wondered what he was working on or what had gone wrong at Rogue.

She turned to find all three MacFarlane men looking at her. It was disconcerting. They were all very attractive, but at least two of them were also dangerous as hell. She doubted Finn would harm a fly, although his intellect was dangerous in its own way.

"So, do you have any more questions?" she asked, looking around at each man one at a time.

"You did great," Finn said kindly. "I think we're ready to go as soon as we have a couple of practice runs with the packaging and the dogs we're borrowing."

"You're borrowing dogs?" she asked.

"Yeah," Connor said, his eyes alight with excitement. "A friend of the family has access to a couple of retired drug dogs. We're going to run the packages by them, see what they can find."

Cian chuckled, his laugh gentle and rich. Lila fought the urge to lean into him. "Connor wants one of those dogs for a pet. He's got a serious hard-on for German shepherds."

"They're amazing, man. Have you seen some of the things they can be trained to do?" Connor asked. "I'd get one to bring me beers when I was watching a game, and maybe hide Jess's underwear so she couldn't get dressed when she was at my place."

Finn snorted. "As if you'll ever get Jess naked at your place again in this century."

"Okay!" Cian's voice was firm. "That's enough. We have company, and business to wrap up."

Connor had the decency to flush. "Sorry, Lila," he said, smiling sweetly.

"It's fine," she answered, not able to help grinning at Cian's younger, lighter double. "I can see the appeal of the dogs." She winked at him.

Cian did his throat-clearing thing again, and Connor stopped smiling and sat up straighter, his brows drawing down.

The next few minutes were spent wrapping up. Lila gathered her belongings and said her goodbyes before heading out to the front of the pub.

Things had changed since she'd gone into the meeting. The place had filled up with an eclectic mix of older neighborhood types and young men who looked like they were in the MacFarlane business— big guys, gun holsters apparent on some of them. Irish accents were scattered throughout the voices around the room.

She ignored some of the appraising looks she got as she made her way through the room and exited, turning the corner around the side of the building once she was outside, heading to the parking lot off the back alley.

It was a chilly night, and Lila's breath misted in the air. Though she'd spent her whole life in Chicago, she'd never been a big fan of cold wind. She pulled her scarf closer around her neck, shivering lightly in the damp night. As she got to her little Nissan Leaf, she had to dig through her bag for the keys, cursing herself silently for being so nervous when she'd arrived that she hadn't put them in the usual pocket.

She heard him only a split second before his arms closed around her, one across her chest, pinning her arms to her sides, and the other around her throat, cutting off the air she so desperately needed.

Lila kicked and thrashed, jamming her heel into his shin and stomping on his foot a couple of times, but he was much bigger than her, and she knew, as she gasped frantically for breath and clawed at his arm around her neck, she wasn't going to win.

"Shh, baby," an accented voice hissed in her ear. "Don't fight me, and it'll go a lot easier for you."

She stilled, her heart pumping at ten times its normal rate.

"You be a good girl for Ramon, and I'll make sure they lube up before they pull the train on you."

Lila panicked, thrashing wildly, making pitiful squealing noises with the little air she could pass through her constricted windpipe. But the man only squeezed harder, and she saw stars on the edges of her vision as everything went darker and her throat began to close completely. Then a new voice came from behind her, and the click of a gun being readied.

"Take your hands off her." She recognized Cian's voice, but it carried a deadly quality she'd never heard before. He spoke softly and carefully, but menace laced every word.

Her attacker loosened his hold.

"I said, *now*," Cian emphasized.

Then the man released her completely, and Lila slumped against her car in front of her, gasping for air, shaking like there was an earthquake rolling through her.

Behind her, she heard Cian giving instructions to her attacker. "On the ground. Facedown. Hands behind your head." His voice was like ice, and she heard the other man swearing in Spanish.

"*Que te jodan, hijo de puta irlandés.*"

Lila's father hadn't spoken a lot of Spanish to her growing up, but even if she hadn't understood her attacker, she'd have gotten the gist of what he was saying from the harsh tone in his voice. She heard the man grunt as something struck him, and finally turned to see Cian standing in his expensive suit, one foot pressed on the other man's neck, a cell phone in one hand and a gun in the other.

"Out back, *now*," he barked into the phone. He slid the device back into his pants pocket, then looked up at Lila. "Are you okay?" he asked, his voice a touch gentler.

She nodded, but when she tried to speak, she coughed, and only a rasp came out. "I think so."

Cian's brow drew down farther when he heard her. "Pull down your scarf," he commanded. She didn't even think before she followed his instructions. His expression went from cold to red-hot anger as he looked at her neck. He dropped to his knees, planting one firmly in the man's back, digging the gun into his head. The man hissed out another profanity.

"Things just got a lot worse for you, my friend," Cian snarled. "Vasquez send you?"

"Fuck you," he spat in English.

The back door to the pub slammed open and Connor and two other men came jogging across the parking lot, guns drawn. Finn followed a minute later, talking rapidly on the phone to someone named Liam. Lila vaguely remembered Liam as the fourth MacFarlane brother.

"What the hell happened?" Connor said as he reached Lila and Cian.

Cian gestured for the other two men to deal with the attacker, then stood. "Looks like Vasquez sent a greeter. He grabbed Lila."

Connor turned to Lila where she was still being partially propped up by her car. He looked ill, his face a mask of horror. "Jesus. I'm so sorry."

She didn't understand why he seemed to be taking it so hard. It was obvious the attacker was tied to the MacFarlanes somehow, but that didn't make Connor personally responsible.

"It's okay," Lila rasped. "I'm all right."

Connor's eyes grew wide as she spoke, and his hand shot out to her throat. He stopped shy of touching her, but fury crawled across his face, and then he turned abruptly, stepping toward her assailant.

Cian stopped him with a hand on his arm. "Not here," he said, leaning in. "Why don't you and the boys take *Ramon* here on a ride for a couple of hours. I'll meet you back at the club."

Connor nodded and pointed to the two men holding the attacker by both arms, then toward the other cars in the lot, indicating they should load him into a nearby SUV.

"Liam's on his way," Finn said, giving Cian a stern look. "He said you don't move from here until he gets here with more guys."

Connor spun to look at Cian. "What the hell were you doing out here by yourself, anyway?" he asked as the other men took the struggling captive away. Someone had produced handcuffs, so the man was partially disabled, and when they got him to the car, Lila saw one of the MacFarlane men pull a zip tie out of his pocket before looping it around the prisoner's ankles.

Cian rolled his shoulders as if sloughing off the previous ten minutes. "It wasn't me who was attacked," he said calmly.

Connor and Finn automatically closed in, keeping their backs to the wall alongside the parking lot, their eyes scanning the lot, but placing themselves between Cian and Lila and the drive aisle.

"Doesn't matter. I assumed you'd be leaving with the same security detail you came in with, but now you're out here alone, and the boys said you told them to have the night off, enjoy a drink."

Cian shrugged. "I was just going home. I didn't need babysitters for that."

Finn crossed his arms and scowled at Cian. "I'm with Connor and Liam on this one. You're the head of the family now. You can't go anywhere by yourself. Look what almost happened." He glanced at Lila. "And it wouldn't have only been your head."

As if the remark had reminded Cian of Lila's presence, he turned to her, his hand drifting to her throat. She held as still as if she were a bunny in the sights of a falcon. He gently stroked the bruised skin with one finger.

"I'm sorry," he said, his voice low. "They've obviously seen you with us before and were waiting to grab you. This is our fault."

Lila swallowed and cleared her throat as his hand fell away. "It all turned out okay," she said, her voice more normal now that she'd had a few minutes of air to breathe. "I knew when I took this job it was dangerous. I think I just need to get up to speed, figure out how to protect myself. I'm not used to having to think about it."

Cian's gaze snapped to Connor. "I want a man with her twenty-four seven until we get this Vasquez thing resolved."

"I don't need—"

He glared at her. "Yes. You do. It's not open to discussion. If I have to get Xavier to insist on it as part of your job requirements, I will."

She stared at him. In all her years of dealing with sexist computer nerds, she'd never had a man try to control her like this.

She snorted, turning and digging through her purse for her keys. "I'll let you know," she said. "Right now, I just want to go home and get some hot tea on my throat."

She heard Cian murmur some instructions to his brothers, then feet moving away. She finally found the damn keys and dug them from the bottom of her bag, punching the key fob to unlock the doors. She'd never leave someplace at night without her keys in hand again. Lesson learned.

"Lila from Rogue." Cian's voice was soft as he leaned against the side of her car, his arm resting along the doorframe so she couldn't open it. "I know your job hasn't ever put you in this kind of situation. I may be a MacFarlane, but I'm not blind. What you do is illegal, but it's never put you in this world. This world isn't virtual. It's very real and very dangerous."

She couldn't look at him right then, her reserves of adrenaline were fading fast. She just wanted to get away from him, go home, break down on her own time, in her own way.

"You need protection." His tone left no room for negotiation, but Lila wasn't the type to accept what she was told to do. She would never have become a hacker if that had been the case.

"I can protect myself." She turned to face him, arms crossed in defiance. She'd lasted all those years with her father. He'd been a responsible addict, but all the same, gambling was a dark and gritty world. She'd made it out. She could handle this herself, like she did everything in her life.

He smiled sadly. "From men twice your size with guns?"

"I'll get my own gun."

He sighed, his eyes dark. His gaze turned to something almost tender, and he leaned toward her so that for a brief moment, she thought he might try to kiss her. And honestly, she didn't know what she would do if he tried.

Then he pulled back, his voice changing to a firm tone.

"You'll get a gun, I'll teach you how to use it, and then you'll learn self-defense. How to fight. Even at your size, you can hold a guy off long enough to scream for help. If you won't take a guard, then at least you'll be better prepared if anything like this happens again."

She wondered how in the world he'd find time to run an organized crime syndicate and still give her shooting lessons, but she shrugged. "Fine, I'll let you know when I have the gun, and I'll sign up for one of those self-defense courses at the Y."

Cian snorted. "I'll have a gun delivered to you tomorrow morning, and you'll learn self-defense from me at the gym my brothers and I fight at." He pulled his phone out of his pocket and shot off a text. "I'll have someone here to drive you home in just a few minutes."

Lila felt her exhaustion morphing to dismay.

"Look, I realize you're used to having everyone follow your orders, but beyond our joint project, I'm not your employee. You can't just…" she sputtered for a moment, "*make* me do things!"

Cian's fingers were warm on her jaw as he forced her to look at him. She'd never known a man who would just touch a woman like that. In the law-abiding world, it would be sexual harassment. In the geek criminal world, the only *touching* would be done via computer.

And maybe it was that shock, the dismay and surprise, that caused her to stand still, allowing him to hold her jaw between his powerful fingertips. Whatever the reason, Lila didn't move as Cian gazed at her, his expression deadly serious.

"I *am* used to people following my instructions. And do you know why they do?"

Lila swallowed uneasily. Now was when he was going to tell her something about concrete shoes and Lake Michigan. She was certain of it.

"Because it's how they stay safe," he finished. "I don't know why you chose the life you have, but it's time you realized it's dangerous. I've never known anything else. I was raised to do what I do. It's in my blood, my DNA." He blinked once, and she saw deep sorrow there for a split second. "I've never had a choice. The good thing about that is I'm an expert. I know how to stay safe. How to stay out of jail. How to stay alive." He smiled briefly and released his grasp on her face. "Now you get to benefit from all my knowledge."

Lila thought about the differences between Cian's life and hers. She'd spent so much of her life operating on the wrong side of the law in cyberspace—starting as a teen to gain her father's attention, continuing on for a brief stint in college to impress professors, then realizing she could earn more as a black hat hacker than she ever could going legit, and deciding to do it to please herself instead of anyone else. Through all of it, she'd considered herself a bit of a badass. She liked the little thrill of being a criminal. She imagined it was what her father felt when he gambled, and as much as she didn't like to admit it, she still yearned to connect with him somehow.

But she was quickly coming to realize that in all those years, she'd never lived like Cian MacFarlane. Her father's gambling was child's play compared to what Cian had seen every day. Her dark web jobs were the tip of the blackmarket iceberg, and Cian lived on the ocean floor. His world was full of guns and blood, men who'd "pull a train" on a woman, and drugs that weren't simply units stored on a server, but crates stored in a warehouse. He'd killed. She knew it. And it crushed her to realize the truth. Lila was a child playing pretend. Cian was the real deal.

A set of headlights pulled up a few parking spaces away, and Lila saw Connor and Finn get out of the SUV they must have been waiting in. They went and spoke to the occupants of the new vehicle, then Connor waved to Cian.

"Your ride is here," he said matter-of-factly. "Give me your keys, and I'll have your car brought to you in a bit. One of my guys will stay outside your place tonight, and I'll be by first thing in the morning—my idea of morning, not yours."

Lila's skin prickled with something. Awareness? Fear? Acceptance? Whatever it was, she knew it was major. The feeling had started the minute she heard about this assignment, and it had grown exponentially every time she saw Cian MacFarlane. As she obediently trudged to the waiting sedan and climbed into the backseat behind two big Irish mob goons after handing her car keys to Cian, she knew nothing in her life would ever be the same again.

**

By nine a.m. the next morning, Cian had spent an hour training Lila how to kickbox. She'd impressed him, her lithe frame moving with ease through the maneuvers he taught her. She'd been wary, of course, and sullen when he picked her up at her row house in the Logan Square neighborhood. But once he'd gotten her in the ring and begun showing her some basic moves, she'd approached it with the same quiet determination she'd shown in her work.

He'd tried not to notice the way her breasts looked in the thin tank top she'd worn, nor how delicate her bones were when she kicked those long legs out. But more than that, he'd worked to ignore how her dark eyes focused on his face when he talked to her. The quiet way she asked the smartest questions he'd ever heard. The serious demeanor she adopted as she watched Liam demonstrate the right way to punch.

Lila Rodriguez continued to fascinate him, and Cian continued to actively ignore that fact with everything he had.

"Where are we going?" she asked yet again as he bundled her into the back of a car and Danny started up the engine.

He narrowed his eyes as he pointed to her seat belt, indicating she needed to put it on. She huffed out a breath in exasperation and did as he directed.

"Is there another word you want me to use for 'shooting range'?" he asked sarcastically.

He saw the tension in her jaw.

"Maybe I have more important things to do."

"Nothing's more important than learning how to protect yourself from guys like that one last night," he countered.

She was stubborn, little Lila. Cian had had her checked out, of course—the daughter of a Korean-American schoolteacher and a Puerto Rican card-sharp, Lila had come by her risk-taking proclivities honestly. While her mother had been the stable provider, her father had been the one who lived to out-smart the opposition, just as Lila did as a hacker.

But even with her father's less than savory ways, her parents had been married Lila's whole life, and her father seemed to be well skilled at taking risks without actually risking what mattered. They owned a home and two cars. He'd always managed to pay his gambling debts, never been in jail, and somehow managed to cheat others out of their money and wind up friends with them at the end of the night.

Meanwhile, Mr. Rodriguez's tiny daughter was turning Cian's entire day upside down.

"You want me to get her set up on the range?" Danny asked as he held the door open for Cian and Lila to exit the car.

Cian knew he ought to just let Danny take care of it. His main guard was perfectly capable of teaching Lila to use a firearm. It would give him a chance to check in on how the interrogation of Vasquez's soldier was going and make some plans for what to do next.

But he'd be damned if anyone else was going to spend that time with her—showing Lila how to load the gun, hold the gun, shoot the gun. Cian was certain if Lila was playing with guns, it ought to be *his* gun she was playing with. He cleared his throat when he realized where those thoughts had taken him.

"No, it's okay," he told Danny. "You can set up on one of the other targets if you want to get some practice in. Or take a break, whatever. I've got this."

Danny looked at him with an amused expression, then nodded before walking them inside.

Once they'd secured a private lane, Cian opened up the duffel bag he'd brought and pulled out the Glock 26 he'd chosen for her.

He held the gun out, and she gingerly lifted it, holding it in both hands, barrel pointed at the floor.

"It's okay," he said. "It's not loaded."

She didn't look convinced, and he smiled. "It's called a Baby Glock because of the smaller size. It should fit your hand better than a full-sized gun and has less recoil. But it's a nine-millimeter, and it'll take down anyone you need it to."

She grimaced and turned it over in her hand, looking at the dull black surface and textured handle.

"It loads with a clip." He pulled one out of the bag and showed her how it snapped into the handle. "And all the safeties are built in, so you don't need to worry about disengaging anything or about it going off accidentally in a purse or something."

"So, there's not an off switch?" Her eyebrows rose nearly to her hairline.

"There is, but the gun sets it for you."

She looked skeptical.

"Here, let me show you." He explained the safety action of the gun, how each component engaged and disengaged as the trigger was pulled and then popped back into place.

"But what if the trigger gets bumped by something in my bag, or jolted by a bump when I'm driving?"

"Come here," he said, holding the pistol out in front of him. He beckoned her to stand slightly in front of him and stepped behind her. "Take the gun." She did. "Hold it out in front of you. Look along the top of the barrel and on to the target. Got it?" She nodded. "Now pull the trigger."

There were a few seconds of silence, as Lila pressed her finger against the trigger. Nothing happened.

"Harder," he said as he leaned down and put his lips to her ear.

The gun fired, and Lila squeaked, taking a small step back and landing against Cian's chest. "Oh my God," she muttered as he chuckled.

"Okay," she conceded. "So it takes a lot to pull the trigger."

"Exactly," he said, smiling as she turned to look at him. "It's somewhere in the neighborhood of five pounds of pull weight to fire it. Not so much you can't do it fast and accurately, but not so little you're going to set it off resting your finger on it or having something bump it in your bag."

She looked at him that same way she had earlier when he'd been teaching her self-defense tactics. Dark eyes, serious expression, mysterious things that swirled beneath the surface. She moved him in some way. He didn't know why or how, but she did, and the fact was, he had no room in his life for someone who moved him.

He took a deep breath and stepped back, then gently pulled the pistol from her grip. "Now," he said. "Let's teach you how to really use this thing."

Chapter Eight

Connor swung his leg back and planted his boot deep in the gut of the Vasquez soldier. The man groaned and retched bile onto the floor of the storeroom at the warehouse they'd taken him to.

"Now, one more time," Liam said, squatting as he pulled the man's head back sharply by his hair. "Where the fuck is Vasquez?"

The door to the room opened, and Finn walked in, followed by two MacFarlane men. He held a cell phone in one hand and had a Bluetooth earpiece in place.

"Yeah, he's right here." Finn glanced at their captive. "Yep, still breathing."

Liam snarled as he shoved the man's head against the concrete floor and stood. "Tell Cian to piss or get off the pot. We're not going to get anything out of this guy."

"You hear that?" Finn asked Cian on the other end of the call. "Yeah. Okay." He wandered back out the door, and the guys who had followed him in looked to Liam for guidance.

Liam spat on the man lying on the floor, then tipped his chin at the door, indicating it was time for all of them to leave.

"Gag him so he can't yell," he told one of the men before leading Connor out of the room.

Finn walked toward them from where he'd been pacing, finishing his call with Cian.

"Now what?" Connor asked. "This has totally screwed up our plans to make peace with Vasquez."

"Not necessarily," Finn answered, that look in his eye telling them he was scheming as usual.

Connor's phone buzzed in his pocket, and he pulled it out, one ear still devoted to listening to his brother. Jess's name flashed on the screen, and he swiped it open.

Connor, it's Carmen. I'm at Holy Cross Hospital with Jess. I found her beaten in her apartment. You'd better get your cheating ass down here. I'm sure this was your fault.

Connor's heart raced as his entire body went stone cold. Where the hell was Ricky? Suddenly, he couldn't breathe, couldn't think, couldn't move. His hand was frozen, clutched around the phone. His mind was a blur of static, and the only thought that penetrated was *he could lose her. Really lose her* this time. And it was all his fault.

"Hey," Liam said as his big hand came down on Connor's shoulder. "Hey, cupcake? What the hell's the matter with you? You're white as a sheet."

Connor swallowed, reality rushing back at him a hundred miles a second. It was like being slammed with an icy-cold wind off the lake, and he sucked in a breath as if he hadn't taken one in several minutes.

He looked down at his phone screen again and nearly vomited.

"It's Jess. She's been attacked. She's in the hospital."

Liam turned and slammed a foot into the side of a wooden crate sitting nearby.

"I thought we had Ricky on her? Where the hell was he?" Finn asked.

Connor shook his head. "I don't know. I just—"

"Vasquez, that motherfucker!" Liam snarled.

He whipped back around and snatched the phone from Connor's hand. Connor ran his fingers through his hair, the backs of his eyes stinging.

"I'll call Cian," Finn said before motioning to the soldiers standing outside the storage room nearby. "Take Connor to—" He looked at Liam, who flashed the phone screen at him, "Holy Cross. Stay with him. Stay sharp. My guess is our friend Ramon was messing with Lila as a distraction for the real business, which was going after Jess."

"They got Jess?" one of the soldiers asked. Jess had grown up with all the MacFarlane employees. Their neighborhood was tight-knit, Irish, and Catholic. Everyone knew everyone else.

"Yeah," Finn said, clamping a hand over Connor's shoulder and giving him a squeeze. "But she's going to be fine." He bent slightly to look into his brother's eyes. "You need to believe that. We all do."

Connor nodded, then swallowed.

"Take care of him," Liam said gruffly to the men. They both nodded and led Connor out of the warehouse. As the cold night air hit his cheeks, Connor vowed silently to make Vasquez pay. No matter what it took, even if it meant his own life, he was going to see Vasquez burn in hell for touching Jess. Burn. In. Hell.

**

Jess was pulled out of a deep and troubled sleep by the commotion at the door.

"You're the one who texted *me*!" a voice she knew nearly as well as her own boomed.

"Well, I thought better of it. I'm sure this was some bullshit that followed you, Connor. You'll just put her in more danger if you're hanging around now. I always said you were bad for her, and this proves it. I'm not letting you in."

"Carmen," Jess called out weakly as she tried to sit up more so she could see across the room. Her left eye was swollen shut, though, so she had a hard time discerning much.

"I had a man assigned to her. I don't know what happened, but please, Carmen…" Connor said, his voice gravelly and desperate in a way Jess had never heard before. "You have to let me in. I don't want to force you, but I will. You don't understand. If I don't see her, I'm gonna lose it."

Jess leaned on one arm to push herself to sitting but forgot about the fractured wrist. "Ahhh!" she shrieked as pain shot up her arm all the way to her shoulder.

"Oh my God, Jess!" Carmen came running across the room and gently helped Jess up, pressing on the electric bed to adjust it, then fluffing her pillows. "Oh, honey, I'm so sorry. I didn't realize you were awake."

Jess gave her a wan smile, but her gaze was pinned to Connor, who was now standing just beyond her friend, utter devastation in his eyes.

"Hey," she said to him softly, glancing at Carmen, who scowled and fluffed her pillow some more.

"I can get hospital security to make him go," Carmen whispered. "Just say the word."

Jess shook her head. "It's okay. We need to talk."

Carmen glanced back at Connor, and Jess could see two of the MacFarlane employees standing on either side of the doorway to her room. Oddly, even though she knew this was Connor's fault, it was comforting to have his guards there.

"You should make him leave," Carmen hissed. "He'll never change, J. I can't stand to think about things like this happening to you again. It's not cool like it was when we were eighteen. It's just dangerous."

Jess cupped her friend's cheek with her good hand. "I know. It's okay. I'm going to be okay. I promise."

Carmen sighed and shook her head. "I'll be right outside the door. You make one peep, and even his goons won't be able to stop me from rescuing you."

Jess chuckled. "Got it."

Carmen swung around, and Jess knew she was glaring at Connor as she pointed a finger at him like a schoolteacher. "Do not upset her, or I will come for your balls."

Connor didn't even flinch as she stormed past him and out the door, shutting it behind her.

He stepped to the bed and sat on the chair placed next to it. He lowered his head to the mattress and grabbed her good hand as his body shuddered. For long minutes, Jess simply stroked his hair as he silently worked to control his emotions. And when he was able to look at her finally, there was a steel in him she'd never seen before. Something hard and cold that nearly broke her heart.

"Where is your dad?" he asked.

"I wouldn't let them call him. He can't see this. He'll go nuts and try to go after the guys himself. I won't let him get himself killed over me." Jess's stomach turned at the mere thought of what Sean would do if he saw her right now.

"And where was Ricky?" he asked.

"He said your dad needed him and that he'd get someone else there as soon as possible. He asked me what I had planned, and I was only going to be at home for the rest of the night. I was working on some billing for the gym."

Connor's eyes grew harder as his jaw tensed.

"He did his job, Connor. And he's been…so nice and helpful. Please don't hold this against him. The guys busted down my front door only about half an hour after he'd left."

"So they'd been watching." He shook his head, defeat hovering around him. "How many?" he asked.

"Two," she answered.

"You fought them?"

"Of course." Her father hadn't owned a boxing gym her entire life for nothing. Jess was skilled at boxing and kickboxing, and she'd put up a hell of a fight before two big men on one average-sized woman had simply been too much. She shuddered to think what would have happened if she hadn't been trained as she was.

"Did they…" Connor's voice caught, and he swallowed.

"No," she said firmly, silently thanking God they'd only beaten and not raped her. "I made such a racket, they had to leave. They knew the neighbors would be calling the cops."

"This was Vasquez," Connor said. "He screwed with us earlier after a business meeting. I think it was to distract us from his real goal, which was proving he could hurt you."

She nodded. The guys had spoken Spanish, and there wasn't much other reason someone would come after her. Her father's gym was in trouble, but they'd paid the MacFarlane protection money every month no matter what, and they didn't owe anyone but the bank. She'd never heard of a bank sending out enforcers.

"God, baby." Conner ran a hand down her bruised cheek. "I don't know how I'm ever going to live with myself."

She sighed, resisting the urge to turn into his hand and let him lie to her more. She knew he was hurting, knew he genuinely cared about her, but Connor was a MacFarlane, and one way or another, something like this was bound to happen to anyone they were close to. It was the life, and as much as she loved him, she didn't want to live it.

She'd seen enough of the lives of the women MacFarlane employees kept around to know it wasn't for her. They were either skanks who wanted the money, or good Catholic wives and mothers, and either way, they stayed in the neighborhood their whole lives, taking what little bits of their men's time and attention they were given without complaint.

Jess's mother hadn't been able to do it. The cooking and cleaning and pretending not to know what the husbands did when they left home every day. The mob wives in their little piece of Chicago spent decades on the endless loop of church, school, and bunco—see no evil, hear no evil, act like your husband never did any evil. Jess wanted more. She wanted a career, she wanted to travel, she wanted to be able to walk around in broad daylight without a security detail. And most of all, she wanted love, and a man who would be not just faithful, but a true partner. In a different life, Connor might have been able to offer her those things, but not in this one.

"You did what you could," she told him sadly. "Maybe now he's gotten his shot in, Vasquez will be satisfied and back off."

Connor snorted inelegantly. "Not a fucking chance, baby. This means war, and he knows it."

"You really think your dad's going to okay a war with Vasquez over *me*?" If she could have rolled her swollen eyes, she would have. The sexist old dinosaur treated women like possessions. There was no way he'd think Jess being assaulted was worthy of a mob war.

Connor paused as if the thought hadn't occurred to him. "Cian will," he answered. "Cian's in charge, and he knows what you mean to me. He'll never let this pass without answering it."

She shut her unblackened eye and laid her head back, suddenly very tired.

She felt Connor's fingers feather over her cheek once again as he whispered, "Just sleep now, baby. I'm right here, and I won't leave you again. You're safe with me. I'll keep you safe no matter what it takes."

As Jess's mind gave up consciousness, she let a momentary fantasy sift through her head—a dream of her and Connor someplace new, just the two of them, and a life without the MacFarlanes.

**

Sergei Petrov put one booted foot up on the crate resting in front of him and leaned down to pull a knife out of his ankle holster.

He began using the tip of it to clean his fingernails, a habit he'd picked up several years ago when he was working in the Ukraine and everything, most of all the people, was filthy.

"You thought it was prudent to leave her alive?" he asked his companion.

Alejandro Vasquez shrugged before leaning against the wall of the loading dock where his workers were moving Sergei's merchandise from one truck to another.

"You said to get them off balance, so that's what I did. I'd rather not kill her until I get my cousin back, right?"

Sergei shook his head in disgust. Both the Irish and the Mexicans had so many complicated family ties. It was always in the way of business, complicating every negotiation, interfering with every decision. They were pathetic and weak. It drove him crazy.

"I was born in the prison camps in Siberia," Sergei said, replacing the knife in his boot as he stood. "My mother worked twelve hours a day carrying water and food to the men who chopped down forests. She doesn't know who my father was since she was raped by four different men before she was pregnant." He paused, one eyebrow lifted as he looked at Vasquez with disdain. "I wouldn't know my cousin from a musk deer in Siberia, and I would never let an enemy get the better of me because of one."

Vasquez put his hands out to the side in a "what can I do?" gesture. "Do you want me to kill the little bitch? I can."

Sergei thought for a moment. "No. Just proceed as you would for now. I need to leave town for a few days on other business."

"And if they attack us?"

Sergei shrugged. "Hit back."

"And if they want to use my cousin as a bargaining chip?"

"Make it a good bargain," Sergei replied.

Vasquez narrowed his eyes at the bigger man. "I got no problem helping out, but I have to say, I'm not sure how you're going to get what you want this way."

This was why men like Vasquez would never be on top. No vision.

"I always get what I want," Sergei said as he strode away.

Chapter Nine

"You hear from Connor yet today?" Cian asked as he watched Liam working out at Sean's gym. His brute of a brother took jabs at a punching bag, dancing on surprisingly light feet around the dangling object.

"Yeah, he's still at the hospital. I don't think we're going to be able to get him to come to work until she's released. I still can't believe the old man pulled Ricky off protecting her."

Cian raised an eyebrow at Liam. Liam was the only one other than their father who'd been there all those years ago. He was the only one who knew what Robbie's initiation for his oldest son had involved. "Really? Doesn't surprise me at all," he answered coldly.

Liam looked uncomfortable and shrugged. "Yeah, guess not." He took another half-hearted jab at the bag before removing his gloves and resting his ass on the edge of the adjacent ring, letting his arms hang over the ropes behind him. "So, what are we going to do about Vasquez?"

Cian watched a few of his guys working out on the other side of the gym. He always let them work out when he did. No sense in making them stand around getting fat if they had a chance to put in some gym time. And he had to admit, most of his men were in great shape. He prided himself on having a fit crew. Liam joked that Cian's worst nightmare was running a crew like Tony Soprano's—a bunch of middle-aged fat guys in bad suits.

"Connor's going to insist we retaliate," Cian said, his attention shifting back to Liam and the question of what to do about Vasquez.

"How the hell can we not?" Liam asked. "He fucked with us not once but twice in one evening."

"His guy's still alive?" Cian asked.

"Yeah. There's someone watching him. We let him eat this morning. He's fine."

"Here's what I want—in Vasquez's mind, Jess was his due for Connor sullying his sister. In my mind, Lila was extra, so we get the soldier to balance the accounts. If he'll agree to that, we'll make peace, and Ricky can *handle* the soldier once the deal is made. It'll give him some satisfaction. I'm sure he's pissed about Jess since she was his assignment."

"He feels like crap," Liam said. "I was afraid Connor might go after Ricky, but he knows there's no reasoning with the old man when he gets something in his head. As soon as Pop let Ricky go, he went to the hospital. Got there about two a.m."

"Okay. I'll have Finn send the message to Vasquez. If Connor's busy at the hospital, maybe that'll keep him occupied until a deal's been negotiated."

"What about the info you have on the informant in the Vasquez ranks?" Liam asked.

"I'll save that to sweeten the deal if he doesn't go for it initially."

Liam shook his head. "I'd still like to get a piece of him. The guy rants about his honor, but who the hell does that to a female civilian?"

"I agree, but with this new project with Rogue, we don't have time for a war right now. I need this to go away so we can focus on the business end of things."

Liam nodded and stood. "Okay. I'm going to go to the hospital and keep an eye on Connor. Since him going off half-cocked is what started all this, I'll try to keep him in line."

"Thank you, I appreciate it." Cian bumped fists with his brother, shot a text off to Finn, and leaned against the wall of the gym for just a moment. He sighed. The exhaustion in him ran bone deep. His head was a tangle of FBI demands, mob wars, and internet sales. He doubted any corporate CEO had more complications to deal with.

"You ready to go, boss?" one of his men asked. Cian gave him a thumbs-up, and the guys gathered their stuff, one of them heading out first to bring the car around.

Back at his condo, Cian took a shower and dressed before pulling out a burner phone from the top drawer of his desk. He dialed the preprogrammed number and waited until Don answered.

"Yeah. What do you have?"

"A load of international laundry. Three years' worth."

There was a pause on the other end. "Yeah," Don answered casually. "Just email me that invoice now."

Cian ended the call, popped open the phone's SIM tray, and pulled the card out, destroying it before also removing the battery, then crushing the burner's case under his bootheel and tossing it in the trash. Next, he pulled out a zip drive from the locked drawer of his desk, slid it into his laptop, and did a click and drag to a shared drive that popped up on his screen. After the file transferred, the drive was unshared as quickly as it had shown up.

Next, he removed the zip drive from his USB port and sat back in his office chair, a tension headache spreading through his skull. He stared at the zip drive in his hand for long moments before grabbing a staple remover sitting alongside a fancy set of pens his mother had given him when his dad retired and he took over the business. He placed the small piece of plastic in the jaws of the staple remover and crushed and twisted until it was thoroughly destroyed, then he tossed it in the garbage with the phone.

Several miles away at the headquarters of Rogue, Xavier watched the footage of Cian making the phone call while he also pulled up the files his hack had copied while they were briefly being transferred from Cian's laptop to the shared drive.

"Oh, MacFarlane," Xavier said, grinning as he opened the files. "You've been a very naughty boy."

∗∗

"What do you mean we're not going to hit back?" Connor ground out as he stood in front of the hospital facing Liam.

"You know I'd love to go after him," Liam counseled. "I'd always rather fight, especially with a pussy like Vasquez who goes after women, but Cian's right about this. It's not the time. This new venture with Rogue means we don't have the resources for a war." Liam leaned closer, putting his hand on Connor's shoulder as his voice dropped. "We'll get him later. I promise."

Connor shrugged off Liam's touch, a fire raging inside him. This couldn't be happening. From his father, he'd expect it, but from Cian? Cian always had his back. Always. His oldest brother was the foundation Connor's life was built on.

When a kid in middle school decided he'd like to take on a mobster's son, it was Cian who showed up at the end of the school day and stood there leaning against the side of the school building waiting for Connor to come out. He'd done nothing more than put an arm around Connor and watched the other kid. As the kid had looked back at Cian, his eyes wide with fear, Cian had talked in a low voice, coaching his youngest brother on survival in the MacFarlane world.

"People will be gunning for you from here on out because they know who your dad is," he said. "You remember you can't ever let them see fear. You are ice, and they cannot melt you. If they throw the first punch, then you punch back hard, just the way Liam's been teaching you at the gym, but your first and best weapon is your cool. You can't be bothered to get scared, because you have the ultimate weapon—you have me and Liam and Finn, and we are always behind you. Together, we are invincible."

Connor shook his head at the memory. Yeah, since he was twelve years old, he'd believed that, but now it looked like Cian had forgotten his promise.

"To hell with later," Connor spat. "There's no way you guys can expect me to make peace with the man who fractured Jess's wrist, her cheekbone, and two ribs." The rage curled inside him, turning his stomach sour and making his head pound. "They could have killed her." His voice dropped to nearly a whisper. "They could have raped her. I will *not* make peace."

Liam's voice was kind, but his words were less so. "You'll do whatever the head of the family tells you. That's how this works, kid. I know it's hard, and you're justified to want revenge, but timing is everything, and it's not the time. Cian's good to us. He wouldn't make a decision like this if he didn't think it was necessary. Finn and I both agree. You're just going to have to be patient for your payback. Maybe in a few months. We'll see."

Connor clenched his fists and stared at the cloudy sky above. Fuck Cian. Fuck Liam and Finn too. They couldn't make peace with Vasquez if he got to the man first. So, he'd do what he had to. It wasn't the first time he'd ignored his older brother's orders; probably wouldn't be the last. All that really mattered was making sure that bastard could never hurt Jess again.

"Fine," he bit out. "Now if you don't mind, I'm going to go take care of Jess, since no one else seems to give a damn."

"Connor, come on," Liam pleaded as Connor stomped off into the hospital. But Connor didn't respond. His thoughts had already moved on to more important things—namely, how he'd find Vasquez and get him alone to do it. Once he'd answered that question, Connor had guns to grab and plans to make. He was going to take down Alejandro Vasquez, and he was going to do it tonight.

Chapter Ten

"That was fast," Cian said as Finn stood in front of his desk at the club.

"Yeah, the soldier we're hosting is Vasquez's cousin. He wants to meet right away."

"His cousin, huh? That puts a different spin on things." Cian leaned back in his chair, considering yet another wrench in his plans. "He's not going to let us use his cousin as the body to even the score."

Finn flopped into one of the other office chairs, looking at Cian from under his unkempt hair. "Nope. He wants him back. I can tell that already."

"Yeah, you know how that's going—his grandmother or Auntie Maria or whoever is in hysterics, telling him if he doesn't get his dumbass cousin back from those filthy Irish, she'll never forgive him."

"Exactly," Finn agreed, "which is why we're going to use the cousin to demand something else in retribution."

"I'm thinking he gives us the slice of territory that runs along Front Street. It's always pissed Pop off the Vasquezes have that. You know how he likes things neat and tidy."

Finn nodded, his expression thoughtful. "And it can never hurt to make Pop happy, can it?" he asked wryly.

Cian didn't let his expression betray anything. "No. It can't."

Strategy agreed upon, Finn left to make the final arrangements for the meeting with Vasquez. Cian sat in silence, watching his screen saver flicker. The feds had been satisfied with the information he'd sent them on some of his family's Cayman accounts, but they'd demanded more, faster. They were becoming increasingly difficult to placate, and he knew it was only a matter of time before they pulled one of his brothers in as leverage. The fact was, they wanted an end to the MacFarlane organization, and that meant every MacFarlane son neutralized one way or another. It was an outcome Cian couldn't allow.

He could tell Vasquez about the informant in his ranks. It might make Cian marketable as the source for Vasquez info instead of MacFarlane info again, but he knew it was only a stop-gap measure. He'd been in denial thinking he could somehow keep the feds satisfied with the bits of intel he'd been feeding them the last three years.

At some point, they were going to make him pay the piper no matter what. They'd thrown out the lure, and now they were reeling him in, and they were good at what they did. They'd studied him ever since he'd agreed to inform. They knew his weaknesses, and they knew exactly how much power he truly had, which was a lot. There might be things his father didn't tell him, but MacFarlane men and MacFarlane business answered to him. His father's retirement had been final, and Cian did everything he could to keep his father out of the loop whenever possible.

He ran a hand over his face, scrubbing at the stubble that was spreading like wildfire. He needed to be smarter than ever now. Things were heating up all over the place, and one slipup could send the entire house of cards tumbling down.

A picture of him with his brothers stared at him from the office wall. It had been taken at Connor's twenty-first birthday, in front of the bar in their dad's pub. Connor had been sneaking booze from the pub since he was sixteen, but that night, he'd marched up and ordered a round for his brothers and every other MacFarlane employee in the room.

He looked at the picture, noticing the way Liam's arm was slung across Finn's shoulders, how Finn leaned his head toward Connor, the proud smile on Connor's face as he held up the bottle of Jameson's. And behind them all, him—arms around the entire pack—the protector, the mentor and boss. The one who'd made sure they stayed safe and healthy and happy. Robbie MacFarlane may have taught his boys how to rule, but Cian had taught them how to love.

He needed the ultimate bargaining chip. He needed a way to make himself so invaluable to the feds, they'd agree to leave his brothers alone for good. His email notifications pinged, and he glanced at the computer screen to see a notice from Rogue.

And that's when it came to him. Cian realized the answer had been there for weeks. It had, in fact, fallen right in his lap, courtesy of Finn and his big ideas.

Cian didn't need another bargaining chip. He just had to leverage the one he had. He'd save his brothers for good. He regretted he'd probably have to sacrifice Lila in the process.

**

The house was dark except for a small light in the kitchen when Lila let herself in with her key.

"Mom?" she called out softly. It was early, only seven thirty in the evening, but she wondered if her mother had gone to bed already.

"In here, sweetie," May Rodriguez called out from the darkened living room.

Lila turned to the right and entered the small room that housed an upright piano, a sofa, and two armchairs. Her mother was reclined on the sofa, a washcloth across her forehead. Lila sat carefully on the coffee table next to her. "Another migraine?" she asked, keeping her voice soft.

"Yes, it came on after dinner, but I think I took medicine fast enough this time. It's getting better bit by bit."

Lila's brow furrowed as she looked at her tiny mother amid the piles of throw pillows and afghans. "That's the third one in a month. I think you should go to the doctor and see what she has to say."

Her mother made a shushing noise. "No, that's silly. I'm fine. I think today was because I accidently ate something with peanuts."

"Okay, if you promise, but if they get worse or more often, you need to promise me you'll get it checked out."

"Of course."

Lila's mother wasn't the type of woman to spend energy worrying about her health or her own needs. She'd been brought to the US as a baby after the immigration laws of the mid-1960s had allowed a wave of immigration from South Korea. The family had been without English, without jobs, and without the large extended family they'd left behind in Daejeon.

Lila's mother had grown to become the family's primary translator, and by the time she was ten or twelve, she conducted all the family's business, making phone calls for her mother, explaining apartment leases to her father, and filling out all the paperwork for her little brothers to enroll in school. It wasn't too much of a surprise she'd grown up to become a schoolteacher. And probably not a surprise she'd married a man who needed her supervision as well.

And as the thought of her father entered her head, Lila gritted her teeth, hating that she needed to bring it up, but it was past time.

"He's been gone a while this time, Mom," she said gently. "Don't you think it's time to file a missing persons report?"

Just enough light slipped in from the streetlights outside that Lila could see her mother stiffen.

"He'll be back," May said resolutely.

Lila sighed and rubbed her temple, wondering if the migraine was contagious.

"It's been six months, Mom. He's never been gone more than a few weeks. Something's happened, and you need to take care of yourself."

"What do you want? For me to divorce him? After thirty years, you think I should just sign a paper and end it because he's gone on a longer trip than usual?"

Diego Rodriguez's gambling had always meant "trips," as her parents called them. Trips to Atlantic City, trips to Vegas, trips to the Santa Anita and Pimlico. He spent his life searching for the next challenge, the next big win, the next fix. Addiction was an ugly beast, and Lila knew she'd been just as guilty of enabling him as May had.

"Something might have happened to him," she told her mother. "Don't you want the authorities to know so they can try to see if he's okay? What if he's in a hospital somewhere and he can't tell them who he is or something?"

"You don't believe that any more than I do, Lila," May chastised. "Your father can take care of himself. He always has. He'll be back. He just found more games to play this time than usual."

The stubborn set of her mom's jaw told Lila she wasn't going to be able to change the woman's mind. Her dad might be rotting in a ditch somewhere, and May wasn't going to budge. And unfortunately, Lila's suspicion was that the ditch scenario wasn't too far from the truth of what was keeping Diego away. The odds of the man having made it as long as he had without getting offed by a bookie he owed or an angry poker opponent were phenomenal. As a student of the odds, Lila knew they weren't in his favor.

But until May was willing to admit her husband was probably dead, there wasn't much Lila could do.

"Okay, Mom, why don't we get you upstairs to bed. I'll bring you some tea and lock up when I go."

May sat up, handing Lila the washcloth. She patted her on the cheek. "You're a good girl to take care of me."

Lila felt her cheeks heat. There was nothing good about her. If only her mother knew the truth.

"You want anything to eat while I'm getting the tea?"

"No. Bring me my tea, then you can go. You should go out, see some friends. Stop worrying about me and start worrying about when you're ever going to meet a man."

Lila rolled her eyes as she helped her mom stand from the sofa. "I spend all day with men, Mom."

"Not the nerdy men, Lila. You need to meet a real man, one who's strong enough to handle you and your big brain."

An image of Cian flashed in Lila's mind, and she tried to control the shiver that worked through her. Somehow, she didn't think the issue was a man who could handle her. No, Lila was convinced she couldn't handle the man Cian MacFarlane was. But there was a part of her that would really like to try.

Chapter Eleven

The moon was just high enough for Connor to be able to switch off his headlights as he turned into the industrial park where Cian was set to meet Vasquez. It had taken a lot of skulking and eavesdropping, plus drinking a few shots with one of Cian's guards to find out the place and time for the meeting, but as he rolled into the weed-choked parking lot, he saw the Audi TT Cian loved parked alongside a black Cadillac CT6 and knew he'd come to the right place.

He quietly climbed out of the car, sliding his hand inside his jacket where the 9mm Glock rested in its holster. He fingered the gun, trying to calm the hum in his ears. Connor had held guns on men, been in a couple of minor shootouts, and plenty of fistfights, but he'd never killed a man before. Tonight, he would, because he'd be damned if Vasquez would get away with what he'd done to Jess.

He quietly walked toward the door to the nearest warehouse, scanning the darkness around the building, watching for shifts in the shadows, listening for the slightest sound that might indicate Vasquez had men waiting to ambush Cian.

As he reached the metal wall of the structure, he turned his back to it, pulling his gun out and holding it ready as he slid alongside the wall until he'd reached the door.

"Your cousin is fine," he heard Cian say just inside. "But I won't just hand him over. You went too far with the girl. We can't let that go without getting something in return."

"Jesus," Vasquez muttered. "You fucking Irish think you can dictate how it's all going to go. I got news for you, this isn't the old world no more, and you can't just take whatever the hell you want and not pay the price. Your *pinche* brother defiled my baby sister, man. He disrespected me the worst way he could. And did I get anything in return? Hell, no."

"Connor's young. He was blowing off steam. We've all done it, and I dealt with him. He knows he did wrong, but he didn't force your sister, and he never came near her again. It's time to let it go."

"So what do you want to give me back, Ramon?" Vasquez asked. "And don't go for broke here, bro. I'm not feeling all that generous."

Cian's voice was calm as he began explaining the boundaries of the new territory he wanted in exchange for what Vasquez had done to Jess. It made Connor's stomach turn. The idea that anything other than the complete annihilation of Vasquez could answer for what they'd done to his girl.

The rage that had been coming in waves for the last forty-eight hours took hold of him again, and he didn't stop to think, just yanked open the door to the warehouse, his gun drawn, trying desperately to fix something that should have never happened in the first place. Something that was all his fault and only he could mend.

Like in a movie, time slowed. He saw Cian turn toward him, his face going pale in an instant. Cian's mouth opened as he yelled for Connor to stop, but he already had the gun trained on Vasquez, who dove toward the floor.

He pressed the trigger three times. Why he'd always remember that, he didn't know, but he would. *Bang. Bang. Bang.* It took only a few seconds and then it was over, his hand falling to his side as Cian reached him and slammed him against the wall of the warehouse, arm against Connor's throat. Connor could feel his air being cut off, and he let the gun clatter to the floor, no need for it now. As Cian yelled at him, Connor stood passively, staring at Vasquez where he lay bleeding on the cold, hard floor.

Somewhere in the back of Connor's mind, he noted that it didn't feel like he'd thought it would— killing a man. The truth was he didn't feel much of anything. The report of the gun still rang in his ears, and Cian was pressing so hard on his windpipe, his vision was black around the edges. But he wasn't too concerned. He'd done what he came to do. He ought to feel something. But he didn't. He really didn't.

"Jesus Christ!" Cian yelled. "How could you? What the fuck were you thinking?"

Connor blinked and realized Cian had released him and was pacing the floor in front of him.

"Is he dead?" Connor asked quietly, still staring at Vasquez's body.

Cian strode to Vasquez and squatted, putting his fingers on Vasquez's neck. After a few seconds, he nodded. "Goddammit, Connor. When will you ever learn?"

"He had to pay. Pop always taught us that. You make anyone who does you wrong pay. He nearly killed her, Cian. How was I supposed to just let that go?"

Cian stood, crossing his arms. "There's more than one way to make someone pay. And a right time and a wrong time to exact payment." Cian looked exhausted. "You've started a war that could go on for years, Connor. You haven't made it better. You've made it so much worse. Jess will be in more danger than ever. So will the four of us and anyone we're close to. You may have just signed the death warrants of a whole bunch of people, and a lot of them are MacFarlane people."

Connor swallowed as the adrenaline he'd been running on for hours started to subside. He didn't want to put anyone else in danger, he'd just needed to make it right for Jess. Make sure Vasquez would never hurt her again.

Cian walked over to Connor and grabbed his face, pressing against his cheeks as he looked him in the eye. "What am I going to do with you?" he asked quietly. "I love you, goddammit, but I'm not superhuman. I can't fix everything you screw up."

Before Connor could answer, a cell phone went off from Vasquez's pocket.

"That'll be Vasquez's men checking up on him. We need to get out of here and prepare. They may try to hit us tonight. Come on." Cian moved to the door, listening for a moment before he opened it. Connor bent down and scooped up the gun, tucking it back in his holster before following Cian out the door.

"Get in your car, drive straight to Pop's house. We'll need to get a plan made right away," Cian instructed.

Connor nodded as he opened his car door.

"Connor." Cian's face was in shadows, but his tone was clear as day. "Don't stop anywhere, don't talk to anyone, don't say a word to Pop until I get there. Understand?"

"Yeah. I got it," he answered. On autopilot, he climbed in the car, started it up, and drove toward his parents' house.

And still, he felt nothing.

**

Cian's tires squealed as he hauled out of the abandoned parking lot heading out of the industrial area. He hit the speaker phone on his steering wheel and called Finn.

"I was just about to check on you," Finn said as he picked up. Cian could hear the noise in the background and knew Finn must be at Banshee waiting for him to come back. "Everything go okay?"

"Connor found out where I was," Cian said.

"What? How?"

"I didn't have time to ask. Things went south very quickly."

Finn knew enough not to ask details over the phone, and Cian wouldn't have been at all surprised if the feds had access to his cell phone calls.

"What do you need from me?" Finn asked.

"Your usual," Cian answered. And that told Finn everything. He was the family cleaner for a reason.

Brilliant, exacting, calm, and collected. Some days, Cian thought Finn had gotten all the sense and Connor all the fire. They balanced each other, but alone, each lacked something.

"I'll get a couple of guys and go right away."

"You need to be really careful. The other side might show up at any point," Cian warned. "Go fast and go safe. Meet us at Pop's after."

Finn agreed and disconnected.

Cian dialed Liam next, instructing him to get their six most experienced men together and meet him at their parents'. Once he was done, he took a deep breath, trying to calculate what he'd need to say to his father to get the best response. He didn't think his father would have a major issue with Connor killing Vasquez, but he'd have a big issue with Connor disobeying orders. Cian had spent almost half his life protecting Connor and Finn from their father's worst traits. He wasn't about to let Connor get a primer now.

When he arrived at the house, several of the men were at the gate, looking extra cautious.

"Connor here?" he asked as he pulled up to the gate and one of the men opened it for him.

"Yeah. He didn't tell us what's happening but said to step everything up a notch."

Cian nodded. "Good. Step it up three or four notches, and I'll be down to talk to you guys as soon as I can."

The man nodded, holding his AR-15 across his body, barrel pointed at the street.

"We got this, Mr. MacFarlane, don't worry about a thing," he assured Cian.

Cian drove on through, noticing Liam had also beat him there and was waiting outside the house, leaning against the side of one of their father's cars in the front driveway.

As Cian got out of the car, Liam stalked over, his face tight with worry.

"What the hell happened?" he said quietly.

"Connor found out where I was and came in gun blazing."

Liam's expression turned to horror. "Please tell me he didn't."

Cian shook his head, his temples throbbing. "He did. Vasquez is dead."

"Son of a bitch!" Liam whisper yelled before kicking one of the tires of Cian's car. "How did he find you?"

"I don't know yet, but it was classic Connor, all emotion, no thought. He probably feels like hell about it now—"

"Like always. For all the damn good it does us. He has to be punished, Cian. You know you can't keep coddling him, or he'll never learn."

Cian sighed. As family enforcer, it was technically Liam's job to discipline Connor and prepare for an attack from the Vasquez organization. The Dublin Devils had been in only one war since Cian was a teenager, and it was long before he took over his father's role. He'd never run the organization during war time, and none of his brothers could even remember when they'd been under siege.

"I hear you, but for now, I want to focus on making sure Pop doesn't find out Connor disobeyed, and getting ready for Vasquez's people. My guess is they'll try to hit fast and hard. I need you to prepare us for that."

The front door opened, and Cian heard their mother's voice. "Cian? Liam? Is that you boys out there?"

"I'll text Ricky, tell him to start getting extra security everywhere."

"Double up whoever's at the hospital with Jess," Cian instructed. Then his mind flew to a pair of beautiful dark eyes, and a long, elegant leg practicing roundhouse kicks. It seemed like it was months ago rather than a day, and Lila was still vulnerable. "And make sure the Rogue girl, Lila, is being watched." Cian tried to sound casual about it, not wanting to admit to anyone that he'd developed some sort of what…a crush? On the woman.

"Done and done," Liam said as he texted madly.

"Boys?" their mother called again.

"Right here, Ma," Cian answered.

"We're coming," Liam said at the same time.

"They should have stopped at three kids," Liam muttered as they walked inside.

All Cian could hope was that they still had four when morning came.

Chapter Twelve

"So, you shot the Mexican?" Robbie asked Connor as he slid a bottle of Connemara across the desk to him, followed by a glass.

Connor glanced at Cian. "Yes, sir," he answered, pouring himself a healthy amount of whiskey.

"You approve that?" Robbie asked Cian.

Cian stood behind Connor's chair, his hands on the back, white knuckling the damn thing. Liam leaned against the door, quiet, but Cian knew his brother had his back like he always did.

"No, but that's on me. I didn't get a chance to tell Connor what we were doing. He heard I was with Vasquez and assumed the worst, came in to protect me."

Robbie looked hard at Connor. "That true?"

"Vasquez was a snake," Connor said, evading the question. "I wouldn't trust him with my dog, much less my brother."

Robbie nodded, taking a sip of his own whiskey.

"So, your first time." He lifted his glass. "*Sláinte*," he toasted.

Connor lifted his own glass and Cian noticed his brother's hand shook when he did. "Drink that all up now," he said quietly, giving Connor's shoulder a squeeze. Connor nodded and drank.

"So we got a war on our hands." Robbie's tone was neutral, which always worried Cian. He preferred when it was obvious what his father was going to do. Cruel or charming, as long as he could predict which Robbie he'd get, Cian could manage him. But the unknown Robbie was always a danger.

"Headed that way," Cian answered.

"You ready for that?" Robbie asked Liam.

Liam nodded thoughtfully. "I already have the guys preparing," he answered. "We've moved any product that was being stored close to Vasquez territory. We're doubling up protection at all the family businesses."

"Defensive, that's all defensive," Robbie said, his jaw set. That told Cian what he needed to know, so he jumped in to preempt the old man and hopefully prevent someone getting hurt.

"Not so defensive since we just killed the head of their organization," Cian said calmly. "The next move really is theirs."

"Bullshit!" Robbie's fist came down on the desk. "You declared war, you make war."

Connor took another long drink of his whiskey, and Cian heard Liam shift behind him.

"Maybe I should have said 'we still have the hostage *and* we killed their boss.' We have the upper hand here, Pop. I don't want to take a bunch of our guys into Vasquez territory and risk lives if we don't have to. If we wait to see how they're going to react, then we can make some better choices about what's next."

Robbie stood, his face red as he stepped out from behind the desk. He moved fast for a man who was nearly seventy and had a heart condition, grabbing Cian by the front of the shirt.

"You listen to me," he snarled. "No son of mine is going to wait around for someone else to make the decisions. You're in a war, you act like a damn general instead of a scared little pussy."

Cian put his hands up, letting his father rage. One punch and he could flatten the old man, but he'd never done it, and he knew it would only make things worse. His hatred of Robbie had passed the red-hot variety years ago. It was cold as ice now, and that meant it waited patiently for the right opportunity. Someday, Cian would finish Robbie, but until then, he played his part.

"All right," he said. "What would you like us to do? Send some guys down there and do a drive-by? Maybe go after one of their storage facilities, set a fire? You tell me. We'll do it." His words were submissive, but his tone was like the ice that wrapped his heart whenever he thought of his father.

Robbie shoved Cian away like so much garbage he couldn't stand to touch. "You hit 'em fast and you hit 'em hard. Finish the hostage, dump him somewhere they'll see him. And knock off some of their other men when you do it. In a war, you never make a move that doesn't include taking some of their soldiers out. The fewer men they have, the less firepower."

Cian's stomach turned at the idea of losing more lives. "You want this done tonight?" he asked.

Robbie snorted in disgust, but Cian could see his outburst had cost him. His skin had paled, and he was breathing heavily. "Yes, I want it done tonight. I want it done two hours ago."

Cian subtly adjusted his shirt collar. "Okay, we'll get right on it."

Robbie's attention turned to Connor. "I'm proud of you for defending your family," he said, cuffing Connor upside the head. "Your brother wasn't half the man at your age." He stared defiantly at Cian, baiting him, looking like he'd welcome nothing more than a chance to take on his oldest son.

Connor nodded awkwardly, and Liam let out a sound of disgust with a muttered "Come on, Pop."

Cian simply strode to the door and opened it, his mind already on his next move. The constant chess match that was his life had no room for bitter old men and their approval—or lack thereof.

"Let's go, Connor," Cian said. "We've got places to be."

Connor stood and walked to the door.

"You'll tell me after it's done," Robbie instructed. Cian nodded, but then his mother appeared in the hall.

"Robert Patrick MacFarlane," she said. "I could hear you shouting in the kitchen. How many times do I have to tell you to calm down or you'll give yourself a full-blown heart attack?"

Cian let his mother slip past him, looking down when she paused to give him a sad smile and a pat on the cheek before she bustled in to fuss at his father more.

Liam and Connor followed him out to the kitchen, where they found Finn waiting.

"Were you able to do it?" he asked Finn.

"Yeah, nobody else showed. It was quick and smooth."

A sigh of relief washed through Cian then. The Vasquez people would know they'd killed Alejandro, but at least the feds and the cops wouldn't have a murder to investigate.

"What happens now?" Finn asked, his voice low as all four men clustered together near their mother's kitchen table.

"Pop wants us to hit 'em tonight," Liam answered, his brow furrowed.

"Is that what *you* want?" Finn asked. Cian shook his head. "Good," Finn said, "because I have a better idea."

**

Cian took a deep breath before stepping out of the car under the street light. "You want me to come in?" Danny asked as he held the car door open.

"No, just wait here." He looked at his man on the stoop guarding Lila's door. "Why don't you take a break?" he said. "Danny will be here. Come back in about thirty minutes."

The guy nodded. "Thanks, Mr. MacFarlane. Can I grab you anything at the Starbucks down the street?"

Cian declined and then walked up the steps to knock on the door of Lila's simple brownstone.

The door swung open, and there she stood in a tight T-shirt, yoga pants, floppy bun, and bare feet. He'd never seen her without shoes. She was even smaller than he'd realized.

"Sorry for the late visit," he said, nudging past her and into the tiny foyer.

"Uh, did you need something?" she asked, still holding the door open.

"Yeah," he answered, moving into the living room. "Why don't you come have a seat?"

She stared at him for a moment, probably something to do with the fact he'd just invited her into her own house, but then she sighed, waved weakly at Danny, and shut the front door before she sat stiffly on the sofa across from the chair he'd taken.

He felt a slight sweat break out on the back of his neck beneath the dress shirt he wore. He'd tried to figure out a way to avoid this discussion, but his choices seemed to be diminishing with each day. He had to either strike the Vasquezes before sunrise or get them to agree to a deal. Finn had provided that proposed deal, not realizing the danger he put Cian in with the idea. Now Cian had about six hours to figure it out, and he needed information that only someone like Lila could get him.

He'd debated going to a stranger, someone who didn't have a vested interest in what he did and with whom, but that was one more loose thread out there he'd need to keep track of. Lila was a fish in his tank already. It would be easier to ensure she kept her mouth shut than it would be some mercenary hacker he'd hire on the dark web.

He leaned forward, elbows on his knees, and gave her his most earnest appeal. Because he *was* earnest; everything he was telling her was true, and he needed her to see that.

"I need help," he began. "I've been trying to negotiate something with the rivals who attacked you and my brother's girlfriend the other night."

"The Vasquez family," she said.

He should have known she'd be up to speed on it. She was smart and had access to vast quantities of information.

"Things between our families have been tense for a long time. And tonight, they snowballed. I'm down to two options—one is to go to war, which will cost lives and money and draw unwanted attention to the business."

She nodded in understanding, pulling her feet up underneath her and relaxing back into the sofa, seemingly lulled by his frankness.

"The other option is to try to trade some information for a peace agreement."

Her eyes widened in understanding. "And you need help getting the information?"

"I do."

They looked at one another for a beat longer, then he broke the gaze, standing and rubbing the back of his sweaty neck as he paced her small living room floor.

"Word has it there's an FBI informant deep in the Vasquez organization." He heard her small intake of breath. "I need to know who that person is so I can trade his name for peace."

He turned and looked at her.

"You want me to hack the FBI?"

He nodded. "Can you?"

She snorted softly. "Of course I can." Then she paused. "But I'd basically be signing the guy's death warrant, wouldn't I?"

He shrugged lightly. He wasn't going to tell her that death would be the easy part of what the guy got. The torture that preceded it would make him grateful for the execution.

She folded her arms across her chest, and he tried not to smile at the frown that appeared between her delicate brows.

"So you need the name of a confidential FBI informant?"

"Yes."

She sighed. "I can probably do that." She moved toward a desktop on the far side of the room.

"There's something else," he added, clearing his throat as she paused midway to the desk. "You might see something—on that list. You might see another name, and if you do, you could do some serious damage to my family." He breathed deeply, leaning back against the wall as he pinned her with his gaze. "You could cost other lives—*my* life."

Her eyes widened as she swallowed so hard, he could see her throat work from across the room. He knew when she got it. Watched as her face went through the full array of responses—shock, disbelief, fear, confusion. Then, as if she'd put on a mask, she nodded once, sharply.

"Okay. I'm going to get to the file you need, and I'm going to step away from the computer, and you're going to look at that file and you're going to get whatever information you need from it. I won't know what's on it—who's on it. I don't want to know."

"This is the part where I'm supposed to threaten you."

"Yeah, I know," she answered, sarcasm tingeing her words.

"I don't give a damn about myself," he said truthfully. "But I care a hell of a lot about my brothers. Everything I do is for them. If anything were to happen to them because of this, I would do what I had to."

She stared at him, and she looked so sad, he almost took it back, almost told her he'd only ever killed one man, and that had been under duress. He couldn't even begin to imagine killing a beautiful, sharp, tough little woman who hacked computers. He was a damned liar.

But admitting he had a weakness wasn't how he played the game, and he'd been playing it a lifetime.

**

Lila tried to control her shaking hands as she sat at her desktop computer. She'd built it herself, piece by piece, insuring it had every single component exactly as she wanted it to be. It was her pride and joy, but now it seemed more like a device to insure her eventual demise.

He'd threatened her. After saying he didn't hurt civilians. But of course, hacking the FBI so he could give information to a rival gangster probably took her out of the civilian category. She wasn't Lila from Rogue working on setting up secure sales systems. No, now she was Lila the expert hacker in the middle of a potential gang war.

Yeah, he'd threatened her, and while part of her was warning her not to ignore it, because he wasn't the head of a ruling crime family for no reason, another part of her simply couldn't believe it. The man she'd come to know was so…decent, she struggled to believe he'd kill her simply because she knew something he didn't want her to.

As she set up the cyber walls she'd need to surround her as she entered the FBI's servers, she took a deep breath, letting it out slowly, willing her heart to settle into a normal rhythm.

Dammit, Lila, she warned herself. Just because he was sexy as hell didn't mean he wasn't dangerous. And truth be told, men like him were master manipulators, letting you see only what they wanted you to. And if anyone should know that, she should. How many times had her father seemed like the caring, attentive parent, only to end up missing her science fair or class play because he was at the track? How many times had he offered to take her for ice cream only to end up dragging her to the track so she could look at stats and odds to tell him which horse to bet on?

If anyone should know how deceptive men like Cian MacFarlane could be, it was Lila.

And yet, there was still a little voice in her head that said he wouldn't actually do it. The way he talked about his brothers, the look on his face when he watched her while she explained technical things to him, the questions he asked when they met for coffee. He'd seemed genuinely interested, not asking the standard questions, but deeper things—like what it was like to grow up biracial, if she was religious, what she liked to do in her spare time. And the way he'd texted her late at night after she'd been attacked.

How is your throat? he'd asked.

Better. But I think I might have a bruise that shows. Scarves for me for a couple of days.

Then there had been a pause, and she'd thought he might have moved on, the obligatory check-in done.

I wish more than anything I could promise you'll never be harmed because of me again, he'd finally added.

It's okay, she'd texted in response. *I'm a grownup, I knew what I was getting into when I decided to enter the dark end of the business.*

You're not even thirty years old yet, and you've been a professional hacker since you were twenty, he'd responded. *There's no way you could have predicted this—my family's business.*

She hadn't known how to answer that, so she never responded. But she'd looked at that message in the dark of her bedroom for hours afterward. Because deep down, as much as she liked to tell herself otherwise, she knew he was right. She'd been twenty, angry, and lost. She'd already broken countless laws on her father's behalf. Erasing his debts with bookies, switching his bets in the records when his horse lost, and scamming online gambling systems on his behalf. And then one day, she'd stood in front of the entire information systems faculty and student body at the prestigious Chicago Institute of Technology and accepted the award for student of the year and her father hadn't been there to see her get it. That was when she'd finally known—he didn't love *her.* He only loved what she could *do* for him.

Her anger over that had been so consuming, she'd dropped out of school, started hacking for personal gain, and never looked back.

Yes, Cian MacFarlane had pegged her in a way no one before ever had. He'd seen she'd never had a choice about what she did. She'd been set on her path just as surely as he'd been set on his. Childhoods and fathers who gave them no alternatives. Men who cared more about their own obsessions than they did their own children.

It was because of the way he'd seen so deep inside her that she was having trouble believing he'd actually hurt her. But wasn't that what manipulators did? Looked inside you, found what made you tick, used it against you. It was what her father had done. He'd known all she wanted was him—his love, his approval—and he'd used it to control her.

Was Cian different? Or more of the same? She gave herself a little shake as a timer told her she needed to get past the current barrier in the system in the next twenty seconds or she'd be booted out and need to start all over again. She focused as the timer ticked down, her heart racing in that familiar way it did whenever she faced a challenge from a system. Ten…nine…Dammit! She reversed the code she'd typed and hammered out another string instead. Five…four… Her screen went dark, then relit almost instantly with the FBI logo. She exhaled a shaky breath. She was into the basic employee system. Now she had to find the file Cian needed. No telling what security clearance level it would require, but at least the first hurdle had been cleared.

She glanced at Cian sitting on her sofa, thumbs flying over his phone screen. Then she shook it all off, focused on the blinking cursor in front of her, and got down to business. Whether he'd kill her or not, he expected her to succeed at this, and the one sure thing Lila had in her life was her hacking. She was one of the best in the world, and she wasn't about to let the FBI or a sexy mobster change that.

**

For the next two hours, Cian sat in Lila's living room as she clacked away on her keyboard, muttering to herself intermittently. He made some calls, scrolled through emails, even went in her kitchen and made them both coffee with the old French press she directed him to.

Finally, somewhere south of three thirty in the morning, she stood. "Okay, I'm in. At least I'm in to one file with the sort of information you want. I can't promise it's the right one, so I may need to look more."

Cian set his nearly empty coffee cup down on the end table and made his way to the computer.

"You'll just double-click on that folder," she indicated, pointing to the screen. "And you should go quickly. They do a security scan at six a.m. Eastern, and it might pick me up digging around in there."

Cian nodded and sat in her desk chair. It was still warm from her body, and something inside him couldn't help but notice that.

She turned away and walked to the kitchen. He heard the refrigerator door open, then a pan being put on the stove. After he double-clicked on the icon, the screen brightened with a list of names, along with series of letters and numbers—some sort of codes.

He scanned the list. What an idiot he'd been. He'd had visions of the list being like a roster—name of informant, organization they were informing on, email address, phone number…something other than first names that were probably pseudonyms and damn secret codes of some sort.

"Jesus," he muttered. "Dumbass."

"You having problems?" she asked as she walked back into the room, the scent of bacon following her.

"Uh, my own stupidity, I guess." He looked at her over his shoulder. "I didn't really consider this stuff might be coded." He scanned down the list. There was no *Cian* there, and thank God, because he had a damned unusual name. "Can you take a look?"

She tentatively stepped closer, standing behind his chair to look at the screen. The back of his neck prickled, and he felt something he knew he couldn't afford to right then.

"Ah," she said quietly. "Not going to be easy to find your guy in all that, is it?"

"No."

"So the trick to these is the patterns…" She leaned over next to him and hit a couple of keys that split the screen, then she began typing rows of letters and numbers that looked like the ones on the FBI's page.

"Your bacon will burn," he said, noticing his voice sounded a little rough as he looked at the strip of skin between her cropped T-shirt and yoga pants. "I'll deal with it. You do what you do." He moved off the chair, striding quickly to the kitchen. Once there, he rolled up his shirtsleeves and flipped the strips of meat, pulling plates out of the cabinet and popping a few pieces of bread in the toaster as well. He'd always liked cooking, and he really needed the distraction.

"God," he heard her call from the other room. "They're so predictable. It's a Caesar cipher. I just need to find the shift value. It'll only take a couple of minutes."

The toast popped, and he slathered on some butter, divided the bacon between the two plates, and added half a grapefruit to each as well. After searching for utensils, he found an entire drawer full of plasticware from takeout packages.

He walked out of the kitchen carrying the food and set her plate on the desk next to her. "You have no silverware," he remarked, one eyebrow raised because he thought it was funny.

She glanced at the plate, then at him and sighed. "I don't cook very much."

He pulled a footstool over and sat on it, balancing his plate on his thigh as he ate.

"What the hell is a Caesar cipher?" he asked around a bite of toast.

Lila absentmindedly plucked a piece of bacon off her plate as she continued to tap out rows of numbers and letters with her other hand.

"It's a fairly simple way of encrypting something. Just imagine if you have two rows of the alphabet and you shift the bottom one four spaces to the right, then take the four leftover letters from one end of the bottom row, move them to the other end, and then substitute letters in the bottom row for letters in the top row."

She grabbed a piece of paper and pen from the drawer and quickly showed him.

"So that's what they've used?" he asked, fascinated at the things she knew.

"Yes, but I don't know how many spaces they shifted, and they've included numbers and special characters, so it'll just take me a sec…" She paused, hit enter, and the screen went wild for a few seconds, spitting out strings of numbers and letters in a frenzy. Then it stopped, two rows highlighted.

"Here we go," she said.

"Did the computer just figure it out?"

"I figured it out," she corrected. "I just set up a quick program to have it run the combinations so it would go faster."

Cian set his plate down on the desk and leaned forward. Her hair smelled like honey, and he couldn't stop himself from taking a deep breath before he focused on the screen where she was now typing madly again.

"Now what are you doing?" he asked.

"Decoding the list for you," she said. "Oh. Except maybe I shouldn't see the list. I can give you the cipher, and you can decode it. We can print it out or—"

"Just do it," he told her. He had neither the time nor the mental energy to solve encrypted FBI informant lists right then, and he'd already admitted to her his name might be there. What difference did it really make?

She swallowed. "Okay."

"Lila from Rogue?" he said quietly, keeping his eyes on the computer screen though he really wanted to look at her.

"Yeah?"

"I'm not actually going to kill you." He couldn't help the small smile that lifted one corner of his mouth as she turned, her face mere inches from his, and stared at him.

"Okay," she said again, her voice thready.

"I have a very complicated life," he continued. "I make hard decisions every day, and my priority is always protecting my brothers. Sometimes to do that, I make unorthodox choices. You can understand that, right?"

She nodded, still staring at his profile. She'd stopped typing, so there was nothing to see on the screen, but he continued to look at it anyway.

"I've trusted you with something because I had to right now. If you choose to tell someone—anyone—it will cost my life, and that in turn will probably cost my brothers their lives, or at least their freedom."

Then he looked at her, and it took every ounce of the self-discipline he was known for to keep from leaning those last few inches and pressing his lips to hers. Her eyes were luminous—dark and shiny. Her skin was flawless, porcelain laid over steel, and her lips were two perfect pillows calling for him to come rest there, release his burdens, lay down his weary soul.

But he was Cian MacFarlane, and he hadn't survived thirty plus years in his world by losing control.

"So, you can tell someone what you learned here today, and you can put me and my brothers at risk. Or you can keep it to yourself. Your choice. Either way, I'm not going to kill you. I don't kill beautiful women who are doing me a favor."

"I don't want you to die," she said, blinking at him for a moment before she broke the spell by turning away and resuming her typing. Something inside him sizzled and sparked at that. The idea that anyone other than his brothers didn't want him to die was refreshing, maybe even inspiring.

"And I haven't learned anything here today," she continued, "except you cook damned good bacon, and the FBI is lazy with their encryption. A five-year-old could have broken that cipher."

Then she grinned and pointed at the screen. "Voilà!"

He looked where she pointed, and there, the third name she'd decoded on the list was Juan, and following it was the name Vasquez. His gaze traveled to the other two rows she'd decoded, and he noted neither included "Cian" or "MacFarlane." He breathed a sigh of relief.

"Now," she said, "it's already five a.m. Eastern. I'm shutting this down before they sweep the system."

"Great," he answered, standing and picking up his plate. "That's what we needed."

He loaded her dishwasher while she backed out of the FBI system, and ten minutes later, they both stood in her foyer, Cian armed with the information he hoped would stop a war, Lila looking tired as hell.

"Thank you," he said as he stood gazing at her, knowing he needed to leave, but not wanting to give up the sanctuary of her quiet home just yet. "I'll have something sent over for your time," he added. "A bonus if you will."

"It's really not—"

"Yeah," he corrected, "it is."

She nodded. "Thank you."

They stared at one another awkwardly for a moment, then he took charge, because that's what Cian did.

"If the circumstances were different," he told her, reaching out and cupping her soft cheek in his big palm, "you'd be my reward for a life done well, Lila from Rogue." Then he leaned down and kissed her chastely on the lips before he turned and left.

**

The sun was rising as Lila fell into bed. She lay in her underwear and nothing else, the sheets cool against her heated skin. She gently ran her fingertips across her lips, the feel of his breath still warm on her skin.

He'd kissed her, admittedly only a whisper, a flutter of feathered wings that was gone before she'd hardly had time to register it. But her heart had raced, her pulse had jumped, and an hour later, her breath still came faster than normal.

"You'd be my reward." Lila had never been special to anyone for anything except her hacking skills. But somehow, she knew that wasn't what he'd meant. No, he'd been talking about her as a woman.

She sighed, unable to stop the small smile that slid across her lips. God, a man like Cian viewing her as a woman—a woman he wanted, no less. It was so far out of her normal worldview, she wasn't sure what to think of it.

Or at least her head didn't know what to think of it. The rest of her seemed perfectly able to think about it—fantasize about it, sigh over it like a schoolgirl with a crush on the sexy older guy in Algebra.

She knew it wouldn't ever happen again, and even if it did, it wouldn't result in anything. But for that one brief moment, as the sun lit up the cold Chicago sky, Lila allowed herself to imagine what it would be like to have Cian's hands on her, his lips skating across her skin, his fingers touching her most achy and tender places, his breath coming heavy as he thrust into her. For just a few brief moments, Lila allowed herself to dream about what it would feel like to be wanted by a man like Cian MacFarlane.

And it was spectacular.

Chapter Thirteen

"You sure you're ready?" Liam asked as he shifted Cian's Kevlar vest, settling it more firmly on his shoulders.

"Yeah, I'm good. Really."

Liam leaned down and picked up Cian's dress shirt off the chair in the tiny office at the back of Banshee.

"I don't like this," he said as he handed it to Cian. "I should be going."

Cian shrugged on the shirt and began buttoning it. "You know it has to be me. Mario Consuelos is never going to agree to a meet with a surrogate. He wants me to recognize him as the new head of the Vasquez organization. That's a huge part of our negotiating leverage."

Liam leaned on the edge of the desk and crossed his arms, causing his biceps to bulge more than usual, the banded Celtic tattoos that decorated them standing out in stark relief.

"Then let me stand with you. Tell him you want seconds there. Pop would never have gone to a meet like this without a second."

Cian snorted in disgust. "Pop would have slit the hostage's throat and tossed him on Mario's front lawn before he blew up a Vasquez warehouse or two last night. Then he'd have eaten six eggs and a rasher of bacon before calling it a day."

"What the hell is a rasher, anyway?" Liam asked shaking his head. "But, yeah, I know he's not really a negotiator."

"You think?" Cian deadpanned.

Liam's brow creased in concern.

"And what if you're too much of a negotiator?" He put a big paw on Cian's shoulder, the weight of his hand comforting in a way Cian couldn't put into words. "You're the smartest guy I know, bro. And the best damn leader this family could ever have. That's why Pop gives you so much shit. He realized it when you were sixteen and all the guys were coming to you with questions about business instead of him. He's always known you were the better leader, and he can't stand it."

Cian smiled wryly at his best friend in the world, the man who always had his back no matter what, the brother who'd given up his entire future to protect and follow Cian. Some days when he looked at Liam, it nearly broke his damn heart.

"But…" Cian said as he pushed his arms through the sleeves of a dress jacket.

"But, I worry you don't see how many people in this business don't *earn* respect the way you do. How many of them lead by fear instead."

Cian's gut turned cold. "You know damn well I lead by fear too, whether I ever wanted to or not."

Liam shook his head sharply. "No. They fear losing your *approval*. They don't fear you'll be vicious. But guys like Vasquez and Consuelos are. They're vicious, and they won't hesitate. They won't bother to weigh the pros and cons and how it'll affect their families. They'll just blow your damn head off."

"You mean the way Connor did to Alejandro earlier?" Cian raised an eyebrow.

Liam shook his head. "Connor's not vicious either. Not like that. He's hotheaded and righteous, but not vicious."

Cian chuckled. "Righteous. That's a big word for you."

Liam flipped him off before pushing away from the desk. Cian gave one last tug to his tie and held his arms out. The double-breasted suit jacket hid the Kevlar well. While there was no reason he shouldn't wear a vest to the meeting, it spoke of mistrust, and he didn't want to set that tone before he'd been able to reel Consuelos in with the bait of a rat's name.

"All I'm saying is…" Liam looked away, taking a breath. "Don't fucking get yourself shot, all right?"

"Hey." Cian squeezed Liam's shoulder. "Don't go soft on me now." He winked. "Do you trust me?"

"You know I do. More than anyone on the planet."

"Then trust I've got this. I'm not going to let Consuelos get one over on me, and you know I'm perfectly capable of defending myself. I kick your ass in the ring at least once a week."

Liam grinned because no one kicked his ass in the ring, but Cian came closer than anyone. He was savvy, focused, and in damned good shape.

"Okay, then, let's go before Danny comes in here bitching at us for being late."

Cian nodded and opened the door to the hallway. One way or another, an hour from now the Vasquez problem would be solved. Either they'd have a deal, or Cian would be dead, because he wasn't going to lead a war, no matter what his father ordered.

**

"So, give me one good reason I shouldn't send my guys out to blow up every member of your family tomorrow," Consuelos said as he stared at Cian across the cracked pavement at the parking lot they'd chosen to meet at. It was on the border between their two territories and designated as neutral.

"I have two things you want," Cian replied levelly as Liam watched from a car twenty yards away. Consuelos's driver was the same distance away in the other direction.

Consuelos spat on the asphalt. He shifted his shoulders, the tight white T-shirt he wore showing his defined pecs and abs. He rubbed a knuckle across his lips, the five thick gold rings he sported catching on a ray from the one working overhead light that left most of the parking lot in shadows.

"My guys want blood," Consuelos said, eyes narrowed. "I'm going to have a tough time explaining it if I let you walk away, bro. Alejandro was *mi primo*, you know? That's family, man. I can't just let that go."

Cian refrained from rolling his eyes. Consuelos had been waiting for years to take over his cousin's territory. His crocodile tears weren't fooling anyone.

"Look, I don't know what happened to Vasquez. I told you, I met with him, he left, that's it." Cian gave Consuelos a dead stare, daring him to contradict the lie they both knew he told. "But I understand it looks bad at the moment, so I've come with a peace offering. I didn't have to. I could have hit you tonight, taken out your warehouse on Canal Street—" Consuelos's eyes widened slightly, telling Cian that, just as Finn had predicted, the Vasquez people had no idea that location was public knowledge.

"But I didn't," Cian continued. He stood with his hands linked in front of his crotch, his legs slightly spread. It was a relaxed stance, but communicated he was serious, not complacent or arrogant. "Instead, I kept your man alive for the last two days even though he assaulted a female civilian who's working for us. Then I went to a lot of trouble to follow up on a piece of information I was given that involves your business."

"Tell me your terms, then, if you have such special information."

Cian shifted slightly, glancing quickly at Liam where he sat in the car, his eyes glued to Consuelos.

"We call it even. The scoreboard is reset to zero. We shake and put things back to the way they were before last summer. We'll stay on our side of the DMZ. You stay on yours."

Cian exhaled mentally. "In return, I'll give you your guy back in one piece and tell you the name of the rat you have in your house."

Consuelos swore softly in Spanish. "Where did you find out about this supposed rat?"

Cian just raised an eyebrow.

"Fucking *pendejo*," Consuelos snapped. "Alejandro was shit for brains as a boss. It's going to take me months to clean house."

Cian nodded. "His priorities were…" He searched for an appropriate word.

"I want something else," Consuelos said suddenly.

Cian didn't move a muscle, just waited silently.

Consuelos paced in a tight loop as he talked, taking out a cigarette and lighting it at the same time.

"Alejandro's second, Gordo, is going to challenge me. He's a stupid fuck, but he had Alejandro's ear, and there's part of the family who want him in charge because he's easy to cheat."

Cian nodded in understanding.

"I want you to make it public you'll negotiate with me and only me as boss. They need to know if they don't back me, they're risking a war with the MacFarlanes."

Cian pretended to think it over for a moment. He could give a shit who was in charge of the Vasquez operations. As long as they didn't go after his family, he was happy to let them have their territory and do their thing. There was plenty to go around.

"Okay," Cian said. "We'll put the word out first thing in the morning."

Consuelos stopped pacing and dropped his cigarette, stubbing it out. "Good. Boundaries stay the same, business goes back to usual. We're even, and you back me to take over for Alejandro."

He put out his hand, and Cian stepped forward to grasp it. As he did, he pulled the shorter man toward him.

"The name you want is Juan Vasquez," he said softly. "You can pick up your soldier at the Briggs Hotel on Halstead, room seven hundred." Consuelos started to pull his hand away, but Cian squeezed tighter, his voice roughening to a growl. "You ever touch a woman under my protection again, and I'll slit you from dick to chin and stake you in your mama's yard to rot in the sun. Alejandro got off easy. You won't."

He pulled back as Consuelos hissed in anger.

"I'll have word out about my support in a few hours," he said as he started toward the car at a leisurely pace. "Nice doing business with you."

**

Cian had grounded Connor. Connor knew his brother had every right to do it. Once again, he'd made a mess, and now Cian, Liam, and Finn had to fix it. But this time, something felt different. This time, he wasn't justifying it to himself or sitting around chafing at his punishment. This time, he knew he'd gone too far. This time, he'd taken a life.

Killing someone wasn't something Connor had ever thought much about. He'd assumed eventually he'd do it, probably in a bigger shootout where it wasn't so immediate and personal, but all the same, he'd always assumed he'd kill at some point. When you were in the mob, that was what you did.

Unlike the Cosa Nostra, the Irish mob didn't have elaborate rules and hierarchies. The MacFarlanes had been high up in the US contingent of the Dublin

Devils since it had been imported along with Robbie MacFarlane back in the 1980s. Now the Devils and the MacFarlanes were synonymous. Without the MacFarlane family, there would be no Dublin Devils.

And because of that, there was never any issue over who would run the organization. As oldest son, Cian was the boss, and the rest of the brothers took on whatever tasks suited them. There'd never been the kinds of tests Italian mobsters had to fulfill—no killing someone to become a "made" man, no pyramid schemes created to funnel money up the chain of command.

In the MacFarlane organization, the family was in charge, all income went to them, then employees were given their pay. Just like in an ordinary business. And all authority rested with them as well. Connor hadn't needed to prove he was worthy of his authority. He was born with it.

But tonight, he'd done something he knew his older brothers had done. He'd killed someone. He'd never asked Cian about who he'd killed or when, but Cian's reputation preceded him. Men talked about his older brother in hushed tones, and no one ever challenged him.

Liam was a different story. Since he was sixteen, Liam had been working to be the family tough guy. Liam had always been…basic. But it was as a teen he'd seemed to evolve into the kind of guy who enjoyed being a threat. He'd begun spending hours at the gym, learning to fight, bulking up, carrying a gun with him everywhere he went, spending hours with their father's enforcers, following them like he was job shadowing.

Connor knew Liam had killed more than once. He'd heard it discussed by the guys, had even heard Cian and Liam argue about it.

Then there was Finn. There was never a question about Finn's place in the family. He was the student, the brain, the one who didn't even need to get his hands dirty. If Finn had ever killed anyone, it was with some sort of top-secret computer program that reached out and choked the person at their desk.

Connor smiled wryly at the idea as he climbed out of the car in front of Jess's house.

"We'll have guys at both doors," his guard said. It was code for *Don't try to sneak out the back*, but Connor didn't mind. He had no intention of going anywhere—unless Jess refused to let him in, which was a distinct possibility.

"Okay, thanks," Connor said before he strode up to the worn front steps. Jess was on the ground floor of the building that had three units like so many old Chicago row houses. One on the second floor, one on the main, and one in the basement.

Her old man had a place just down the block. She could have lived in one of the other units in the house he owned. He rented out the other two flats, but she'd wanted her independence, to feel like she'd left home, so she'd moved down the damn street. Connor thought it was the dumbest thing he'd ever seen, but since he hadn't offered to have her move in with him, he really couldn't say much.

He felt queasy at the memory of his selfish, immature self two years ago. He'd moved out of his parents' house the minute he'd started getting a salary from the business at eighteen and never looked back. When he started dating Jess, she'd been working at the gym doing bookkeeping and other office stuff for her dad and living at home. She wanted some kind of independence, and he'd been unwilling to take their relationship to the next level—because he was a stupid little shit, he thought, knocking on the door.

He waited, his head tilted toward the door, listening for footsteps.

"Who is it?" Her voice came through the flimsy wood.

He leaned his head on the door. "It's me, Jess," he said softly, his heart so desperate to see her, he thought he'd die from it.

She opened the door slowly, chains still in place, and looked out at him, her bruised face beautiful and broken. It nearly choked him.

"Hey," she whispered.

"Hey. Can I come in?"

She nodded and shut the door to remove the chains. After she'd let him in, Connor stood in her tiny hallway and just looked at her for a moment. She smiled uncomfortably. "Almost as pretty as yesterday?" she asked. "Everything's starting to turn purple instead of just red."

He swallowed, following her into the kitchen that took up the back end of the house, while the living room was at the front.

"Do you want something to drink? I have some beer, or, you know, coffee or whatever."

He leaned against the kitchen counter as she nervously dug around in the refrigerator.

"I should be waiting on you, Jess," he said softly. "You just got out of the hospital."

She shut the fridge and paused for a moment before turning around, pinning him with her swollen gaze.

"Why are you here?" she asked.

"I had to see you."

"It's okay, Connor, I forgive you. You don't have to carry a bunch of guilt about this. What happened, happened. The sooner we move on, the better. And the less we're seen together, the safer, I guess." She walked across the room and flipped the switch on the electric kettle.

"I'm not here because I feel guilty," he said. She narrowed her eyes at him before turning back to the cabinets, pulling out tea and mugs. "I mean, of course I do, but it's not that." He paused, taking a deep breath. "Jess," he whispered. "I did something I can't take back. I finally went too far."

He saw her shoulders tense, and she leaned her good hand against the countertop, her head dipping as she let it hang between her shoulders.

"Don't, Connor, okay? I know I shouldn't care anymore, but I do, and I… Just don't tell me about her. You're a free agent. You shouldn't feel like you need to confess to me. And I don't want to hear it. I *can't* hear it. Not now. I've had all I can take for a few days."

He was across the kitchen, standing behind her in a flash, his head bent over hers as he spoke roughly into her ear.

"There is no *her*, I swear it. That's not what this is about. I told you I love you, and I meant it. I don't give a shit about other women." He gently took her shoulders and turned her so he could see her face where a single tear rolled down her cheek.

"I was so angry about what they did to you. I couldn't stand the idea of Vasquez not being punished. Cian was going to negotiate, and I was so…" He ran a hand through his hair.

"Oh God, Connor," she whispered. "What did you do?"

He knew he couldn't tell her. If he was ever crossways with the cops and they questioned her, she'd be at risk. She'd have to testify against him, and his father wouldn't hesitate to put a bullet in her to keep that from happening. But she was his moral compass, and he couldn't live if he kept it from her.

He compromised. "He'll never touch you or anyone else again."

Her eyes grew wide, and she gasped slightly. Then he told her the rest.

"But it doesn't feel good," he admitted sadly. "In fact, it feels like it might eat me alive."

She didn't say anything else, just wrapped her arms around his shoulders and held him as he buried his face in her soft hair.

**

Jess held on to Connor and felt him shudder in her arms. Goddammit. This man. This man was actually going to be the death of her if she wasn't careful. But she loved him so much, she thought she might burst with it some days. No matter what she said or did, her heart couldn't seem to let go of him completely.

She took his hand and led him away from the kitchen and toward the bedroom.

"Jess?" he asked as she pulled him to the bed.

"I'm tired," she said. "Can we talk here?"

He nodded, and they lay down as he pulled her into his side and stroked her hair.

"Are you okay?" she asked.

"I don't know," he answered honestly. Her heart cracked a little at his tone. He sounded like a lost little boy. And in some fashion, that was what Connor had always been to her. Still a little boy in certain ways, a jaded man in others. But always lost. Caught in a lifetime of following his older brothers, hoping for someone to notice him, praise him, help him.

She knew she suffered from that age-old affliction of women confronted with beautiful, damaged men—she'd thought she could fix him. But she'd come to terms with the fact she couldn't. No one could fix Connor. As long as he was a MacFarlane, he'd be lost, no matter how hard she loved him.

And she did. She loved this man more than her own life.

"You did what you had to," she said softly, her hand curling around his waist in the dark. His T-shirt was warm and soft, the skin beneath even warmer, and while Jess was too tired and too hurt to think about more than holding him, her mind stored the feeling for later when she'd be without him again.

"I was afraid Cian's negotiations wouldn't keep Vasquez away. All I could see was the way you looked when I walked into that hospital room."

"It's okay," she consoled.

His voice cracked as he said the next words. "Who have I become?"

"Someone who protects the people he cares about," she answered, lifting her head to look at him fiercely.

"What if there was another way…what if Cian knew what he was doing? God." He raked his free hand through his hair, clearing his throat painfully.

Jess rested her chin on Connor's chest and put steel in her voice she didn't necessarily feel. "You're a good man, Connor. It doesn't matter what your family does, it doesn't matter that you're not perfect. I know you, and you're a good man. Please don't ever doubt that."

His hand found her hair, and he stroked it softly, the repetitive motion seeming to soothe him. "I haven't been good to you, baby."

She squeezed her eyes tight to hold the tears at bay. "It took both of us to get here," she finally admitted. "I was pulling away, I knew deep down I couldn't keep on. I should have said something to you. Maybe then, you wouldn't have…"

"Don't you dare," he snapped, his voice hoarse with emotion. "Don't you make this your fault. Yeah, you were pulling away—because you didn't want this to happen. Strange men breaking into your house and attacking you, a boyfriend who comes home with blood on his hands, in-laws who might end up in maximum security one day. You pulled away because you're too smart for all this, Jess. I knew it, and I should have let you go. Instead, I tried to avoid it by going to someone else."

She sighed. Jesus, they were a mess.

"You need to know…" He took a deep breath. "I didn't enjoy it…with her. I'm not just saying that. I hated it. I hated myself. I'd change what I did with her before I'd change what happened with her brother."

Jess closed her eyes and pictured her happy place—a beach, sunshine, happy children playing nearby, her ID card from an important job lying on the towel next to her, and a man, her man, smiling down as he leaned in to kiss her. And he didn't have Connor's face. He couldn't have Connor's face.

Jess clung to the only man she'd ever loved, even as she knew it couldn't be his face in her future.

**

Several hours later, Connor sat up in the dark, a jolt of adrenaline rushing through his head. He took a few breaths, calming himself, listening carefully for any-thing out of the ordinary. When it seemed quiet, he pulled his phone out of his pocket and fired off a quick text to the guys outside. When they confirmed all was fine, he lay back down on the bed and rolled to one side, looking at Jess's small form next to him.

They'd fallen asleep with all their clothes on after talking for hours. It had been the closest to the old them Connor had felt since he'd ruined it all. It was also the first time in his life he'd ever wished to be someone other than who he was—other than a MacFarlane. Because he knew he'd never be with her like this again. At the age of twenty-four, Connor had only now learned the full truth about what it meant to be him.

He'd learned when you were a MacFarlane, you couldn't afford to love anyone.

"Hey." Jess's sleepy voice pulled him out of his thoughts.

She rolled onto her side and threw one leg across his in such a familiar way, it made his whole chest ache.

As her head settled in the cup of his shoulder, he tipped his face down and kissed her forehead.

"Just go back to sleep, baby," he whispered.

But her hand snaked out, sliding under the hem of his T-shirt and into the waistband of his jeans.

"Jess?" he asked, swallowing down the lightning-fast arousal that shot through his body.

"One last time," she murmured as she leaned up and began to kiss his jawline.

"You don't have to do this," he said.

"I know." She stopped, gazing down at him in the dark. He couldn't see her eyes, but he could hear the sorrow in her voice. "I want to."

"I'm so sorry," he whispered as her lips came down over his.

She arched into him, her T-shirt sliding up as he slipped his hand along her smooth stomach.

Their tongues tangled, and Connor felt that familiar squeezing of his heart, a racing in his gut, and the hardening of his shaft. There was no one like this woman. Everything about her, from the silk of her skin to the scent of her hair to the tiny gasps she made when he reached her nipples and rolled them between his fingers seemed designed to fit him perfectly. Like the lock to his key, Jess was meant for him and him alone.

"I love you," he whispered as he traced her bottom lip with his tongue.

"I love you too," she answered, her fingers pulling at the button of his jeans.

He slid her T-shirt off and stared down at her bare chest in the darkness. Her breasts were full and lush, and his pulse raced as he traced them with his index finger. She was like a goddess. Perfection laid out beneath him, and he knew he didn't deserve her. Not a word from her lips, not a touch from her fingers, not a taste from her tongue. Yet, here he was, being given one last moment with her. He'd go to church tomorrow and he'd give thanks to the Holy Mother, but in the meantime, Connor would make sure Jessica O'Neil never doubted how much she truly meant to him. He slid his hands beneath her yoga pants and stroked her core, eliciting a moan from her.

"This is all about you, baby. You are everything. Let me show you."

And under cover of the dark, while his brothers risked everything to fix his mistake, Connor MacFarlane said goodbye to the love of his life the only way he knew how—with the slide of skin, the slick of sweat, and the whispered regrets of a man who'd never stood a chance. Because he'd been born to a life that had no room for things like love or women like Jess.

Chapter Fourteen

Sergei slipped out of the passenger side of the SUV, gesturing for his man to stay in the car. "*Zhdi zdes'. Eto ne zaymet mnogo vremeni,*" he told him. It wouldn't take long because he only needed two words to speak to the Mexicans—*cash* and *MacFarlane*.

He walked to the door of the auto body shop and pounded. When it opened, a stocky man in chains and leather greeted him.

"You need somethin'?" he asked, blocking Sergei's entry to the small office beyond.

Sergei could take the guy out with one well-placed punch, and his fingers itched to do it, but he controlled himself.

"I need to see your new boss. Tell him the Bratva would like to discuss some business we previously had with Vasquez."

The man nodded, whispered something to someone standing behind his left shoulder, then continued to block Sergei's way.

In a few moments, Sergei heard someone say, "*Toma sus armas. Déjalo entrar.*"

"He says—"

"I know what he said," Sergei snapped. He removed the gun beneath his left arm and dangled it in front of the guard. His gaze dared the man to try to check him for more. The guard shrugged, then stepped aside.

Fool, Sergei thought. He still had a knife in one boot, a gun in the other, and a syringe in his back pocket with enough heroin in it to send Consuelos to his grave in about five minutes.

He was led by a second guard to the work bays for the repair shop behind the office. The odor of motor oil was strong, and Latino rap vibrated around the concrete room that housed some tools, a lowrider with the hood open, and Consuelos with two more guards. Sergei tried not to smirk. He'd come in alone, and Consuelos still felt the need to keep a small army around.

"I wondered how long it would take you to show up," Consuelos said, lounging against the door of the lowrider. The orange flames that decorated the trunk contrasted violently with the glittery green paint. Sergei couldn't help but wonder why the Mexicans couldn't drive Third World dictator cars like everyone else in the business.

"Good to see you again, my friend." Sergei gave him a slow grin. "I hear congratulations are in order."

Consuelos shrugged lightly. "It's sad but true. My cousin Alejandro has disappeared, so until he resurfaces, I'm doing what I know he would have wanted and stepping into his very large shoes."

"How kind of you," Sergei murmured. "Word is you have the support of the MacFarlanes."

Consuelos nodded. "I've met with Cian MacFarlane. He and I have an understanding."

"And does that understanding involve anything your cousin and I had previously arranged?" Sergei's tone implied it had better not.

One of the men in the room shifted, and Consuelos stepped away from the car, walking slowly to where Sergei stood. Consuelos leaned forward and gave him a feral smile as he quietly spoke in Sergei's ear. "Our understanding is simply that things remain status quo. I won't ask questions about where my cousin Alejandro has gone, and MacFarlane supplied me with the name of someone who might not be loyal to *mi familia*."

Sergei nodded. "I see. As long as we're discussing things that will remain status quo, I assume you know the details of my arrangements with your organization?"

Consuelos nodded.

"I expect those to be honored," Sergei demanded, his voice as cold as he could make it.

He had to hand it to Consuelos, the new leader was tougher than Vasquez had been, not as ego driven. His response was murmured so the men in the room wouldn't hear all of it, but his voice was strong and his intentions clear.

"I very much want to honor them. However, given the newness of my position, I'll need some assistance in return."

Sergei cocked an eyebrow, waiting.

"As I said, Mr. MacFarlane was kind enough to tell me there is a rat in my house. While I normally would dispose of the rodent myself, it would be better right now if I didn't create any dissension among the men."

Sergei nodded. Transfers of power were never easy or simple.

"I would like you to take care of the problem for me; then business between us can resume as it was under Alejandro."

Sergei wasn't often pleased. He wasn't often much of anything, but this pleased him, because it was easy, and not many things in his world were. Making one Mexican mobster who'd been informing disappear? Piece of cake.

"Give me the information," Sergei said, removing his phone from the inside pocket of his leather jacket. "It will be done in twenty-four hours."

Consuelos flashed him a mouthful of white teeth. "Thank you." He snapped his fingers, and one of his men produced a cell phone. They traded numbers, and Sergei quickly received a text with the name Juan Vasquez along with an address. He nodded to Consuelos.

"I'll be seeing you soon, yeah?" Consuelos said as Sergei strode toward the door.

"You'll see me when you see me," he answered.

As Sergei climbed into the car, he looked at the name and address Consuelos had texted him and sighed. He swiped the screen of his phone and held it to his ear. "I've just met with the new leadership of our friends from Mexico. You have a something to take care of it." Then he disconnected and sent the name and address on.

As he settled in for the drive to his Gold Coast apartment, he sighed in satisfaction. Sergei liked easy solutions, and this had been one of the easiest.

**

The bottle crashed against the wall as Robbie MacFarlane took a menacing step toward Cian.

"Pop," Liam said quietly, warning in his tone.

"Get out," Robbie growled, his face red with rage.

Liam started to protest, but Cian interceded. "It's okay. Pop and I need to talk in private," he said, never taking his eyes off the old man.

"You sure?" Liam asked.

"Yep. Go see if Mom has any dinner cooking. I'll be out in a bit."

Liam muttered something about being close by and shuffled out of the office.

The minute the door closed, Robbie was on him. His fist connected with Cian's jaw, snapping his head to one side. He had to hand it to his father, he knew how to throw a punch. But Cian was a pro at taking them, and he gave himself a thumbs-up for not letting it knock him off his stance.

"You done?" he said blandly as he stared at his father.

Robbie shoved a finger in Cian's chest. "I told you to make fucking war," he snarled.

"And I decided to avoid killing off a bunch of our employees, including possibly your own sons, and negotiated a peace that cost us nothing. No territory, no business, no lives."

Robbie's finger continued to press into Cian's chest, and he smothered the urge to grab the old man's hand and crush it like a piece of newsprint.

"You didn't *gain* us anything either, which is the point of the war. It's a once-in-a-lifetime opportunity to gain new territory and slow down the competition. You want a prize for leaving us no worse than we were yesterday?"

"Actually, I want a prize for putting up with *you*," Cian snapped. He hardly ever let his father bait him, but damn, this was over the top.

Robbie's eyes grew feral with rage. He took the last step, putting himself chest to chest with his oldest son. "You've been a pussy your whole life," he said, his voice low and dangerous. "You proved to me how weak you were that night, and you still are."

"Yet, you turned over the business to me," Cian replied, as he held his hands out to his sides the way he always did to keep from hitting his father. He'd promised his mother years ago he wouldn't kill the old man, and he kept his damn promises. It was the only honor he had to hold on to at this point.

"And I can take it back."

"Can you?" Cian stepped away and moved to lean a hip against his father's large desk. He'd never pushed this far before, but the stress of the last forty-eight hours and the absence of Liam's moderating presence was making him feel reckless.

Robbie didn't say anything, but his face was mottled red and his fists opened and closed at his sides.

"I think you realize you couldn't take things back even if you had your health. The men are happy, everyone's profiting, things are safer than they have been in years." He stared at his father the same way he'd stared at Consuelos a few hours earlier. "I'm a better boss than you could ever hope to be, and that's what this is really about."

169

Robbie strode back to his desk and sat, a hard glint in his eyes.

In spite of his best efforts, Cian felt the sting of bile in his throat, a foreboding spreading up his neck like lightning.

Robbie slowly slid open the top drawer of his desk and pulled out an eight-by-ten photo, looking it over for a moment and smiling before he slid it across the desk.

"See, you may *think* you have the loyalty of the men and your brothers, but you don't have the balls to do what it takes to stay in control."

Cian looked at the photograph, and his heart froze. There, clear as day, was Liam, straddling a body, blood staining the dead man's chest, a gun in Liam's hand as he pointed it at the corpse and stared down.

"I have others. Of all your brothers," Robbie said smugly. "Photos of Liam carrying out a hit, or Connor handling a packet of product, or Finn meeting with one of the FBI's most wanted. It doesn't much matter which one hits the feds, it'll bring it all down around your head."

Cian had known a lot of cruelty from his father over the years, and until that fateful night when he was eighteen, he'd endured it and worked twice as hard to be what his father wanted. As in many families, he'd gotten the worst of it as oldest son, but as a child, he'd only wanted to make Robbie proud, so he'd doubled down every time, vowing never to disappoint Robbie again.

Then on his eighteenth birthday, it had all come to a head in one blood-filled night. That was the night Robbie had pushed Cian too far. The night Liam had started on the path to becoming an enforcer. The night Cian had vowed he'd end Robbie MacFarlane if it was the last thing he ever did.

But while Cian was accustomed to Robbie's cruelty, he'd never dreamed Robbie would do anything to risk the business. And make no mistake, his sons and the business were one and the same to Robbie.

"You'd send your own sons to prison just to prove a point?" Cian said in shock.

"No, I'd send 'em to prison because they're your weakness, and I know it. It's my insurance policy. The kind of insurance you never saw coming because you think if *you* wouldn't cross that invisible line, then no one would. It's the kind of insurance policy you've always been too scared to take out yourself."

"And what the hell do you *want*?" Cian asked, his voice raspy in the quiet office.

"You'll do what I say when I say. I don't give a damn about the day-to-day. I'd have never handed it over if I did. But when I say go to war, you go to war. When I say expand territory, you expand. You don't ever dare defy me again, because you may think you're running this ship, but I can sink the whole motherfucking thing."

Cian's lungs were tight, and keeping his breaths even was a challenge, but he'd be damned if he'd let the bastard see him fall apart. He could do that later when he was alone. For now? For now, he'd play along, but tomorrow, he'd figure out a way to put an end to this thing with Robbie. It was past time he took care of the biggest loose end his life had.

Chapter Fifteen

"Something's happened," Don said as Cian slid into the backseat of the sedan with its tinted windows and stale cigarette odor a few days later.

"I assume it pertains to me?" he answered, not removing his sunglasses as he stared at the two federal agents.

"Indirectly."

Cian waited. It had been four days since the night Connor had murdered Vasquez, since Cian had brokered peace with the Vasquez organization by trading the name of the informant ratting them out. He'd been expecting this little powwow with Don and company. He'd also been very hopeful it would restore him to his former position as the only informant between the two organizations so he could stop handing over so much information about his own family.

"We had another source of information," Don continued.

Cian nodded slightly.

"But it appears we don't anymore."

Cian's mouth formed an "o" of feigned surprise.

"We don't know how our source was discovered, but we're sending the word out to all our other informants. Watch your back. Be extra careful."

"And to think, all this time, I thought you didn't care."

Bruce flipped Cian off.

"Is that it? I have other things to do."

Don's forehead creased. "That's it, but you need to know, this doesn't change our arrangement with you. We're still expecting more information on the MacFarlane organization. The deal for you and Connor stands, but only if you give us what we want. Otherwise, we come after all of you."

Cian's head blossomed with a sudden headache. Every time he thought he had it all under control, more piled on. Here he was, with both the FBI *and* his father threatening to lock up his brothers. He was nothing but a pawn in an endless battle to outsmart the other side. And he was determined to outsmart them all, but damn, he was tired.

"I want that deal for Connor," he said, thinking it was even more necessary now than before. If the FBI ever suspected Connor had offed Vasquez, there'd be no way he could get his youngest brother out safely. "What do you need to get the ball rolling so we can get him and his girlfriend into witness protection?"

Don looked at Bruce, who shrugged lightly. "The rest of the trail. It's all fine and good to give us the location of the laundered funds, but we need proof of what the money was for in the first place. We need photos, communications, documentation."

"Okay," he agreed, thinking about all the sales through the Rogue site, and trying *not* to think about Lila Rodriguez. "That's going to take a few weeks, but I'll get it." He lowered his sunglasses to peer over the tops. "But as soon as I hand that over, you'll give Connor and Jess the immunity and the protection?"

"You have my word," Don replied.

"And how do I know you'll keep it?" Cian asked.

"You don't, but what other choice have you got?"

What Don said was true, so Cian kept moving, putting the possibilities he couldn't control out of his mind as he reached for the handle and opened the car door. A split second before he stepped out, Don spoke again. "MacFarlane."

Cian turned and looked at him.

"You'll never take that witness protection for yourself, will you?"

Cian smiled sadly and shook his head. "I'll never make it out of this," he said. "I was lost a long time ago. But Connor's not."

✱✱

Lila sat in front of the computer screen and watched the orders begin to roll in.

"So, everything's doing what it's supposed to?" Connor asked from his chair on the other side of the desk.

"So far, so good," she answered. She'd been relieved to find the information she'd dug up for Cian had seemed to solve his problem with the Vasquez people. The guards outside her house had been removed, and a week later, she was back to feeling like her life was at least somewhat normal.

Well, normal if you didn't count that kiss. Which she was trying really hard not to.

"I'm sorry I have to sit here and stare at you. I know you're perfectly capable of handling whatever on your own. In fact—" He got distracted briefly by something on his phone. "Since I'm not a computer guy like Finn, I couldn't help you even if you needed it."

"So why are you here?" she asked, giving him a small smile. He was like a younger, less haggard version of Cian, and she couldn't help but find that appealing.

"Let's just say I did something really dumb, and my punishment is spending a lot of time here at the office doing not much."

Well, that was fantastic. "So sitting here with me is considered punishment with you guys?"

He flushed slightly. "No, I didn't mean it that way at all…I…"

She laughed softly. "Relax. I'm kidding. I understand what you meant. You're keeping a low profile."

"Yeah. That."

She looked back at her screen, trying not to think about what kind of punishment Cian might consider giving her. She found her imagination moving away from torture of the deadly kind to torture of the orgasmic kind. She rolled her eyes internally. Stupid girl.

"Well, we have about eighty orders now, and it looks like the payments have been processed just fine. The system seems to be running smooth as glass," she told Connor.

"Really? Eighty orders in half an hour? Where did they all come from?"

She clicked a few keys. "All over—some in California, a few in the South, a bunch from Nevada and Ohio."

"I know I've been listening to all the info about this project since Finn thought it up, but I don't think I ever considered how anyone would know the stuff is for sale on Rogue in the first place. It's not like we can advertise or anything."

Lila clicked a few more keys, shutting down the screen running the data for her. Then she closed the lid on the laptop.

"We give it exposure on the Rogue site, and then word of mouth, dark web searches, that kind of thing. There are people trolling the internet looking for pretty much everything. If you offer it, they'll find you."

Connor nodded. "You're all done, then?"

"Yep. We'll download the orders at the end of each day and send them to your guys in packaging."

"I hope we can keep up with them," Connor mused. "If not, I'll have to work on tweaking the system and maybe setting up two locations to do packaging."

Lila had always been amazed by how serious the MacFarlane men were about their work. She didn't doubt that Connor would be able to handle whatever the new market they'd created threw at him. He was young but smart and, like all the MacFarlane brothers, serious about his obligations.

Lila looked at Connor again and wondered what Cian had been like at his age. Did he smile easier? Was he more carefree? Since the kiss he'd given her before leaving her house a week ago, she'd tried her best to put him out of her mind, but with his younger double sitting across a desk from her, it was tough.

"So, who is it that grounded you? Does your dad decide that stuff or Cian?" she asked.

She really shouldn't be fishing for any stories she could hear about Cian, but since when had Lila ever let what she should do interfere with what she did do? It was a terrible trait she'd picked up from her father. The same place she'd picked up all her terrible traits.

Connor sighed. "Cian handles the day-to-day. So, yeah, it was him. It's usually him."

Her eyebrow rose. "Do you get in trouble a lot?"

He chuckled. "It makes it sound like I'm a four-year-old, doesn't it? But to answer your question, no. I really screwed up this time, though. I deserve whatever he throws at me."

She watched him, seeing a deep pain in his eyes, even though his smile was still peeking through.

"Is he tough on you? Cian, I mean." *Stop, Lila*, a voice in her head said, but it apparently had no connection to her actual voice.

His gaze shot to hers, and she felt her face flush. She needed to temper her interest in the mob boss. Connor was more likely to think she was informing on them than the truth—she had a burgeoning crush on his tortured criminal of a brother.

Connor's expression grew deadly serious. "Cian has been more of a father to me in my life than my actual dad. He's the best man I know, so if he says I fucked up, then I did. And if he says I need to sit with my ass in this chair and answer the phone and watch you work for the next ten years, then that's what I'll do."

He shook his head slowly. "Honestly, I don't deserve him. He'd do anything to protect me." He cleared his throat awkwardly. "I only hope I can be the kind of man he is someday."

Lila's heart pumped a little harder, flutters tickling her stomach. The tone in Connor's voice was so loyal, so sure, she felt something inside her shift. No one who was truly bad could inspire that kind of affection. He might be a criminal, but could it be Cian was actually a good man? She cleared her throat, trying to push thoughts of Cian away.

"Well, if it's okay with you, I think I'm all done here, so I'll go."

Connor stood and stretched at the same time. "Great. Thanks for coming to let me see it launch."

"Of course. And you know if you have any questions, you can just call me, right? I mean, or Cian can…or Finn. Whoever."

Wow. That hadn't lasted long.

Connor looked at her appraisingly, a smile playing around the corners of his mouth. Dammit, she'd overplayed her hand, he could totally tell she was thinking dirty things about his brother. "Sounds good." He smirked.

She rushed out the door and could hear him chuckling as it shut behind her.

God. She really needed to get over this thing— whatever it was. A man gave her a two-second kiss and she lost all sense. Maybe she needed to date more. Obviously, she was feeling desperate, because Cian MacFarlane was about the worst possible love interest a woman could conjure.

She reached the parking lot behind the club and opened the door to her car, climbing in and locking it tight before she even put on her seat belt.

Her phone buzzed, and she saw Xavier's name flash on the screen. She stared at it for a moment. Hackers didn't call; they messaged, texted, emailed, whatever written form of communication was convenient. They didn't like talking to actual people, or they wouldn't be hackers. In fact, the only reason Xavier's number was even in her phone was because he'd called her to offer her the job years ago. He'd never called her since, and she sure as hell hadn't called him.

"Hello?" she answered finally, brow furrowed as she looked out the windshield at the cracked pavement of the parking lot.

"Where are you?" he asked without identifying himself.

"I've just left the launch meeting with our newest clients," she said. She might not talk on the phone much, but she knew enough not to say names. You never knew who could be listening.

"Good. Everything start up fine?"

"Yes, orders rolling in and the system working smoothly."

"The oldest one—he likes you," Xavier said abruptly.

Her chest did more of that little tickling thing that was entirely unacceptable. "We've worked together fine, if that's what you mean."

"Mm, there's something more there. The way he looks at you."

She leaned back against the car seat. Xavier was like a gossipy college girl. Lila hadn't been that girl even when she'd briefly tried college.

"What's your point?" she asked, completely losing patience.

"I want you to keep your eyes and ears open for me. Make an effort to spend as much time with him as you can without arousing his suspicions. Since he likes you, it shouldn't be that hard. Listen to what he says, watch what he does. That's all."

Lila's eyes narrowed. Why did it feel like every man in her life wanted her to do something for them? And always something dangerous and wrong. She snorted. Gamblers, hackers, mobsters. No matter what they looked like or how much they paid, they were all really the same man—her father.

"You do realize who he is? I'm not real interested in winding up in the lake."

She heard Xavier clacking on his keyboard and wondered if he'd forgotten she was there.

"Hello?"

His reply was distracted, as was his custom. "Just watch, listen, and report," he said.

Then he hung up.

Lila stared at the phone for a moment before tossing it on the seat next to her in frustration. What the hell was Xavier's deal? He'd been progressively weirder and ruder the longer they'd worked with the MacFarlanes. Even for him, he was acting bizarre. Was he in some sort of trouble with the family? Maybe he'd borrowed money and owed them? Was that why he'd struck this deal?

Something told Lila she really needed to know more than she did, and nothing was more inspiring to a hacker than the need to solve a puzzle. She started up the car and headed for home. Xavier was a hacker too, one of the best in the world. Finding out his secrets wasn't going to be easy, but if anyone was up to the task, it was Lila.

⁎⁎

Cian leaned on the edge of the boxing ring and watched Liam and Connor sparring. Liam was bigger, of course, but Connor was fast, dodging and weaving with skill.

"That move drives Liam nuts," Finn said as he walked up and stood next to him.

"Yep. I think he referred to Connor as an annoying gnat last week."

"Why aren't you out there?" Finn asked.

Cian hadn't even bothered to put on gym clothes. He just didn't have it in him to punch anyone today. He had enough frustration built up, but the energy required to take the swing might just kill him.

"Not up to it today," he said. "You going to get in a workout?"

Finn wasn't much interested in boxing, but he was an expert in martial arts, and Liam knew enough to spar with him and give Finn a workout.

"I have a session with my sensei later," he answered. He tipped his chin toward the ring. "How's Connor doing?"

Cian shrugged lightly. "He's being remarkably cooperative." He glanced at Finn. "I think he might have finally pushed the recklessness far enough he's going to grow up."

Finn nodded sadly. "Had to happen sooner or later. I'm sorry for him, but if it keeps him from getting killed in the long run, it was worth it."

"Thank God we were able to fix it," Cian added, shaking his head in disbelief. "I really thought I wasn't going to be able to save him from this one."

"You know," Finn said quietly, "if any of us could make it out of this whole life, it would be him."

Cian's gaze snapped to Finn. "What? What do you mean make it out?"

Finn shrugged. "Don't you ever think about it? If we hadn't been Robbie's sons, what would we have done? What would life be like if we weren't MacFarlanes? I think if anyone could do something else, it would be Connor."

Cian swallowed, his throat suddenly thick. "Because he's the youngest?"

"Because even after what happened the other day he has the most of that thing the rest of us haven't had since we were teenagers—hope."

Cian was definitely out of hope for himself, but he'd never given up hope for his brothers, and now with Connor's future nearly secured by a witness protection deal, his efforts needed to turn to Liam and Finn.

"So," he said as casually as possible. "What would you do if you had hope? Or if you hadn't been born a MacFarlane?"

Finn was silent for a few moments, then a smile crawled across his face. "I'd be a private detective," he said. "I love surveillance, figuring out the clues about why people behave like they do, and the forensics could be pretty kick-ass."

Cian chuckled. "Sort of the other end of being a fixer."

"Exactly," Finn said, his eyes aglow with excitement. "I'd like to try to outsmart other guys like me."

Cian turned to him and gazed at him seriously. "You know if I could make that happen for you, I would, right?"

Finn gave him an odd expression. "Make something happen for me that would take me away from the rest of you?"

"If it's what made you happy, then yes."

"Yeah, I know. But I'm happy where I'm at too. You can't take on the world, Cian. You didn't get to choose this any more than the rest of us. It's not your fault."

Cian turned back to the ring. "Sometimes it doesn't matter whose fault something was. It only matters that someone can fix it."

Movement to the right of the ring caught his attention, and he saw Jess leaning against the doorframe of the office watching Connor and Liam spar.

"Too bad you can't fix that," Finn murmured.

"Yeah," Cian answered quietly as Jess noticed them and quickly went back to the office. "Too bad."

Chapter Sixteen

Nodding to the guy standing guard outside his parents' house, Cian quietly let himself in. It was four o'clock on a Wednesday, which meant his mother had taken his father to mass at St. Pat's. The hour and a half of an empty house was exactly what he needed.

His father had caught him off guard the morning after he'd negotiated the deal with Consuelos. But Robbie didn't realize that while he might be the more brutal of the two of them, Cian was every bit as wily, and he wasn't about to let his brute of a father out-maneuver him.

He quietly walked through the house, heading to the back hallway where Robbie's office was.

He opened the door to the dark paneled room, his eyes resting for a moment on the leaded glass that decorated the top half of the windows in the elegant room.

He went to the desk first, even though he knew Robbie would have moved everything. After he shimmied the lock on the desk drawers and confirmed what he already knew, he moved to the safe in a hollowed-out section of wall behind the credenza. The combination that Robbie had used since Cian was a child had been changed, but it didn't take long for Cian to crack the new one. The old man had only so many numbers he could use for something like that.

The safe held guns, cash, and some documents that Cian had no doubt were more of Robbie's famous insurance against certain people. But it didn't have anything pertaining to his brothers. He closed it back up and replaced the heavy piece of furniture in front.

He stood, arms crossed for a moment, thinking about where else his father would keep a safe box. Then it came to him. The place least likely would be the most likely.

He made his way to the second floor of the old house, walking by the bedrooms that had housed him and his brothers growing up, all four of them still decorated as if the boys had moved out the day before. He'd once caught his mother sitting on the bed in Finn's room, quietly weeping. When he'd asked her what was wrong, she'd said that she missed them. "But we see you every week, Mom," he'd told her, putting an arm around her.

"No," she'd corrected, "I miss ten-year-old you."

He reached the last room before his parents' suite and opened the door into the dark, cool space. Flipping on the light since the blinds were closed, he was greeted with another blast from his past. How many hours had he spent sitting in this room, doing homework or playing with toys when he was small? His mom loved to quilt, knit, and cross-stitch. This room had been her refuge, the place she went when his father had business associates over, or her four rambunctious boys had driven her to distraction. It was also the place she made the boys sit with her—one at a time—when she wanted to be able to supervise them closely.

To the best of his knowledge, Robbie had never set foot in the sewing room while Cian was growing up, but he was willing to bet he had in the last week.

Cian started by looking along all four walls, under the sewing table and along the window seat. Next, he tackled the built-in cubbies that held scraps of fabric, felt, yarn, and batting.

When that didn't yield results, he moved to the walk-in closet where there were stacks of quilts, some partially finished, some waiting to go to the church auction and the Catholic charities home.

As it was, he almost missed it, but just before he turned to leave the closet, he noticed the imperfection in the back corner. He flipped on the flashlight on his phone and shone it on the spot. It was clear where the carpet had been sliced open, a square that had then been put back into place.

Cian's pulse ratcheted up as he knelt and took out a pocket knife to lift a corner of the sliced carpet. It lifted easily, and a moment later, he'd removed the square entirely. There was a manila envelope underneath. He lifted it out, tearing it open along the top with his knife.

Inside were a series of incriminating photos of his brothers along with a USB drive. Cian took a moment to shuffle through the photos. They'd all been taken by someone there in the moment. Obviously, his father had one of the men recording their activities. It was a problem Cian couldn't fix. Technically, they worked for the family, and officially, Robbie was still the patriarch of that family. Firing anyone would only leave a disgruntled enemy at large. And he certainly couldn't have the whole staff killed.

No, Cian might have found this round of insurance, but he was willing to bet Robbie had more in reserve, and Cian had a problem. He couldn't afford to leave his brothers vulnerable. So he'd have to double down. Just like he always had with Robbie. Only this time, he'd be doubling down with outside help, and that was going to make all the difference.

**

The motorcycle idled smoothly as Connor sat under the big oak tree kitty corner from Jess's house. The streetlight overhead was dim and cast shadows that helped him be discreet. But it was still a risk. He knew a peace had been brokered. Consuelos had more than enough to do asserting his newly acquired authority. He wasn't going to be coming after Connor or Jess anytime soon.

Yet, Connor couldn't let go of the worry and fear that plagued him now. He'd always known she could be harmed by his enemies, but he'd also always arrogantly thought he could protect her. That somehow his name and family would be enough to keep her safe.

The truth was, it had been something of a game to him. Being a mobster was the grown-up, exciting, dangerous thing his father and brothers did. He'd never thought about anything other than joining them, and when he did join the family business, it all had a gritty glamour to it that appealed to his immature need for entertainment.

But then he'd blinked, and Jess was in the hospital. He'd blinked again, and a man was dead at his feet. In that one day, Connor had learned the biggest lesson of his life—it took only a fraction of a second to kill someone. And no one could be protected every fraction of every second of their lives.

They were all vulnerable. Finn, Liam, Connor himself—even Cian. And now, Jess as well.

The porch light at Jess's unit turned on, and the front door opened slowly. Connor quickly shut off the ignition on the bike, slipping back farther into the shadows.

Jess came and stood on the front porch, arms crossed as she peered into the dark where he stood. A moment later, she turned and went inside, but just as the door closed behind her, his phone pinged from his back pocket. He pulled it out and looked at the message.

Why don't you come inside? It's going to get cold out there.

Shit. Guess his surveillance skills weren't worth much.

He considered getting back on his bike and riding away. Away from his family, away from Chicago, away from Jess. But then his phone pinged again.

I have leftover stew and soda bread. Come inside and eat.

He sighed, swinging his leg over the bike and stuffing the keys in his front jeans pocket. He looked around carefully before entering the house, and when he went in, all the lights but the kitchen's were off.

In the kitchen, Jess was already setting out a plate with dense soda bread on it, and stew was reheating on the stove.

"You want a beer?" she asked casually, not turning to look at him.

"No, I'm good."

He sat at the kitchen counter, watching her as she moved around the room, stirring the stew, slicing more bread, filling glasses with ice and water. Neither of them spoke.

A few minutes later, she set the food down in front of him and sat on the other stool, a plate in front of her as well.

"You cook this for your dad?" he asked, knowing she often took dinners over so old Sean wouldn't starve on his own.

"Yeah, I gave the rest to him, but it was my grandma's original recipe, not the one I usually cook, so I wanted to keep a bit for myself, see what I think of it."

He nodded and lifted his water glass. "Looks good," he said. "*Sláinte.*"

"*Sláinte,*" she repeated, gently bumping her own glass against his.

The beef was tender, and the potatoes were buttery. Connor ate thinking it might be nearly as good as his mother's traditional stew. He hadn't realized how hungry he was until he took the first few bites, but then he shoveled it in until he'd finished every last drop and also plowed through three thick slices of bread. As he pushed the plate away and sighed, he looked up to find Jess watching him.

"What are you doing here, Connor?" she asked.

Her black eye was healing well, the bruising now yellow and green rather than red and purple. The cast on her wrist had been replaced with a lighter Aircast that she could remove when she needed, and he knew in another couple of weeks, he wouldn't be able to see she'd been hurt at all.

But he'd know it anyway. He didn't need to see her bruised and battered to feel the shock and pain of it all over again. It was indelibly etched in his mind, burned into his memory, seared into his soul.

"I had to make sure you're okay. I worry about you—I can't stop worrying about you."

She stood from her stool and took his hand, leading him to the living room sofa. After they sat, she spoke slowly, carefully. "I worry about you too."

He ignored her words. "I know you'd worry about your dad, but I think—" He paused, his chest tight with pain. "I think you should go—leave town, start over again somewhere else."

Her eyes were sad as she gazed at him. "Is that what you want?"

He stood and walked to the window, peering out between the curtains, checking the surroundings, looking for unusual cars or people hiding in the shadows like he'd been doing an hour earlier.

"I want you to be safe, Jess, and I'm not sure you ever can be here again."

"I thought he can't come back—you handled that…"

He spun, eyes blazing with emotion. "Yeah, Jess, I did. I handled that—permanently. But you think he's the only one? You think there won't be ten others just like him over the next ten years? I'll never be safe. No one who's around me will ever be safe. It's always going to be like this, and I think—" He ran a hand through his hair in frustration. "I think that's finally sinking in." He sighed, his whole body sagging in defeat. "I'll never be safe. You'll never be safe."

Connor reached the sofa in two strides and knelt in front of her, his hands on her knees, pleading with her, desperate for her to understand how badly he needed her to be safe and happy even if it wasn't possible to be that with him.

"Unless you leave," he finished. "If you go somewhere else, disappear, start fresh away from me, away from my family and this neighborhood."

She started to answer, but he put a finger against her soft pink lips. "I'll take care of your dad. I'll make sure he has what he needs, hire a bookkeeper for the gym, pay off the debts. You know I'd never let anything happen to him. And he'll be happy as long as you're happy. It's the truth."

She grabbed the finger he held against her mouth and wrapped her fist around it before planting a tiny kiss on the tip.

"Then come with me," she whispered.

He stared at her, disbelief washing over him.

"What?"

She released his hand and looked him in the eye, solid, strong, determined. Maybe this Jess had been there all along and Connor was too self-absorbed to see her.

"Come with me. Tell your family you don't want to do it anymore, and we'll leave. We don't need their money or their help. I've got a little money saved up—enough for a couple of months' rent. We can get jobs, an apartment, be normal. Make friends, go to the movies, sleep on futons until we can afford a real bed. We can be like everyone else, Connor. Just come with me."

Connor stared at her, his heart racing, throat dry. Leave? Just leave? The thought had never crossed his mind—until last week. Until the night he'd held a gun in his hand and watched Alejandro Vasquez lying in a pool of blood. In that moment, he'd thought maybe it was inevitable. Maybe if you stayed in this life—the life of the MacFarlanes—it was only a matter of time until you faced a kill-or-be-killed moment. A slice of time where it seemed the only way to protect the people you loved was to take someone else's loved one away.

"I can't—"

"You can," she said, firmly.

"My dad would never allow it," he murmured.

She let her fingers drift through his hair where he kneeled in front of her. "But Cian would. Cian would let you go. He'd even help us, I know it."

"I shouldn't be here, Jess. I shouldn't be risking someone seeing us together. I shouldn't be stringing you along. I should let you go, make you leave."

"And I shouldn't be letting you in. I should be furious with you, or scared of you, or at least smart enough to stay away from you."

They gazed at one another, a thousand words passing between them in silence.

"If I went, you would come?" he finally asked.

"Yes," she whispered.

"God, Jess." He reached up and ran a finger down a silky strand of hair, slow and easy. "Do you know how much I love you? I don't think I realized until I saw you in that hospital bed."

He moved onto the sofa next to her, wrapping an arm around her shoulders and drawing her close. "Where would we go?" he asked, settling in with her soft curves against him.

"Someplace warm," she murmured. "Florida or California."

"How about Hawaii?" he asked.

"The farther, the better."

"Yeah," Connor agreed, "it's going to have to be very far away."

Chapter Seventeen

Xavier watched the screen in front of him as Liam MacFarlane lounged on the sofa in his bachelor pad. So far, his surveillance of Liam had proven the second MacFarlane brother to be a complete bore. He worked on his giant muscles, screwed a different floozy every couple of days, and watched a shit ton of MMA on TV.

A message flashed in the top corner of his screen, and he clicked on it. The oldest MacFarlane brother was online, so Xavier clicked over to see what he was up to.

He sat up straighter, pressing several keys until his screen showed what he wanted it to. Cian's laptop was transferring a file to an encrypted server.

"Bingo," Xavier murmured as he intercepted the file and downloaded it to his own machine. The moment the transfer was complete, the file disappeared off Cian's drive. He flipped on the camera that allowed him to see Cian. The stylish mobster was texting someone on a cheap burner phone. When he was done, he removed the SIM card and destroyed it before tossing the phone in the trash.

Xavier opened the file he'd stolen. It contained photos, a timeline, and spreadsheets. It didn't take him long to see that the spreadsheets were mirror images of each other except for the dollar amounts on them. Money appeared between one and the next, money that was undoubtedly being laundered.

"You've obviously struck a deal with our friends," Xavier muttered to himself. "But are you tossing your own family to the wolves?"

He had a hard time believing that, but really, it didn't matter for his purposes. He needed capital, and Cian was handing it to him on a silver platter.

He watched as Cian sat back in his desk chair, staring at the computer screen with a look of exhaustion. A few seconds later, he stood and walked to his door. Xavier couldn't see who was there, but Cian followed them out, leaving the computer camera focused on an empty room.

He tapped a pencil on his desk for a moment. He was getting closer. He could feel it. And when he had the last piece, he'd make sure the MacFarlanes gave him exactly what he needed. If Cian was lost in the cross fire, he didn't much care. Liam was next in line, and he'd be a lot easier to manage than his older brother. Xavier clicked back to the image of Liam in his living room. He had his shirt off and was still sprawled on the sofa, his oversized muscles and tattoos dominating the space. Yes, Liam was a thickheaded moron. Xavier relished the idea of leaving the MacFarlane business in his hands. Cian be damned.

**

Lila's fingers flew across the keyboard as page after page opened, layering her screen with billions of bytes of information.

She flipped between pages, closing one out as quickly as she opened another, her mind sifting through, eliminating one thing as rapidly as it saved another to dig into later. Drilling down to the true Xavier wasn't easy, but Lila had a growing burn deep in her gut that told her it had to be done.

It was odd that she'd worked for the man for so many years and never thought twice about him or his motivations. She'd thought she knew him—your above-average outlaw hacker. She'd been around guys like him since she was a teenager. But his obsession with Cian, the way he'd been acting since they started working with the MacFarlanes—something about that wasn't like anything she'd known from him or guys like him before. Lila's sixth sense was ringing like a doorbell, and she needed to let the information in.

If she were being honest with herself, it was scary. These men were all scary, and while she'd always thought she was tough because of her father's under-world associations, she was rapidly learning there was an entire criminal element that went way beyond anything she knew. If she had any sense, she'd keep her head down and ignore all of it. But there was something else there, something beyond her innate curiosity, and it was hard to admit.

She liked Cian MacFarlane. Not just in the obvious he's-sexy-as-hell way, but in a genuine, he's-a-good-guy way. Which he wasn't. Yet, her gut kept saying it anyway. It didn't make any sense. It was at odds with everything common sense told her, but regardless, she liked Cian MacFarlane. A lot.

And because of that, she couldn't allow Xavier's odd behavior to go unchecked. She had to know if he was a threat to Cian.

When her phone buzzed, she barely glanced at it, but then stopped when she saw Cian's name flash. *Speak of the devil.*

She closed out of the page she had just opened, minimized several others, then picked up the phone, reading the text he'd sent.

Do you have time for another special assignment? I could use your help.

She sighed, her gaze darting to the computer screen and back to the phone.

Finally, she answered. *When do you need this?*

As soon as possible.

She looked at the computer monitor one more time, then hit a key that cancelled all the pages that were open, killing them one by one until there was nothing left but her screen saver—an anime kitten that reached out as if it was going to touch you with its paw over and over again.

Meet me at the Starbucks, she typed into the phone. Then she grabbed her tablet and bag and went to see the mobster she couldn't seem to shake.

**

"Mr. MacFarlane has a table in the back," Danny said as he met Lila at the door.

"How's that new app I made you?" Lila asked as she smiled at him.

"It's really great," he replied, ushering her through the crowded coffee shop. "It works exactly like I wanted. Tracks all my steps and the money I spend in one place. You should sell it. You'd make a ton."

She grinned. "You know, I just don't want to spend the time, but if I ever did, I'd name it the Danny app and use a caricature of your face as the avatar."

They were both laughing as they reached Cian's table, and he stood to greet them, looking at Danny with tension showing in the lines around his mouth.

"Is Louis at the back?" Cian asked, gesturing to the other chair so Lila could sit down.

"Yes, sir," Danny answered, sobering immediately when he saw Cian's expression.

"Good. I'll text when I'm ready to go."

Danny nodded to Cian and gave Lila a quick wink before he made his way back to the front of the restaurant.

Cian sat and leaned back in his chair, giving Lila the once-over. She pretended to ignore him as she took off her jacket and opened her bag to remove the tablet.

"I didn't realize you and Danny were such good friends," he said slowly.

She glanced at him as he stared her down from across the tiny table, a shiver running through her from head to toe.

"I created a little app for him. He was complaining about having to use several different ones to get everything he needed, so I made him one with all the features he wanted combined."

Cian blinked at her. "You can do that?"

Her brow wrinkled. She'd hacked the FBI for him and he was impressed with an app? *Poor man*, she thought. He had no clue about technology.

"Yeah, I can do a lot of stuff."

"I bet you can," he murmured as he took a sip of his coffee.

"Why did you call me here?" she asked, trying to ignore the way his remark made her feel. "Because I know it wasn't to talk about my three-day-long friendship with Danny."

Cian cleared his throat and sat forward. His blue eyes bore into hers, and she blinked back, trying to keep her mind focused on the job he was going to give her.

"I need more information, and it has to stay between us again."

She nodded and waited. It was one of her most useful qualities, the ability to wait people out.

A barista called out a drink order, and she realized she hadn't gotten anything to drink, and unlike all the other times they'd met here, Cian hadn't offered her anything. He was either very distracted, or…something. She didn't know what, but it made her feel gloomy.

"I need you to look for information on my father," he said quietly.

"What kind of information?"

He glanced around, his long finger absentmindedly circling the tabletop. "Everything. Anything. Financial records, the records of his arrest three years ago, the case the FBI was building against him, who he talks to every day, where he goes, what he spends."

Her heart beat a few times extra. As much as she tried to ignore her client's dealings and motivations, there could be only one reason for this line of questioning—he was planning a coup. Taking the organization away from his father. And what would happen to the old man after that? Would Cian have him killed? Was he capable of that? Did she want him to be? Did she want him not to be?

"Is there something in particular you're hoping to find?" she asked, her jaw tight.

He shook his head slightly. "You don't need to worry about that. Just hand it all over to me, and I'll sift through it."

She nodded, suddenly more frightened by what he'd just asked her to do than anything else he'd requested to this point.

"Will the bonus I paid for the last job be adequate? Don't hesitate to ask for more."

"No. That was more than generous," she said. She'd taken a delivery of ten thousand in cash the morning after she hacked the FBI.

"How soon can you get this done?"

"It probably won't be hard, but there will be a lot of places to get into. It'll take time."

He nodded sharply. "Okay, I'll check in with you in a few days, then."

He went quiet, scanning the store with a thoroughness that spoke to how often he did it. She realized he was nearly always on alert, looking at his surroundings, keeping his back to walls, watching the door to any room, his body language relaxed but also ready to move at any moment.

She couldn't say what possessed her to do it, but she suddenly reached across the table, putting her hand on his and twining their fingers together.

"Are you okay?" she asked, her voice rougher than normal.

His blue eyes looked at her from under the shock of dark hair that always fell over his brow. He idly rubbed his thumb across her knuckles. "I will be," he said. "Thank you for asking." Then he was standing and picking up his coffee cup. He looked down at her expectantly.

"I think I'm going to stay here and do some work," she told him, feeling slightly rebuffed by his cool response.

"I'll leave Danny here. He'll walk you to your car. It's going to be dark soon."

"You really don't need—"

"Lila. Danny's staying."

She nodded.

He watched her for another moment, then gave his head a small shake before walking away. As he left, Lila's sense of foreboding grew. Cian might think he needed information about his father, but Lila's gut told her he needed information on Xavier more, so she decided to start with that. But first, she ordered two cups of coffee, one for her and one for Danny. It was going to be a long night.

Chapter Eighteen

Robbie MacFarlane sat at the massive desk in his home office and considered his life. For the most part, he was pleased. He'd risen higher and achieved more than he'd ever dreamed was possible.

Raised in Dublin in the 1950s and '60s, he'd gone from living in a single room with his ma and three younger sisters in the Mount Pleasant tenements to running a small gang of boys working for the Dublin Devils in the streets of Ranelagh. In his early twenties, when he'd been offered the chance to go to America as the Devils began their slow and calculated expansion, he'd known it was his chance to break out of the cycle of poverty his people had been in for generations.

America was the land of opportunity even in the 1970s, and Robbie had made every use of those opportunities. He'd risen through the ranks by being unyielding and merciless. Other gangs had known not to cross him, and other Devils had known not to turn their backs on him.

Now, at sixty-eight he sometimes wondered why Lady Luck had changed her mind and decided to kick him in the ass. His heart condition had sidelined him, and while his beautiful bride Angela Milligan MacFarlane might think it was a blessing in disguise to have him out of the business, all he could think was that God had it out for him.

After forty-plus years of working to amass power and fortune, Robbie was stuck in a body that had betrayed him, with an heir who was doing the same. Cian had never had what it took to be Robbie's replacement.

The kid was plenty smart, and he'd gotten the Milligans' height, with Robbie's thick hair and blue eyes. Robbie had always been popular with the lasses, and he knew Cian was as well. All his boys had become good-looking men in fact, strong and imposing. Even Finn, the biggest disappointment of them all, was able to handle himself in a fight. At sixteen, the kid had once karate punched someone at school so hard, the victim had been sent to the emergency room with a broken nose, cheek, and eye socket. Robbie had bought Finn a pint at the pub that night, he was so proud of him.

But no matter Cian's assets, he was lacking the one thing he needed to maintain the Devils' dominance in an increasingly competitive world—Cian wasn't a killer.

Being a killer meant you were willing to do whatever was necessary to win. It meant if you had to tie a man to a chair and burn him with a hot poker for a few hours to make your point, you did it. It meant you didn't hesitate for anything or anyone. Whether it was keeping records on enemies so you could blackmail them or knowing when a rival was having a family gathering so your attack could do the maximum damage, if you were a killer—like Robbie—you never hesitated.

Robbie looked through the window at the roses his wife had planted outside. Cian had warned him all those years ago he'd get revenge, and now Robbie was afraid that was exactly what his oldest son intended to do. He knew Cian didn't always tell him things about the business, knew he ran things how he wanted and kept certain pieces of information from Robbie.

But until this whole Vasquez business, Cian had never openly defied Robbie. He'd never blatantly ignored an order from his father. Robbie couldn't let it pass—*wouldn't* let it pass. Which was why he had to leverage that which Cian loved most. And that had always been his brothers.

Robbie didn't want to put his own boys in prison, but, like the killer he'd always been, he'd do what he had to. Only now Cian had stolen the photographs Robbie had asked Danny to take.

Robbie fisted the picture of Cian and the other three boys taken a few years ago when he was in hospital. They were all around Robbie's bed, two on either side, leaning down and smiling. But in Cian's face, Robbie recognized the look—anger. Yes, his oldest son had been angry with him since the kid's eighteenth birthday. And it was obvious that wasn't going to change.

He needed a new way to remove Cian from the equation. If he could keep the other three boys around so they could continue to run things under his direction, that would be preferable.

Robbie tapped his finger on the arm of his desk chair. What else did Cian love enough Robbie could use it to break him? He turned and picked up the phone on his desk, swiping to open the contacts list. He hated damn technology, but the boys had told him he couldn't use a landline anymore and expect anyone to take him seriously.

He found the number he wanted and tapped it. He might use the smartphones, but he sure as hell wasn't going to text where everything you ordered was recorded for anyone to see.

"Yes, sir?" Danny answered on the first ring.

"I need to talk to you," Robbie ordered. "When can you get here?"

Danny gave him an ETA, and Robbie disconnected the call. He'd figure it out. Somewhere, there was something or someone he could use against Cian. It was just a matter of finding it. Once he did, Cian would come to heel. The kid was weak, after all. He always had been.

**

Cian squinted at the computer screen in his office at Banshee. His vision was blurring from exhaustion, but he'd been putting off the regular work to deal with one crisis after another. He couldn't ignore the new internet sales, and that meant looking at the numbers. Luckily, they were better than anyone could have foreseen.

He sighed as he rubbed his forehead. At least one thing was running smoothly.

"Hey," Connor said as he peeked around the partially open door.

Cian motioned for him to come in. "Where've you been?" he asked, minimizing the spreadsheet.

Connor shut the door behind him and sat in the armchair on the other side of the desk. "I was checking on the packaging for the Rogue product," he answered.

"Sales are going wild. Packaging and distribution running okay?"

"Yep. I brought in a few new people to handle the increased demand, and the system seems to be running fine."

"Good." Cian looked harder at Connor. His brother was nervous. It was obvious. *Shit.* What now?

"So, can we talk?" Connor asked, elbows resting on his knees.

Cian sighed. "Yeah. What's going on?"

Connor looked down at his hands where they hung between his knees. "I've, uh, been spending some time with Jess."

Cian nodded. "I know you're still torn up about the stuff with Vasquez, but Consuelos isn't going to come after us again. You can trust me on that. Jess is safe."

"For now," Connor said, shooting his brother a look that said Cian needed to quit blowing sunshine up his ass.

"Okay." Cian waited.

"I love her so damn much," Connor said softly.

"I know, man. And it was scary, but she's okay. You're okay. I'll make sure it stays that way."

When Connor's gaze met his again, Cian saw something there he'd never seen in his youngest brother's eyes before—cynicism. Connor had grown up. He wasn't the same kid he was a few weeks ago.

"I know you'd stop at nothing to keep us safe, but I also know there are some things you can't control."

Cian didn't answer, because as much as it tore him up to admit it, Connor was right.

"Jess and I have been talking. There are things we want to do, you know?"

Cian's throat was thick. "What kinds of things?"

"Normal things. Live together. Travel. Have friends. Go places in public."

"You don't do those things now?" Cian asked. He knew the answer, but he wasn't ready to concede quite yet.

"You know we're not like other people. Jess—she doesn't want to live this way. And after what happened, I can't blame her."

Cian scowled at the top of his desk. What the hell was his brother trying to get at?

"What do you want, Connor?"

Connor's gaze met his, and there was a steel there Cian had never seen before. A new determination that made his heart swell with love.

"I want out."

Cian froze, not even blinking as he stared at his youngest brother and the world shifted around him. Yes, he'd planned to get Connor out with a witness protection deal, but he'd thought it would only work if Connor was choosing between that and prison. He'd never in a million years thought Connor would voluntarily opt out of the life.

How wrong he'd been.

Connor leaned back in his chair, turning his eyes to the ceiling. "I can't believe I'm saying it, but I want to leave Chicago, take Jess, and go somewhere new. Get a regular job, live together, pay for our own shit, get married. I want kids and bills and friends."

He cleared his throat. "I know it means I might not be able to see you guys as much, or that I couldn't see Mom and Pop at all, but…" He shook his head sadly. "I don't think I can live like this anymore, Cian. And I know I don't want to live without Jess."

Cian nodded, so damn much pride swelling inside him, he wasn't able to speak for a few moments.

"Well, damn," he said, his voice rough. He chuckled softly. "Wasn't expecting that."

"I know. I'm sorry."

"No, don't be. I've always told you to come to me with anything. This is exactly the kind of shit I was talking about. It's a surprise, but I'm glad you're talking to me."

"Pop will never agree to it," Connor lamented.

"Yeah, and that doesn't mean you can't do it, but it'll require some significant planning."

Connor's gaze grew sharp. "You'd let us?"

Cian smiled warmly at his baby brother, that kid who'd snatched his heart twenty-four years ago and never given it back.

"I've always told you I only want you to be happy and safe. If we can figure out a way to do that, then we'll do it."

"And Jess too?"

"Of course. You won't be happy without her, so she's a big part of the equation."

They both sat quietly for a moment. "You can't tell anyone, not even Finn and Liam," Cian cautioned.

"Okay."

"And I can't make it happen overnight. I'll need to figure out the details."

Connor nodded, a smile spreading across his face.

Cian ran a hand through his hair. "And there's no questioning how I arrange it. When it's all set, I'll come to you, and you'll do what I say, understand?"

"Yes. No questions, no arguments. And Jess too. She knows this means leaving her old man, but she's ready."

"You can tell her not to worry about Sean, I'll make sure he's taken care of."

Connor's voice was hoarse as he gazed warmly at Cian. "I knew you would. How will we ever thank you?"

Cian didn't hesitate. "By having a great damn life." He stood and walked around the desk as Connor stood at the same time. He pulled him into a rough hug. "I'm so proud of you, I can't put it into words. Hang tight, and I'll fix this."

"Thank you," Connor whispered. "Thank you."

After Connor left his office, Cian sat alone while the sounds of the club coming to life filtered into the dingy little room. The scents of dust, old papers, and stale cigarettes lingered in the air as he closed his eyes for a moment and, for the first time in almost over a decade, felt maybe it had been worth it. Maybe. If he could get Connor out of this life, away from Robbie for good, he'd be one step closer to redeeming his blackened soul, one step closer to finally paying penance for his worst sin.

His mind traveled back to the night of his eighteenth birthday. That was the night he'd realized he'd never earn his father's approval. It was the night he'd learned his father was more monster than man.

Robbie started Cian and Liam in boxing as teens, making sure they knew how to fight their way out of virtually any situation as well as how to burn off their sexual energy. On their sixteenth birthdays, he'd gotten each of them their own guns and taught them how to use them. But he'd promised their mother he wouldn't let them work in the family business until they turned eighteen.

On Cian's eighteenth birthday, Robbie took him and Liam out to celebrate. He bought them a good Irish dinner at the pub, gave Cian his first official bottle of Connemara, and then said they could come do a deal with him. Liam was there to watch, Cian to practice what it took to be a real leader.

Cian was excited, pumped with fantasies about impressing his father with what he knew about business. Unbeknownst to Robbie, Cian had been reading about negotiation, investments, and entrepreneurship for months. He was ready to blow his father away with his ideas and enthusiasm.

But he never had a chance, because Robbie wasn't interested in business but in power, and power was something Cian hadn't studied.

After the birthday dinner, Robbie took Cian and Liam to one of the family's warehouses, and when they arrived, Cian's godfather, Dylan, was just regaining consciousness.

Dylan had been one of the original men sent over from Dublin with Robbie. He'd served Cian's father and their family for three decades, killing for them, fighting for them, and being a friend. He'd been the best man at Robbie's wedding to Angela and godfather to Cian. He was valuable, and more than that, Cian loved Dylan. Which was why Robbie chose him.

"What the fuck!" Cian shouted when they walked into the old warehouse and saw Dylan duct taped to the chair. "Uncle Dylan! What happened?"

"Don't touch him," Robbie ordered. Cian turned from where he was about to release Dylan and was stunned by the evil that flared in Robbie's gaze.

"What's going on, Pop?" Liam asked warily.

"Rob," Dylan said, his tongue thick from drugs. "*Ní thuigim…*"

No, Dylan *hadn't understood.*

"*Géill dom*," Robbie had told Dylan. *Forgive me.*

Cian's heart raced, his mouth turning dry as he realized what was about to happen.

Dylan realized then as well, and he'd *taken it like a man*, just the way Robbie liked.

"Why?" he asked calmly.

"Because you need to be Cian's first," Robbie answered. "Get your gun out, Cian."

Cian's heart raced faster. He only *thought* he knew what was coming. "What are you talking about, Pop?"

"Do what you're told."

Cian's hand shook as he removed the gun from the back of the waistband of his jeans. He held the gun out to Robbie like an offering.

"Not me," Robbie growled, "you."

No, no, no. "Me *what*, Pop?" He heard the desperation in his own voice, and from the corner of his eye, he saw Liam's gaze widen.

"You're eighteen now—a man—and if you expect to make it in a man's world, there are times you have to do things you might not like. It's better you learn this now."

"Pop!" Liam said in horror. "It's Uncle Dylan."

Dylan hung his head then, taking one long, shuddering breath.

"No." Cian said it with more vehemence than he'd ever used with his father. Too bad it was the wrong answer at the wrong time.

Robbie reached over and grabbed Cian's forearm, squeezing it so hard, Cian gasped, his jaw tightening. Robbie lifted Cian's arm and pointed the gun at the back of Dylan's head.

"Pull the fucking trigger."

"No!" Cian shouted hoarsely, wrestling his arm away, his stomach nearly catapulting out of his mouth. "Why the hell would I hurt Uncle Dylan?"

"Because I'm your father and your king, and you *will* do as you're told!"

"Cian, son," Dylan said softly, turning his head so Cian could see the side of his face. "It's okay. The Lord will forgive you. It's not your choice."

Cian knew Dylan's Catholicism had always disgusted Robbie. "Religion," Robbie had once said, "was best left to the women. No God helped me climb out the slums of Dublin and become filthy rich. That was all me and my gun."

"Pop, I'm not going to shoot Uncle Dylan," Cian said, turning away from Dylan and desperately trying to shove the gun back in the waistband of his jeans.

But Robbie had also always told his boys that "you lead by example." So he drew his own gun, pointing it at Cian.

"Fuck!" Liam shouted as Cian froze, the muzzle of Robbie's gun an inch from his forehead. His life didn't flash before his eyes. It simply flew away, like his soul and his heart, and everything he'd ever thought he knew about his family and their lives. Because while Cian had always understood his father was a bad man, he'd also always thought the badness was only for other people, never for the family. Now he knew different, and his world was changed forever.

As they stood, staring at one another, Cian finally saw the deadness in his father's eyes. The darkness, the violence, the hate. He stared at Robbie, and Robbie stared at him. No one moved, the only sound in the room Dylan's heavy breathing where he sat slumped in the chair now, resigned to what came next.

"Pop," Liam said, his voice small and shaky.

"Shut up," Robbie snapped, never taking his eyes off Cian, who was motionless. "You expect to be me someday?" he asked, his voice low and deadly. "You think you deserve to inherit this business? The money? The power? You want all that to be yours? Then you'd better learn how to do what a king does, because there's no room for pussies when you're at the top."

Cian swallowed hard as Robbie pulled back the hammer on his gun. The sound seemed to echo through the warehouse.

"Do it," Robbie said, his voice low and dangerous. "Or I will."

Without making a conscious decision, Cian felt his own head slowly shift from side to side. Then he opened his mouth, and one word came out, the rattle of a dying man. "No."

Robbie looked almost pleased for a moment, but then, like a rattlesnake striking, he jerked, and Cian blinked. When his vision refocused, Robbie held the gun to Liam's left temple. The blood rushed so hard through Cian's ears, he didn't even hear his father say, "What about now?"

Cian slowly raised his arm to one side and pointed his gun at the back of Dylan's head. His gaze was still fixed on Robbie's as he rasped, "I'll make you pay if it's the last thing I do." Then he pulled the trigger, and Dylan slumped forward, the back half of his skull blown to bits.

Chapter Nineteen

The alarm blared an obnoxious siren sound, and Lila jerked up, knocking an empty plate off the desk and wrenching her neck at the same time.

"Ow! Dammit!" she cried out as she reached for the mouse and frantically clicked on the screen to get the alarm to turn off.

Once the alarm was neutralized, she blinked as her world came back into focus. She'd fallen asleep at her desk after spending much of the last thirteen hours digging through everything online Xavier had ever touched.

And damn, that was a lot of stuff.

She rubbed her eyes, then stiffly stood and went to the kitchen, where she made coffee and grabbed a granola bar before heading back to the computer.

She opened the file with all the information she'd gathered in her all-nighter.

Pages and pages of records spread out in front of her eyes. Bank accounts, real estate contracts, applications for patents, incorporations, a divorce she'd never heard about, and then the random mentions—places he'd been tagged in social media posts, some old high school tech competitions, his three semesters of college transcripts.

She maximized the last thing she'd been looking at the night before, an account in the Caymans that appeared to be where he put a good chunk of his assets.

She began coding, string after string of the stuff until she was able to crack into the bank's actual site. Using Xavier's purloined account number, she drilled down until she got to his account records.

At first glance, the account looked to have very little activity. A set of deposits each month, and a few scattered withdrawals. Then she noticed all the deposits were in the same amount.

"Who's paying you, and what are they paying for?" she muttered as she followed the trail of the codes for the deposits. They were made via phone and always sent from the same place, an account based in Moscow. The transfers weren't on the same day of the month, but with her affinity for patterns, it didn't take Lila long to see they took place every twelve days.

She clicked to another page and pulled up the record of Xavier's mobile phone calls. She scrolled to one of the dates of the bank transfers. Hunting for area codes outside Chicago, she found two that day. She repeated the process for several other days, correlating the bank transfers with calls outside of Chicago. While none of the phone numbers were an identical match, each day he received a transfer, there was also a call to the 917 area code. She googled it—*Brooklyn.*

"Okay, how do a bank account in Moscow and someone in Brooklyn fit together?" she whispered as she kept digging.

There was a lot about hacking computers that was complicated and mysterious to all but the most tech savvy, but it wasn't entirely magic. Sometimes Google was your friend.

She typed in *Moscow, Brooklyn, money, hacking, crime*, and hit enter. The third entry read: *Russian gangs of New York*. She clicked the article, then began branching out from that. Fifteen minutes later, she had a sick feeling in her gut.

The Russian mob had been heavily active in Brooklyn for a generation or more. They had their fingers in every criminal enterprise a creative mind could conjure—drugs, cybercrime, extortion, racketeering, human trafficking. The list went on and on.

"Oh, Xavier. What the hell have you gotten yourself into?"

Over the next two hours, Lila became an expert on the Bratva. Their activities, their assets, their expansion plans. And that was where the picture began to come together. The Russians had been working to expand into Chicago for years. In fact, they'd been making headway a few years earlier—right around the time Robbie and Liam MacFarlane had been arrested for trafficking. But then the tides had shifted, and the MacFarlanes had come out on top again.

Lila felt lightheaded when she finally turned away from the computer after her extensive research. She might not know all the details, but she had a pretty good idea of what was going on. In fact, she was willing to bet Rogue's whole deal with the MacFarlanes was for a single purpose—destroying the Dublin

Devils so the Bratva could move in. Xavier must want information on Cian so he could help his Russian friends plan how to take Cian out. And she guessed there would be a bust involving the drugs the Devils were selling via Rogue similar to the bust that had landed Robbie and Liam in jail.

She paced her small living room, memories of Cian sitting in her space that one night still fresh in her mind. His big, solid frame taking up so much space, the quiet way he waited so patiently for her to crack the FBI's servers. Cian cooking bacon in her tiny kitchen, the despair he'd worn when he realized the FBI didn't just keep a list of names and addresses for informants.

She laughed softly to herself as she stopped pacing and flopped onto the sofa. Cian had sat right here. He'd watched her with those icy-blue eyes, and he'd told her one of his deepest secrets. She picked up her tablet and clicked on one of the pages about the Bratva she'd looked at earlier. A horrific murder scene covered the screen, and her stomach flipped. Instead of the body in the photo, she saw Cian. His beautiful dark hair caked in blood, his chest splayed open like the corpse on the page.

Lila wasn't sure what it was she felt about Cian MacFarlane, but she knew there was no way she was going to let Xavier succeed. In the last few weeks, she'd learned about the mob. They weren't all created equal, and Cian MacFarlane was the cream of the crop. He was a drug lord, a criminal, and a man who killed other men. But he was also a conscientious, decent leader who could instill fear and respect in equal measure, a man who was capable of mercy and love.

You only had to hear him talk about his brothers to know it.

And a single kiss from him could send a girl's mind reeling for days.

No, Xavier had better think again if he thought she'd sit back and let him bury Cian MacFarlane. Cian might not be able to rely on many people, but she wanted to be one of them. She would find a way to protect him. Her skills had been wasted on her father, but Cian was worth it. Cian might even be worth something more.

**

"Nope, we're not there yet," Don said as he stood looking at Cian in a large empty airport hangar. "When we have enough for an airtight case, then we'll take care of him."

Cian's jaw set as he took a deep breath.

"Wrong," he said, steel in his voice. "I won't give you anything else until you get Connor and his girl-friend out."

From the corner where he stood smoking a ciga-rette, Bruce chuckled. "It's funny how you keep for-getting we're not your lapdogs, MacFarlane."

"Look, Cian," Don said, "It's not my choice. I'll never be able to get the higher-ups to approve it if we aren't ready to file charges against you, and I'm not going to blow years' worth of investigation by filing too soon. I want this thing ironclad. I want the Devils out of business, and I'll make sure you and Connor get free of that, but I have to build the case first."

Luckily, Cian wasn't as stupid as his father thought. He'd come with insurance. He stepped closer to Don. "Can we talk privately for minute?" he asked in a low voice.

Don nodded before tipping his chin at Bruce. "Be right over here." He led Cian to the far side of the hanger, next to a forklift and some hydraulic jacks.

"I'm going to reach into my pocket," Cian said. Don nodded his approval.

Cian extracted the paper, holding it out to Don. The agent scanned it quickly, a twitch in his left cheek the only reaction he had to it.

"I didn't think you had it in you," he finally said.

"I've been hearing that a lot lately," Cian answered. "Guess you should all quit underestimating me."

"You're a real son of a bitch."

"No need to bring my sweet mother into it." Cian took the sheet of paper back, returning it to the inside breast pocket of his jacket. "The good news for you is I have every intention of giving you the information you need for the case. I just want an advance on the payment—Connor and Jess get out in the next forty-eight hours. New identities, an agreement not to prosecute for any crime that might be associated with him up to and including the day he vanishes, and he gets wiped from the federal database."

"Jesus, can I get you your own island as well?" Don spat out.

"As soon as he's safely on his way, I'll remove that money from your bank account as quickly as I put it there, and no one will be any wiser. But if you'd rather take the bribery rap, go for it. I'm guessing your wife and daughter would miss you, though. And it's a real drag when they freeze all your assets with cases like this. Makes it hard for your family when they lose the house, can't get any credit, can't afford a lawyer for you…"

"Fuck you."

Cian just gave him a cold smile.

Don ran a hand through his hair. "Fine. Connor and the girl get out."

"Forty-eight hours," Cian said.

"I'll have the new IDs delivered tomorrow, along with plane tickets."

"No," Cian interrupted. "I don't want them in one of your witness protection houses. They'll have enough money to get started and the new identities. That's all they need. They just want to be normal kids, and as long as my father can't track them and you aren't coming after them, they'll be fine."

Don shrugged. "Fine, whatever you want. The IDs are solid. Your old man won't be able to dig them up, and I have no use for Connor when I still have the rest of you here."

"Good. That's what matters," Cian responded. "Nice doing business with you."

Don snorted before he set off across the warehouse. He said something to Bruce, and they both stomped out.

Cian slowly walked to the door, listening until he heard their car start up and drive away. Then he took his phone out of his pocket and dialed Connor's number.

"Hey," Connor answered.

"What we talked about the other day in the office?" Cian asked.

"Yeah?" Connor's voice was tense.

"It's done. Bring Jess to the office day after to-morrow at four. Pack whatever you'll need. I'll have everything ready for you."

"Oh my God, are you serious?"

"As a heart attack."

There was silence for a beat, then Connor's voice came through, strong and sure. "Thank you."

"Be happy, Connor," Cian answered. "And run far."

Chapter Twenty

Connor and Jess entered Banshee through the back door and made their way to the office Connor had spent so much time in over the last few years.

The club had been a gift of sorts for Connor when he turned eighteen. Cian had wanted him to have a way to learn about running a business. So he'd bought a nightclub, made Connor a full partner, and hired a manager to teach Connor how to run it. In the six years since they'd purchased it, Connor had learned every piece of the business, from ordering liquor to keeping the books to overseeing a renovation of the bathrooms and kitchen.

He realized now that Cian had made sure he learned something legal in the midst of all the illegal. Yes, Connor could manage a distribution network of drug dealers, but he could also manage a nightclub, and probably a restaurant or bar too. He had skills and knowledge that would take him beyond the Dublin Devils and into the world he and Jess were about to enter.

Connor stopped when he reached the office, looking around at his three brothers sitting there. This, he hadn't expected.

He stared at Cian, questioning what was happening.

"Come on in," Cian said. "Close the door."

"Hi, Jess," Finn said. "Nice to see you all healed up."

"Thanks," she answered, squeezing Connor's hand. He felt how nervous she was, and while he knew his brothers would never hurt him, he hoped this wasn't some sort of intervention and Cian had tricked him into coming.

Cian stepped out from behind the desk. He looked at Liam and Finn. "What happens in this room during the next half hour can never leave it. You may not understand what I've done, and you may not agree with it, but you have to trust me that it's for the best, and you have to promise you'll never breathe a word of it to a single soul for the rest of your lives."

Liam snorted. "Who the hell do you think we are? Jesus, Cian, as if you even need to ask."

Finn just looked concerned. Jess squeezed Connor's hand so hard, it started to go numb, so he leaned down and kissed her gently on the cheek, then whispered, "It's okay, just relax."

"I need your word, Liam," Cian persisted.

"God. Yes. Of course. I'm insulted, but of course."

Cian ignored Liam's temper and looked at Finn, who nodded solemnly.

He leaned back against the desk. "About a week ago, Connor came to me with a request. I thought it over and decided I agreed with him. I've set up what he asked for."

"Which is?" Liam interjected.

"Connor and Jess want to leave Chicago."

"What?" Liam jumped up from his chair, while Finn crossed his arms, brow furrowed. "What the hell, kid?" Liam asked, eyes flashing as he turned on Connor.

Connor took a deep breath. He hadn't known Cian would have Liam and Finn here. He wasn't prepared for how to talk to them about this, but now he had no choice.

"It's what Jess and I want," he said, his gaze pinned to Liam's. "We've talked it over, thought about it a lot. I know the sacrifice I'm making, and I know it means—" He cleared his throat as emotion dealt a blow to his diaphragm. "It means I won't be seeing you guys for a very long time. But we feel like it's the only way to have the life we want. If I saw another option, I'd take it, but I don't."

"Another option is to quit being a drama queen and get back to your life," Liam snapped. "No offense, Jess, I'm really sorry for what Vasquez did to you, but that problem's solved. You don't need to worry about it anymore, and Connor, you don't either. You're being fucking ridiculous."

Connor narrowed his eyes at his biggest brother before looking over to Finn. "And do you feel that way too? Like Jess and I should just 'get over it'? Get back to the status quo?"

Finn gave a small smile. "I think there's more you're not telling us," he answered.

Connor nodded, swallowing through the thickness in his throat.

"I don't want to do it anymore," he said firmly. "I don't want to live the life anymore. I want to be a normal guy, you know? Go to work. Come home. Take my wife out to dinner. Watch my kids play soccer."

"Be in debt up to your eyeballs and bored as shit for the next forty years?" Liam asked disdainfully.

"Okay," Cian interceded. "Jess? Can you excuse us for a few minutes? Maybe you could go up front and have the bartender get you a drink. He's setting up for tonight. We don't open for a few more hours."

Jess looked to Connor, who kissed her on the forehead. "It's fine," he said. "Place is as safe as you can get, and Jimmy will make you anything you'd like."

"Okay," she answered before giving Liam a dirty look.

As the door closed behind her, Cian turned to Liam. "Look, you don't have to understand it, but Connor's not made this decision lightly. He's in love, and he's young, and he's asking for the opportunity to choose a different road."

Liam rolled his neck and shoulders then huffed out a long breath before turning to look at his baby brother.

"You really want to leave us? Go live like a paper pusher or a construction worker? You won't have money, you know."

"He'll always have money," Cian interjected. "As long as I'm alive, he can have money anytime he needs."

Connor looked at Cian, unsure what to say to that. It hadn't been part of the plans he and Jess had made, but it added some security.

"I don't care about the money—I'm going to work. I know I've leaned on the family all these years, but I can take care of Jess and me. I'm not a child, and I'm not stupid." He turned to Liam, hoping to make him understand, desperate to have his blessing. "I know Jess isn't in any danger right now, but this whole thing showed me how easily it can happen. No matter how careful we are, no matter what we do, it can all fall to pieces at any second."

Liam didn't have a response to that.

"You could get married, protect Jess that way," Finn added softly. "Mom's lived a nice life all these years."

"I will marry her, but Jess doesn't want to spend her whole life going between church and the house with guards around her," Connor answered. "Mom and Pop are old-school. I don't see any of you guys bringing women into your lives for more than a night. I'm the only one of us who's ever had a relationship. Why do you think that is?"

"Because there are more women than time," Liam snarked. Connor kept staring at him until Liam looked at Cian. "You feel like that? Like you haven't stuck with anyone because it's too dangerous?"

Cian sighed. "How the hell am I supposed to find time for something like that? And if I did, then what? Connor's right. What woman in this day and age wants to live like Mom? She's practically a shut-in, and Pop too, now he's not managing things. They do stuff in the neighborhood and at church, and that's pretty much it."

"Yeah, but Mom's never wanted more than that," Liam protested.

"And if she did, how would it work?" Cian asked back. "What if she were twenty-five and had a job she'd spent years going to school for? Would she bring guards to work with her? What about kids? I guess they'd have to go to St. Pat's because that's the only school in town where we can station our guys on the street outside the front door like Pop did when we went there."

Liam's expression turned somewhat desperate. "Finn?" he asked.

Finn shook his head. "They're right. I know we've never talked about it, and I don't think about it a lot, but they're right. I can't imagine many women today would want to live the way we do. It's one thing for them to spend a night with some guy who seems dangerous and bad, it's another to live like us."

"I really thought we were all on the same page here," Liam said. "I don't want one woman, I want as many of them as I can get. I thought the rest of you felt the same."

"The point isn't what we all feel," Cian corrected gently. "It's what Connor wants. He doesn't want this. I can understand that. Can you?"

Connor watched Liam warily. He was on his way out the door no matter what, but damn, he didn't want his last interaction with his brother to be like this. He'd thought he would slip away and leave Cian to tell them all what had happened, but now he was here facing them, he knew he needed Liam's blessing.

"I can understand it," Liam said finally. "I'm going to miss the hell out of you, but I can understand it."

Connor exhaled the breath he'd been holding for ten minutes and said, "Thank you."

Liam turned to Cian. "How's this going to work?"

Cian picked up a manila envelope from his desk. "I have new identities for you both," he said. "There's a car registered in your new name sitting out back— California plates. There's also ten thousand in cash in here, and the number of an offshore account that's in your new name with another hundred and fifty thousand. If you need more—"

"Jesus, Cian." Connor shook his head. "I'm not going to need more. I'm not even going to touch what's there."

"You never know when you might run into problems. What if you or Jess get sick or hurt and need to go to the hospital? What if you get in a car accident or—"

Connor stepped closer to his brother and put a hand on Cian's shoulder. "Thank you," he said softly. "Thank you for always making sure I'm taken care of. Thank you for helping me do this, and for cleaning up my messes. I'm not going to need the money, because you showed me how to be a man. How to do these things for the people you love. I love Jess, so I'm going to take care of her. I'm going to make you proud."

"You already have," Cian replied before grabbing Connor around the neck and pulling him close so their foreheads touched. "You're doing the right thing," he whispered. "And I'm beyond proud of you."

"There's one thing you've left out," Liam said, clearing his throat. Connor and Cian pulled apart, both turning their gazes to him. "What are you going to tell Pop?"

Cian sighed. "I've thought about it a lot. There's no good solution, but my best is to use the one leverage we have with him—Mom."

"Explain," Finn said, a frown on his face.

"We can't tell them Connor's been killed. Pop would insist on seeing the body. We can't tell them he's vanished because Pop would turn the city upside-down looking for him and start a hundred wars in the process." The rest of the brothers nodded. "But if we tell him Connor's run, he'll go nuts trying to find him, and while I don't think he could, it's a risk I'd rather not take."

"So how do you keep him from hunting me down?" Connor asked.

"By going to Mom first and explaining why you left. If she's on board with your plans—with your dream to have a regular life with Jess and babies and all the things Mom cares about most—she'll tell Pop he can't look for you. And then, even if he does, he won't do it with any enthusiasm. It'll be a half-assed attempt at making himself feel like he's in control. He won't really want to find you, because he'd have to admit to Mom he'd defied her wishes." Cian looked at each brother in turn. "She's his one weakness."

"Mom will never get over Connor leaving without saying goodbye," Finn remarked sadly.

"But he's going to leave her a letter," Cian added, turning around and picking up a pen and piece of paper off his desk. He handed them to Connor. "Tell her what you've told me. Tell her how you feel about Jess. Tell her who you're going to become. She'll understand. And she'll help protect you from the biggest threat—Pop."

Connor nodded, not able to speak for the moment.

"Okay," Liam said. "I guess you'll need a few minutes to write that, and then you're going to get in a car and start fresh."

"I'm having a hard time with the idea I might never see you again," Finn added.

Connor scratched the back of his neck and gave them all a wry smile. "Yeah, I try not to think about that part too hard."

"You'll see him again," Cian vowed as he looked at Finn. "You'll all see him again, and when you do, a lot of things will be different."

Liam's head tilted in question, but Cian wore that look they all knew well—it said *don't ask, because I won't tell."

Ten minutes later, Liam and Finn had moved bags from Connor's car to the new one, Cian had spoken to Jess about what her father needed and reassured her he'd make sure Sean was taken care of no matter what, and Connor had written a very difficult letter to his mother that his brothers would deliver in a few days when he and Jess had had plenty of time to get far away.

The actual goodbyes were short, done in the crowded hallway near the back door to the club, with only the MacFarlane brothers and Jess there. And as Connor stood with one arm around Jess's shoulders and the other around Finn's neck, he looked at Cian and Liam and recorded every tiny detail about that moment in his heart.

Later on, he'd lie in the dark wherever it was they were going, and he'd remember the feeling—the feeling he'd taken for granted most of his life, that of being part of a greater whole, of being something more than just Connor. He was a MacFarlane, and no matter what name he went by, he'd always keep that in his heart.

"You need to go now," Cian said, giving Connor a gentle slap on the cheek.

"Yeah, I know." Connor sighed and released Finn, then he kissed Jess on the temple.

"*Slán abhaile*," Liam said, his voice thick with emotion. *Be safe.*

"*Slán abhaile*," Connor answered. And then he turned and gently directed Jess out the door ahead of him. He didn't look back, because he knew if he did, he wouldn't go. He didn't break down, because he knew if he did, he'd never stop. Connor walked to his new car, got in, and drove to his new life, because if he didn't, he'd never forgive himself.

**

The next three days, Cian, Finn, and Liam rearranged the family business. They decided to split Connor's duties managing distribution between Finn and Liam. Liam already handled the security aspects of distribution, and Finn had ideas for more efficient ways to handle getting product onto the streets.

"Why didn't you ever suggest any of this before?" Cian asked after Finn explained the ideas to him while the three of them sat at a table next to the windows in the swanky restaurant at the top of the Chicago stock exchange building.

Finn shrugged. "It was Connor's gig. I didn't want to step on his toes. He needs—needed—to have his own territory. It's gotta be hard being the youngest of four, you know?"

Ricky was standing in the corner behind them, and he tapped his earpiece, listening for a moment before he leaned closer and bent down, speaking quietly. "Mrs. MacFarlane is in the elevator on the way up."

The three brothers looked at each other and grimaced. Cian knew none of them wanted to break their mother's heart, but they'd put it off as long as possible. If Connor didn't show up at their parents' house soon for a meal or something work-related, both of their parents would start questioning his whereabouts.

The lunch went as well as could be expected. Angela cried quietly, then read her letter, tears streaming down her face as she nodded.

"Mom?" Cian asked when she was done. "Are you going to be okay?"

"Yes," she said, her voice gaining strength with each word. "I'm going to be okay because Connor and Jess are going to be okay. He's meant to do this, I feel it. It's what God wants for him, and I can't fight that. I don't even want to."

There was a collective sigh around the table as Cian relaxed for the first time in days. Then Angela MacFarlane surprised them all.

"Now," she said, straightening her spine. "How are we going to keep your father from going after Connor and dragging him home?"

Cian's gaze shot first to Liam, whose eyes were wide with surprise, then to Finn, who only shrugged.

"Actually, Mom, that's kind of why we met you here instead of at the house."

"You know he's going to lose his mind, don't you?" she asked, taking a sip from the wine they'd ordered for her even though she rarely drank.

Yes, Cian knew the old bastard would lose his mind, and while he didn't look forward to the fallout, he also took great pleasure in besting his father.

"We were hoping you could help with that," Liam added.

Angela sighed. "I wish you boys had told me about this before he did it."

"Yeah, but then you'd have had to act like you didn't know what was going on."

"You think I can't act?" Angela huffed. "You forget, I've been acting like I have no idea what you all do for a living for over three decades."

"Jesus, Mom," Liam choked out as he swallowed his whiskey wrong.

Cian cleared his throat awkwardly.

"My point is," Angela continued. "If I'd known about it earlier, I could have done something to prepare your father—subtly, of course. Now we're just going to have to spring it on him and endure what comes next."

"I'll handle that," Cian stressed. "It was my decision, I enabled it, and I'll be the one to take the blame with Pop." No way was he allowing Robbie's wrath to fall on the rest of them. It had been his decision. It was his burden to bear.

Angela's eyes grew damp again. "Do you really think that's the best idea, *mo grá*? I think we should present it as a group."

Cian gave her hand a squeeze and sighed. Some people might have blamed his mother for allowing Robbie's abuse, but Cian knew she was as much a victim as the rest of them. Robbie MacFarlane was a tyrant, and an entire city suffered his abuse.

"Mom's right," Liam said. "No way you're taking the blame for this. I could have stopped him that afternoon, and I didn't. I listened to what he wanted and what you guys thought about it, and I decided to let him do it. Since then, I could have told Pop so he'd send people out after Connor. I didn't. This was as much on me as you."

Finn and Angela both nodded. "If I'd known beforehand," Angela said, "I wouldn't have made him do anything differently. This is what he wants—" She held up the letter, giving it a small shake. "He deserves the chance to live his life how he wants. But your father won't see it that way, so we'll all have to buckle in for the ride and hope the stress doesn't kill him."

Cian didn't have to say Robbie's death was the least of his worries.

**

"This was you," Robbie snarled, his face a mask of rage as he jabbed a finger in Cian's face. "Your weak fucking leadership. You didn't have the balls to bring your brother to heel, and now he's wandering around with some piece of tail instead of here helping his family like he should be."

"Robert!" Angela snapped from her seat on the sofa where she sat with Liam on one side and Finn on the other. Cian rested an arm against the fireplace in his mother's living room and stared with dead eyes at his father. It was a stare he'd perfected since that first time on his eighteenth birthday. And he dreamed of the day when he'd be able to use it for the very last time, the day when his father was finally gone.

Robbie barely spared Angela a glance before he started in on Cian again. "You think you can keep him from me? You think whatever bullshit IDs you got him can hide him? I'll find who supplied them, and they'll tell me exactly what name he's using now. I'll drag his ass home and make sure the woman isn't ever a temptation again."

Angela stood stiffly. "Robert Patrick MacFarlane," she gasped. "You will not speak about my future daughter-in-law this way!" She marched over to where Robbie stood. "I know this hurts you." Her voice turned watery. "But we have four strong, independent sons. And they've kept your business running smoothly. We have more money than anyone has a right to, and what matters is that Connor is healthy and happy. He'll come back to us when he's ready, but until then, I want you to let him be."

Robbie's glare continued, his gaze darting between Angela and Cian. At last, his color began to return to normal, and he cleared his throat. "I'm sorry for swearing, *mo chridhe*," he said. He turned to Cian, then Liam and Finn. "I'm ashamed of you all," he said, his voice husky. "I didn't raise you to treat family and the family business like it's a choice. You do what your family needs you to, and Connor should have been told that. Out of deference to your mother's wishes, I won't go after him—now. But in six months or a year, I promise nothing. Because I'm only accepting this temporarily. Connor has obligations here, and I won't allow him to shirk them forever."

Cian didn't move a muscle. Let the old man rage. He'd never find Connor. Cian had made sure of it. But just to be sure, he needed to push Lila harder for dirt on Robbie. She'd said it could take a while, but that excuse could only be tolerated for so long.

"That's fine," Angela said softly, stroking Robbie's arm as she held his hand. "You've had a shock. Let me get you a drink, and you can relax with some rugby on TV for a bit. I'll see you boys at Sunday dinner," she instructed before whisking their father out of the room.

"Holy shit," Liam muttered when they'd left.

Cian pushed off the fireplace mantel. "It could have gone worse."

"Yeah," Finn grunted darkly.

"And when he gets bored and decides to go after Connor in a few months?" Liam asked.

"One thing at a time, brother," Cian answered. "If you ever take over all this mess, you'll learn that real fast. When you've solved a problem for today, then you move on to the next one. Because the problems never end."

Chapter Twenty-One

It was seven forty-two on a Thursday night when Lila finally confronted Xavier. She'd avoided speaking to him for nearly a week once she figured out he was working with the Russians. What she'd learned was bigger and badder than she was comfortable with, but she knew the longer she waited, the more likely he was to do something that would put Cian in danger.

She came into the office and spent all Thursday afternoon working on updates to Cian's business. And she waited for her only coworker to leave, enabling her to speak privately with Xavier.

While there were plenty of dark websites operating from laptops in people's basements, Xavier had always had a front for Rogue. He rented a small office in a run-down office park with a sign out front that read: "Elite Software Specialists." It enabled him to launder enough money to look like a legitimate businessman. Hackers or "programmers" coming and going at all hours of the day and night didn't trigger any warnings at all to the property owners, and while most Rogue staff worked from wherever they wanted, Lila and a few others had always been in Chicago, so they came in to the office when it suited them.

As the door closed behind Lenny, a man who'd worked at Rogue for at least three years and never spoken a word to Lila other than "Hey," and "See ya," she shut down her laptop and stood. She'd spent most of last night in bed, trying to think about how she'd approach Xavier, but as nothing had come to her, she decided she had to get it over with. She knew as much about Rogue as he did, and she doubted he wanted her to quit because he was being a greedy bastard.

Once he knew she was on to him, Lila was certain Xavier would give in and extricate himself from whatever he'd gotten mixed up with. Or, at the very least, he'd find a way to do it without damaging Cian MacFarlane. She felt certain he didn't want her to tell Cian what he was up to.

"Yeah?" Xavier asked without looking up when Lila entered his office.

"We need to talk," she said, leaning against the doorframe.

"Okay." He kept clacking away at his keyboard.

"I need you to look at me while we do," she demanded.

Xavier froze, his gaze swinging to hers. He lifted his hands off the keyboard. "Whoa, sorry. Didn't know this was something so important." His tone was mocking, and, coupled with what kind of guy she was rapidly learning he was, it pissed Lila off no end.

"Yeah," she said, eyes narrowed. "It is important. I want to know why you asked me to watch Cian MacFarlane."

"Maybe I don't trust him," Xavier said, leaning back in his chair.

"Maybe I don't trust *that*," she answered, one eyebrow raised.

Their stare down lasted a few seconds, then he gave her his best imitation of a smile. Xavier rarely smiled, and when he did, it was entirely socially awkward. Until now, Lila had always found it funny. Now it seemed somehow mostly gross.

"I give you a lot of freedom in your job," he began. "But that doesn't mean I'm not still your boss. I asked you to do something, and it's hardly any different than when I ask you to monitor someone online. We do it all the time."

"But it doesn't usually make me feel like you're whoring me out," she snapped.

"I didn't tell you to have sex with him, for fuck's sake," he muttered. "Just keep tabs on him. What's the difference if it's in person or online?"

"It's different," she replied. "Trust me."

He narrowed his gaze, watching her for so long, she nearly cracked and told him to forget she'd mentioned it, but then something else flickered in his gaze.

"Oh, don't tell me you've fallen for him." Xavier tossed his hand up in the air in frustration before standing and stalking around the desk. "You have, haven't you? You fell for the big sexy mobster, and now you feel too guilty to inform on him. And you think you need to protect him from what? Me?"

Her blood pressure spiked. How dare he act as though she was the one in the wrong here. "I know you're taking payments from the Bratva," she said, her voice soft but deadly.

Xavier stopped, cocked his head, and looked at her thoughtfully. "I've always liked that about you, Lila. You're smart, and you don't pull punches."

"You're not denying it." Her anger ratcheted up more.

He shrugged. "What's the point? You've obviously seen the offshore account and the deposits." He half sat on the edge of his desk, nothing but a few feet between them.

"And your intent is what? To destroy the Dublin Devils so the Bratva can finally take over Chicago?"

He shook his head, a sad smile on his face. "Oh, Lila. The thing about being smart and pulling no punches is that it can lead you to things you're not supposed to know."

Suddenly, Lila's fury was replaced by something more disquieting. A shiver traveled through her as she watched his face morph from amused to cruel.

Before she could move, he was on her, grabbing her long hair in his fist and yanking her head back. He pulled her over to the desk, where he picked up a trophy made of thick glass in the shape of a triangle. He held the sharp point to her throat, pressing until she coughed.

Lila breathed hard, so shocked by the attack, she didn't resist. But as she stood with her neck awry, a large chunk of glass held against her larynx, she knew she couldn't let him kill her.

"I am glad you came to me with this, though," he said. "It could have created some real problems if you'd told your new man candy."

Lila tried to shift, but Xavier only pressed the glass in harder.

"Now, here's how this is going to work—"

Lila remembered one of the moves Cian had taught her in their self-defense session and brought her elbow back as hard as she could, but not into his midsection, into his crotch. As she shifted to hit her target, the glass cut her, and she felt something in her trachea give way, but she didn't stop, spinning as he released her with a cry and doubled over.

She dove for the door, but even though he was bent over, he reached out, grabbing her around the thighs. She flew forward, landing hard on her front, midway through the doorway.

"You bitch!" Xavier snarled as he pulled on her legs to regain control. She kicked and gasped, loosening his hold enough that she could roll onto her back. Partway up on her elbows, she kicked hard at his face. And in a moment, it was over. She connected with his nose, which burst, spraying blood everywhere, but the force of it threw his head back against the doorjamb. There was a horrifying crunch, then he collapsed forward, landing facedown on her ankles.

Lila screamed hoarsely, scrambling to get away from him. She panted, on her knees a few feet beyond where Xavier lay, motionless, the back of his head and nose both spilling blood that slowly pooled beneath him.

"Oh my God, oh my God," Lila chanted to herself. Blood dripped down her neck and into the V-neck of her T-shirt, ending up in her cleavage. She stood on shaky legs and stumbled to the front of the office, locking the main door and then grabbing her phone from her desk. She pulled up the contacts and pressed the Call button.

"Lila from Rogue." His deep voice came over the line, and Lila began to shake so hard, she almost dropped the phone.

"Lila?" he said again. "Are you there?"

"Help," she rasped out.

His voice turned from teasing to sharp in a second. "Where are you? What's happened?"

"Rogue office. I think I killed him." Her voice was barely a whisper, and the blood from her cut was beginning to soak into her shirt, turning the lavender cotton a reddish brown. All she could think was, *it will never come clean*.

To Cian's credit, he didn't ask who was dead, and he didn't sound surprised, just efficient and in charge. "Are you safe there?"

"I think so. I locked the door."

"Good." She could hear him moving and snapping orders to people around him. "Stay there, don't answer the door for anyone but me, don't call anyone but me. Can you do that, Lila?"

"Mm-hm," she said, panic setting in.

"Lila," he said, low and soothing. "Whatever's happened, it's going to be okay. I promise."

"Hurry," she said before she disconnected and sat down halfway between Xavier's body and the front door, pulling her knees up to her chest as she shook with sobs.

∗∗

Cian watched as Danny knocked lightly on the glass door to the generic office suite. All the offices opened onto the sidewalk in the strip park. Exposed. Not Cian's favorite setup, especially when he didn't know what had even happened, but there was no way he was going to get a call from Lila asking for help and not answer.

Danny turned to him, questioning. "Let me," Cian said, stepping forward.

"Not liking this, boss," Louis said from beside him.

Cian grunted an answer as Danny stepped aside. He leaned his head toward the door and knocked a touch louder. "Lila," he said quietly, "it's me."

He heard the click of the bolt sliding, and then the door cracked open. As soon as she saw it was him, she pulled it wider, and he stepped through, barely clearing the threshold before she pinned herself to him, burying her head in his chest while she kept her arms wrapped about her middle protectively. His open overcoat partially concealed her, and he wound his arms around her in a bear hug, tipping his chin to his guys, who followed him in.

"Go see what the situation is," he instructed. As they moved to the back of the suite, he murmured comforting words into her hair. "It's all going to be okay now. I promise. Whatever's happened, we'll take care of it." His chest ached as he held her for the first time. The feel of her small frame tucked into his was life altering.

Danny came back, his face saying more than even his words. "We got a body," he said. "The nerd guy she works for. Face and head wounds."

Cian nodded, still protecting Lila. "Call Finn and have him get over here right away. See if there's a back entrance he can use, and then put one of you out back and one in front."

Danny nodded before disappearing into the back of the suite.

Cian gently guided Lila to a cubicle in the front corner of the room where no one could see her and vice versa. He sat in the biggest chair in the tiny space and, without a second thought, pulled Lila onto his lap. He shifted to get comfortable, then set her back a few inches so he could finally look at her face.

His brave little hacker. She was shaking like a leaf. He'd never touched her like this, but it felt so natural and right, he didn't hesitate for even a moment.

He pushed back the hair that hung alongside her face, obscuring his view of her. And that was when he saw it—ugly dark bruises on her throat, along with a slice directly across her larynx, blood still oozing from her mottled skin. Rage erupted so hard and fast, he had to take a steadying breath, but even then, when he spoke, his voice was smooth and cold, like ice.

"What the hell did he do to you?"

She gazed at him, her eyes heartbroken. His heart raced. *No.* Anything but that.

He had to clear his own throat to say the next words. "Did he…?"

His eyes grazed over her face and down to her chest, her arms, searching for other signs—torn clothing, blood, more bruises—but she interrupted. "No. No, it wasn't about that. He was trying to kill me, or maybe keep me until the Russians got here, I'm not sure."

Cian's head spun with incomplete information and the obvious raspiness of her voice. So much worse than when he'd saved her from the Vasquez guy. Her larynx was obviously seriously damaged.

"Russians? Lila, you need to start from the beginning."

And she did. She told him Xavier had been out to destroy his family from the beginning and she'd figured it out, then she'd confronted him with her suspicions and been forced to fight for her life because of it.

Once she'd described it all, he melted into the chair, pulling her as close as possible, one arm wrapped around her hips, the other around her back, his hand reaching into her smooth hair. She pulled her knees up, tucking herself into his big body as tightly as she could.

He didn't reprimand her for putting herself in danger, nor for not telling him about the threat immediately. The fucking Russians were after him now too. He closed his eyes for a moment. Thank God Connor was out. Things were going to get worse, and he couldn't imagine what he'd have done if anything happened to Connor.

He needed to get Finn and Liam safe next. It wasn't going to be good enough to keep them out of prison now. He had to get them out of the life entirely. Not something he'd have a hard time convincing Finn to do, but Liam was another issue all together.

He turned his attention back to the frightened woman in his arms. "You're a fighter, Lila," he said softly as he heard doors opening and closing and hushed voices at the back of the suite. Finn was here getting to work. "You did the right thing calling me.

We're going to handle it all. My brother's the best fixer there is. No one will ever know what's happened here. You can relax."

"What about Rogue?" she asked. "Everyone at Rogue will notice he's disappeared. We can't just pretend he's still here."

Cian thought about it for a few moments before answering. "How many people at Rogue have ever seen or spoken to him?"

"Four of us. The four here in Chicago who use this office sometimes."

"So everyone else only hears from him online?"

She tipped her head to look up at him. He could feel her gaze on his face like the heat of the sun.

"Right," she answered. "He's just a signature on the internet to all but a few people at Rogue."

"Okay, so I think he needs to put out a message detailing his leave of absence and leaving you in charge."

Lila's gaze was assessing now. He seemed to have snapped her out of any lingering trauma. "You're thinking no one has to know he's gone."

"I think Xavier has a personal crisis of some sort. Something that's called him away—maybe it's family, maybe it's legal trouble that's forced him to hop a plane out of the country. No one's going to doubt that, are they? He'll leave you in charge. Rogue will continue as normal."

"Or…" she paused. "It just so happens that I've spent a lot of time recently discovering his every movement online. I could *be* Xavier for a while." She paused, her brow knitted in thought. Cian resisted the urge to run a finger over that soft skin and smooth

the tiny wrinkle away. "Eventually someone will fig
ure it out, though," she finished.

"Of course they will," he answered with a slow
smile. "But it won't be right away, and when they do,
we'll have already established that he disappeared, and
no one will ever know if he was snatched or ran. And
sure as shit, no one's going to be calling the police.
No one Xavier associated with wants to be scrutinized by the cops."

Lila nodded, wincing as the motion caused her
pain.

"Dammit," Cian said, concern furrowing his
brow. "We need to get you to a doctor."

"We can't." Her eyes widened in horror. "They'll
call the police to report my assault."

He smiled warmly at her. Her eyes were so beautiful, dark and decadent. "I have a doctor who can take
care of you. He's top notch, no hospitals, no police."

She nodded then, and he stood, sliding her off his
lap and onto her feet, but keeping ahold of her, tucking her under one arm as he walked them into the
bigger room.

"Stay right here," he instructed, then showed her
Danny was standing on the other side of the front
door, keeping them safe.

He strode to the back of the suite and found Finn
there, supervising a couple of their guys removing the
body.

"Hey," Finn said, his face serious. "It looks like
there was quite a struggle. He died from a blow to the
head." Finn pointed to a place on the doorframe of
Xavier's office, where blood and hair were still
lodged.

Cian snarled. "Asshole attacked her, and she fought him off. It was accidental. She was just trying to get away. He nearly sliced her throat open first."

"Jesus," Finn murmured. "She's such a tiny thing."

"I'll explain everything that went down later, but I need to get her to Dr. O'Reilly."

"Yeah, of course," his brother said, giving him a slap on the back. "Don't worry about any of this. There's a fair amount of blood, but it's localized. We've already gotten the name of the property owner, so we can dig up dirt on him to hold on to in case we encounter any trouble, but I don't think anyone's going to ever know it happened here. Should clean up sparkling."

"Good. But don't dump him yet."

Finn looked at him assessingly.

"We may have use for him. Keep him on ice."

"You got it, but don't leave him around too long, even I can't guarantee no one will find him."

Cian thanked Finn, grabbed Louis, left Danny to help with cleanup, and poured an increasingly exhausted Lila into the SUV. As he arranged for the doctor to meet them at his penthouse, he looked over at her pale face and drooping eyes. And for the first time in his adult life, he wondered if he might have a reason to want to survive along with his brothers.

Chapter Twenty-Two

"I've given her a sedative so she'll get some more restful sleep," the doctor told Cian when he came out of the guest room at Cian's apartment. "Should wear off by morning."

"And her injuries?" he asked.

"Some damage to her larynx, but nothing that's compromised her breathing. Shouldn't be permanent. I've given her a round of antibiotics just in case any sort of infection were to develop in her trachea, and left some painkillers, just a few days' worth. She shouldn't need more than that. Also, I gave her some butterfly stitches for that cut. Mostly, she should rest her voice, drink and eat whatever feels okay on the injury, and stay away from whoever did that to her."

Cian realized Dr. O'Reilly normally dealt with MacFarlane men who'd been hurt in fistfights or gun battles. He'd probably never treated a woman for the MacFarlanes, and Cian was surprised to hear the protectiveness in the old doctor's tone.

"Trust me," Cian said, "he won't be anywhere near her again."

The doctor looked at him sharply, then shook Cian's hand and left. Cian walked down the hall to the small guest room. He quietly pushed the door open and leaned against the doorframe watching her sleep, her small frame finally looking peaceful and relaxed.

Cian had always had a thing for brunettes. Starting with Molly Reilly in ninth grade, he'd had a string of perky brunettes on parade in his teens and twenties. At first, he'd been happy to find girls who'd have sex with him, and not so happy when they'd wanted him to take on obligations that seemed onerous to a nineteen-year-old guy whose father expected him to oversee a dozen men, keep his younger brothers out of jail, and fetch and carry on a whim.

As the years went on and Cian continued to live at the beck and call of Robbie, things like women became tertiary. Protecting his brothers was always first, keeping Robbie from doing something rash was second, and getting laid somewhere after all that. By his mid-twenties, he never had anything other than perfunctory one-night stands. Owning a nightclub, it was simple to find partners, and his office at Banshee became the site for the vast majority of his sex life.

He shook his head as Lila murmured something and shifted in her sleep. God, did he even know when he'd last gotten laid? He really shouldn't be dealing with Lila when he was probably primed to jump anyone who was willing.

But as he took one last look before shutting the door, and his heart did that thing it did all the time around her, he knew it wasn't just because he wanted a good, hard screw. No, Lila from Rogue did something to him. Something he didn't have time for, couldn't afford, and sure as hell wasn't allowed.

But damn, she was something.

He went the rest of the way down the hall to his own room. He had to be honest with himself, he wanted her something awful, and honestly, Cian was getting very tired of putting everyone else first. There was a voice inside his head screaming to get its due. A part of him that wasn't nearly so noble as what he tried to portray. The truth? Yeah, Cian wanted Lila Rodriguez. Had wanted her since the day he first laid eyes on her, and now she was a few feet away, vulnerable, needing him in a way that made him feel powerful.

"You don't have to sleep with her to save her, asshole," he muttered to himself. In fact, Lila would be safer if she was far away from him. Maybe that was what he should do—get her a nice place with Wi-Fi on a beach somewhere and send her away. Things near him were only going to continue to heat up—the feds, his father, and now the Russians. Cian's life was nonstop danger. How could he conceive of pulling Lila into that? Whether he was involved with her or not, he'd bring her nothing but trouble.

Then there was the other issue—the one where he needed to give up Rogue to the feds, and Lila would almost certainly be caught in the net. He'd thought about it over and over, and Rogue was the best way to give the feds something significant without doing damage to his brothers. If Cian could work out immunity for Liam and Finn, then he could hand the feds full access to the Rogue information, and given what he knew Rogue sold and to whom, the MacFarlane portion of it would only be a tiny fraction of what the feds found. Cian could simply wait it out, and whatever consequences fell on him and Robbie, he'd take them.

Except he was struggling with the idea of Lila going down with Rogue.

So yes, she'd be better off on a beach somewhere. He could make that happen. He didn't like the thought of never seeing her again, but he did like the thought he drifted off to sleep with—Lila on a beach, smiling at a man who loved her. He knew he'd never be that man, but he put himself in the spot anyway. It was a dream, that was all. Cian knew dreams didn't come true for guys like him.

**

Lila woke slowly, confusion clouding her head for the first few moments. Then it all came back to her, Xavier trying to kill her, the wet crunching sound as his head struck the doorframe in his office, calling Cian. Heat suffused her cheeks as she remembered him holding her, stroking her hair, telling her everything was going to be all right.

Her throat was raw and sore, and when she touched the skin on her neck, she felt the scab that had formed there. The memory of that chunk of glass pressing against her larynx made her stomach heave, and she had to take deep breaths to calm the rising panic.

When the wave of hysteria had passed, she rolled to one side to sit up, and every muscle in her body screamed in protest. She felt like she'd been beaten. "Because you were, Lila," she mumbled.

Once she was upright, she stood and looked down at her clothes. She'd slept through the night in jeans and a plaid flannel shirt Cian had lent her so she could remove the bloody T-shirt she'd worn. She slowly walked to the adjoining bathroom and saw Cian had been kind enough to place a toothbrush in its wrapper along with some toothpaste on the counter. After brushing her teeth, rinsing her face, and finger combing her hair, she ventured out of the room and followed the smell of coffee that permeated the hallway.

She saw him before he saw her. He was standing in the kitchen with his back to her, a pair of sweats hanging low on his hips, shirtless, with bare feet.

She sucked in a breath as she looked at the tattoos that wrapped around his back and shoulders. Two huge wings, fanned out across his shoulder blades, and between them was a Celtic knot. The wings were in shades of blue and green, subtle, and variegated. Script flowed along each of the three parts of the knot, and as she walked closer, she saw they read, *Liam*, *Finn*, and *Connor*. His brothers. He had his brothers' names tattooed on his back.

He hadn't turned around because he was wearing earbuds, and she couldn't help but wonder what music he liked. She realized that each time she was with him, he became less the cliché of a mob boss in her mind, and more a real person.

As she entered the kitchen, she heard him humming quietly along with whatever he was listening to. He was rinsing something in the kitchen sink, and she noticed bacon already sitting on a platter, and a waffle maker next to it cooking two large waffles.

She knocked lightly on the countertop, but he didn't hear her, so she reached out and touched him gently on the elbow.

He moved so fast, she didn't even have time to scream, although she doubted her throat was capable of it. He pinned her to the refrigerator, one hand holding her wrist next to her head, the other arm across her midsection so he immobilized her other arm and her entire torso at the same time. They blinked at each other a couple of times then he said, "Oh shit," and released her before ripping the ear-buds out of his ears.

"I'm sorry," he said, watching her warily. "Are you okay?"

She took a deep breath and tried to ignore her racing heart. Nodding, she gave him a small smile. "Yeah, it's all good." Her voice sounded like she was a pack-a-day smoker. "I should have found a better way of letting you know I was here. I'm sorry."

"No." He stepped back, giving her more room that she wasn't even sure she wanted. "I'm sorry. You didn't do anything wrong. I'm just—" He ran a hand through his hair in frustration.

"Cian?" she gingerly touched him on the arm again. "It's really fine. I'm fine."

He looked at her, and something in his face softened, pulling on her chest, making all her aches and pains seem less somehow.

"You never use my name," he murmured, his gaze roaming her face. "I like the way it sounds on your lips."

She swallowed around the raw pressure in her throat, not sure how to answer him. He saved her the trouble.

"How is your throat? Are you in a lot of pain? You should drink something. I sent the guys out to get a bunch of different stuff, so you can choose anything that sounds good."

He gently pulled her away from the refrigerator door so he could open it to show her an entire shelf full of smoothies, sodas, carbonated waters, noncarbonated waters, iced teas, and juices. She tried to smother the smile that wrapped around her lips. He'd gone to a lot of trouble to make her comfortable.

"Um, how about this one?" She pointed to a cucumber-flavored water. "And maybe some coffee?" She wasn't sure if the heat would be tolerable on her throat, but damn, she wanted the caffeine.

He got her drinks set up at the kitchen island, and she climbed onto a stool, running her hand across the smooth marble countertop as he continued preparing what looked to be a full breakfast for her.

"Do you always eat all this in the morning?" she asked.

"No, but I don't always have a guest who was assaulted the night before and needs to get her strength back," he answered.

She sipped her cucumber water, relishing how cool and soothing it felt on her ragged throat.

"Tell me how you really are," he commanded as he poured more batter on the waffle maker.

She thought about it for a moment. "I'm sore everywhere, but I feel decent."

"And in your head?"

She took a deep breath, doing an assessment of her own mental state. It certainly wasn't fragile enough that she didn't notice every little movement of his pecs and abs while he moved around the kitchen. Yeah, given how mesmerized she was by his body, she'd have to say she was psychologically fine. Well, it was all relative, but yeah.

"I'm okay," she told him, setting the water aside and taking a small sip of coffee. "Ouch," she rasped before drinking more water.

"That heat hurts?"

She nodded.

"Don't worry, I can fix it for you." He took her coffee cup off the counter and went to work, pulling things out of the cabinets and the refrigerator. A minute later, he turned back around and presented her with a tall glass of iced coffee swirling with rich cream. She took a tentative sip, and it was subtly sweet, with a hint of cinnamon and chocolate.

"Oh my God, that's good," she said in surprise. He grinned at her and removed the last waffles from the iron, adding them to the serving platter along with a bowl full of blackberries.

The waffles and bacon were barely tolerable on her throat, but she was able to get some berries down better, and all her coffee and water.

"You're too thin to go without eating," Cian said with concern. "I have some protein shakes. I think you should drink several of those a day until you can eat more than one corner of a waffle and half a slice of bacon."

She chuckled. "Have you always had this motherly tendency?"

He grinned at her, and it was so stunning, it stole her breath. "I'm the oldest of four boys. My brothers need constant mothering."

"Well, I promise not to starve to death." She looked around at the clean, crisp decor of his luxurious apartment. "I should get out of your hair. I'm sure you have a lot to do today. I don't know how I can ever thank you for what you did last night." She realized in that moment, she was beholden to him—a mobster. She ought to be concerned about that, but given everything she was dealing with, she couldn't gather up the energy.

"You don't need to thank me, Lila. I'm honored you came to me, and I'd rather you not go back to your place for a few days. We need to make sure the Russians Xavier was working with don't come looking for him and find you in the process."

Her poor heart raced with a surge of adrenaline. "You said no one would be looking for him."

He gave her a pitying look. "I said we could delay them by a few months, but if the Russians really are after MacFarlane territory, then they'll show up eventually."

"And if I'm the one left in charge of Rogue, they're going to come straight for me, aren't they?"

He looked miserable. "Which brings us to something I want to discuss with you this morning."

He led the way to the big leather sofa that was placed by a bank of windows overlooking the street forty stories below.

Lila sat, folding her feet under her.

Cian stood by the window, looking like a dark angel lit up by the morning sun.

"I don't know why you've made the choices you have—to pursue hacking for a place like Rogue rather than a legit security company or something. But I know for certain you never signed up to work with people like me." Self-recrimination soaked through every word.

"While we didn't realize it at the time, Xavier dragged you and other Rogue staff into a completely different level of danger. You may have had to worry about feds before, but now you have to worry about—" He paused, frowning. "People who will kill you rather than put you in prison."

She held her breath, waiting to see where he was going with this.

When he continued, his voice was nearly as rough as her damaged one. "I don't want anything to happen to you. It doesn't make sense, I've only known you for a few weeks, and I deal with people who disappear all the time, but you're not part of this world, and I don't want you to be destroyed by it."

Lila looked down at her hands, tears threatening in the face of his raw honesty. On the surface, it seemed like Cian was what she was used to—like Xavier, like her father. Men who used her for her talents but didn't really care about her as a human being. But more and more, he was proving to be different, and that scared Lila worse than if he'd been more of the same.

"I can give you a fresh start," he said, walking over and sitting on the coffee table so he was knee to knee with her, leaning into her space, all his bare skin mere inches from her fingertips. "I know you're able to get yourself a new identity, but I can give you an offshore bank account, and a private jet out of the country to someplace tropical with no extradition agreements. You can start over. Get a legitimate job, or just invest wisely and hang out on the beach."

She blinked at him. "What's the catch?" she asked warily.

He shook his head in confusion. "Catch?"

"Yeah, what do I have to do? Let you launder money through my bank account? Do occasional hacking assignments? Be your mistress? How do I earn this fresh start?"

His eyebrows shot up to his hairline, and he burst out with a surprised chuckle.

"My *mistress*?" he asked, and Lila felt her face heat with a blush. God, why the hell had she said that? Of course a man like Cian MacFarlane wouldn't be looking to *her* as a mistress. *Idiot, Lila, pure idiot.*

She gathered her dignity as best she could with him preventing her from stomping off across the room.

"Sorry, I realize that suggestion is ridiculous. I just meant how am I going to have to debase myself to get this amazing fresh start you're offering?"

Cian seemed to find her anger entertaining, and rather than backing up like she wanted, he leaned closer, his elbows on his knees. She refused to be cowed, so she glowered at him. His gaze turned thoughtful.

"First of all, Lila from Rogue," he said, his voice low and velvety. "If I had mistresses, you'd be my first choice for sure."

Her heart nearly pounded out of her chest.

"But secondly, I don't exploit women. I was raised by a good woman, and while my father has a lot of faults, treating my mother poorly wasn't one of them. MacFarlane men don't hit women, they don't disrespect them, and they don't exploit them."

He reached out and ran one finger softly down the side of her face, stroking her cheek, sending tiny sparks of electricity straight to her chest. Then he took a deep breath as his eyes drifted closed for a moment. When he released it, he sat back, and it was all Lila could do not to follow him with her entire body as if they were connected by a string, chest to chest, heart to heart.

"The fresh start is yours to take, no conditions. You'll never have to speak to or deal with anyone from my family or organization ever again."

Lila's head spun with the possibilities, even as something inside her sank in disappointment. But her practical side quickly took over, and she assessed the advantages, the disadvantages, the dangers and risks, along with the fact Cian MacFarlane had said she'd be his first choice for a mistress.

Cian watched her and waited, always patient, always observant.

"Can I think about it?" she asked, not able to clear her mind enough to make a decision right then.

"Of course. But in the meantime, you stay here. Deal?"

She nodded, not sure if being in such close proximity to him for an extended period of time was going to help her decision-making abilities.

"Now," he said, smiling. "I bet you'd like to get fresh clothes and some of your other things."

She agreed, grateful for the reprieve from life-altering decisions and the tumbling that was going on in her tummy.

"Good. Let me get dressed, and we'll take you to your house so you can pack."

As he walked away to his bedroom, Lila decided shock had finally set in, because she was actually considering saying no to his offer. It was absolute insanity, which would make sense, because Lila had become progressively crazier since meeting Cian. And now?

She wasn't sure if she was ready to leave him. Not even for a beach and a fresh start.

Chapter Twenty-Three

Sergei looked around the former industrial space. It was wide open, with high ceilings, brick walls, and concrete floors.

"We can have interior walls built where we want?" he asked the Realtor. She was one of those typical American women—tight business suit, high heels, hair that didn't move, and twenty extra pounds packed beneath the Spanx he knew she wore.

She fluttered thick eyelashes at him, and Sergei briefly considered fucking her against the brick walls, but then she opened that mouth with the overpainted lips and that thought, along with other things, shriveled.

"Absolutely! The property owner wants the tenant to have the freedom to transform the space into whatever you desire."

Sergei grunted at her and slowly walked around the room again. As he counted off paces to get an idea of the size of things, he mentally calculated how many he'd need to store here. Maybe ten to fifteen at a time? If he held auctions once a month, he could clear inventory to almost zero every thirty days and then restock.

"And the owner is out of state?" he asked.

"Yes, but I manage the property, and I'm here for anything you need at any time. We're very conscientious about our customer service. If you need maintenance or a repair done, we can have someone out within the hour."

Sergei snorted softly. If that were true, he'd have never chosen this particular property management company. But regardless, he wouldn't be asking for any maintenance, and he doubted Chloe here would be stopping by otherwise. She was notoriously lazy, and the property owner was an eighty-year-old man who'd retired to Boca Raton years ago.

"I'll take it," he said, giving her a smile guaranteed to send her skipping back to her office in the wilds of Naperville.

"Oh, that's wonderful!" she chirped. "Let's go to the car. I have all the paperwork. If you have a check, I can process this today, and you can start moving in tomorrow."

He had better than a check. He had cash. *Lots* of cash.

"I can pay in cash," he said, looking at her with a challenge. "Will that be a problem?"

Chloe smiled even bigger. "No, that will work just fine."

Yes, thought Sergei, this *was* going to work just fine. And it was going to work right in the MacFarlanes' backyard. Filthy Irish pigs would never know what hit them until it was too late.

**

Connor stood on the balcony and looked out on downtown San Diego. The sun was setting over the water a few blocks away, and the sky was an amazing shade of orange mixed with pinks.

He heard the door slide open behind him and re-strained his first instinct to put his hand on his gun. There was no gun strapped to his torso now, though he still had a few stashed around the place, but he was working to develop new habits, and Jess was helping him.

"Hi," she said as she leaned on the railing next to him, resting her head on his shoulder. "It's beautiful, isn't it?"

He kissed the top of her head. "Not as beautiful as you," he said.

"Kiss-up," she murmured.

"Just telling it like I see it," he answered, the smile that had graced his face for the last two weeks spreading into a grin.

"I just heard from that temp bookkeeping service," she said. "They hired me."

He turned and pulled her into a hug. "That's great, baby. I'm so proud of you."

"Right?" She smiled up at him. "I've never had a job anywhere but with my dad, but those fake reference letters your brother gave us worked."

He gazed at her, his brow furrowing. "No, those are required, but if you didn't have the knowledge and hadn't aced the interview, they would have never hired you."

She smiled back. "It'll be fun to see what it's like to work in real offices, and I love that I'll get to move around every couple of weeks. I'll meet so many new people."

Connor's heart nearly burst with the joy in her voice.

"And then at night?" he murmured, burying his nose in her hair as she pressed against him from chest to toes.

"At night, I'll bring all my new friends to your pub while you're managing, and after that, we'll come home, and you'll sex me up until I have to get up for work again."

"Sounds tiring," he chuckled.

"We're only young once," she answered, glowing.

"You'll always be young in my eyes."

She laughed and smacked him on the chest. "Now, I'm going to go look online to see what people are wearing in offices. I'm going to need work clothes. Will you come shop with me in the morning?"

"Of course," he answered. "Do your research, and then I'll take you out to dinner to celebrate."

She bounced back inside, shutting the door behind her. Connor watched as she went into the kitchen and pulled out the small laptop they'd invested in. Cian's new life package had included a special email account that Lila had secured for them. It was anonymous and untraceable, sending any messages through a random sequence of servers before it landed, making it impossible for anyone to track the location of the source of the messages.

He'd received one message at the address so far, and it was nothing but ten numbers—a phone number.

He reached into his pocket, pulled out the burner phone he'd purchased earlier that day, and punched in the numbers from the email.

"Hello?"

"It's me," he said.

"Damn." Liam's voice was thick with emotion. "It's good to hear you."

"Same here," Connor answered, surprised at the bittersweet emotions that rolled through him.

"How are you? Is everything going like it should?"

Connor looked at the fading sun and the lights of downtown San Diego blinking to life. "Yeah, it's going exactly like it should. There's a pub. I have a role there. And my roommate has a place too. An office. She's really excited." He tried so hard not to say too much, but he wanted to let Liam know how happy they were.

"I'm proud of you both," his brother answered. "No problems?"

"No, man. I've been very careful, but no sign of anything."

"Good. Just remember when you start to relax is when you're most at risk."

Connor nodded. Liam had always taught him that. Never let your guard down when you feel like you should, keep it up longer than that, and then longer still.

"Yep," he answered. "I'll remember. I learned from the best."

Liam snorted. "Then get rid of the device you have, and I'll send you a new number in a couple of weeks, yeah?"

"That'd be great."

"We decided we'd take turns holding on to it, so you'll get somebody different every time."

Connor smiled, imagining his brothers arguing over who got to talk to him and finally developing a complicated system for passing the phones around.

"Good. I wouldn't want to get stuck with you every time," he joked.

"Dick," Liam said good-naturedly.

"Love you too," Connor answered.

"*Slán abhaile*," Liam said softly.

"*Slán abhaile*," Connor answered, then the call disconnected. Liam had probably started a timer the second Connor said hello, because eventually, in spite of whatever fancy rerouting he knew Cian would have had Lila put on the call, the signal could be tracked. The longer they talked, the longer it gave someone else to follow the trail of breadcrumbs from cell tower to cell tower, around the country or the world, until it landed on Connor's exact location.

Connor removed the SIM card and crushed it, then put the rest of the phone in his pocket to be disposed in a trashcan on their way to dinner. He took one last look at the sun as it sank into the Pacific. *Freedom.* It came with a price, but a price he'd pay again and again. He'd never tasted anything quite like it. It tasted like life.

**

Lila sat up in bed, something making her heart race. She listened carefully in the heavy dark that shrouded the room. Then she heard it again, the sound of feet on carpet. Her heart thumped hard, but she silently climbed out of bed, phone in hand as she made her way to the door. She peered out the crack in the doorway, ready to have an armed Russian leap out at her. But instead, all she saw was a soft light from the room two doors down—a small workout space where Cian kept a treadmill and weights.

She tiptoed down the hall, sounds of heavy breathing and soft grunts coming from the room.

When she peeked around the corner, Lila's heart did a flip. There was Cian, shadow boxing in the full-length mirror that covered one wall of the room. He was naked from the waist up and wore only shiny compression shorts from the waist down. He bounced on the balls of his feet, his hands shooting out in a pattern over and over again. His breath came short and fast, and once every three or four punches, he'd hit harder, grunting softly as he did.

She watched him, breathless, forgetting she was violating his privacy, she was so intrigued by the choreography of what he did. It was beautiful, even though she knew in real life, boxing was a horribly violent sport. But the way Cian did it, the grace with which he moved, jabbed, floated over the floor, it was like a dance. *Amazing*.

As if he sensed her presence, his gaze in the mirror shot to the doorway. Lila nearly ducked and ran back to her room, but it was too late.

"I'm sorry," she said, quickly. "I heard sounds and just wanted to make sure everything was okay."

"No, I'm sorry, I didn't mean to wake you." He turned and faced her, his skin glowing with a light sheen of sweat that made her want to touch it.

"I'm sleeping really lightly these days. It doesn't take much to wake me."

He gave her a small smile. "Well, since you're here," he said, crooking one finger at her.

She did as he directed without a second thought. She should be worried about that, but somehow, she couldn't be bothered.

When she got into the room, he motioned for her to face the mirror, then came up behind her. She was wearing a tank top with no bra and a pair of yoga pants, and she suddenly felt self-conscious.

He stood behind her and put his hands on her arms. "Remember what I taught you that day at the gym? Show me what you got, Lila from Rogue," he said in a low, husky voice.

She lifted her arms and made small fists.

"Good," he rasped, positioning her arms and holding on to her wrists, his big biceps pressing against her shoulders as he did.

Her breath was shallow and rapid as she watched them in the mirror.

"Now, there's a rhythm to it," he coached. "It's one, one, two." He moved her arms in punches—left, left, right.

"There you go," he said, his voice dropping lower, eyelids heavy.

Lila felt the same heaviness, in her core, in her arms, in the way her breath dragged through her like she couldn't quite get enough in.

He continued to move her arms in soft punches like she was a doll, but his head dropped to the crook between her neck and shoulder, and he buried his nose in the strands of hair that rested there.

"Lila," he whispered, his voice as hoarse as hers. "You should go now, while you have the chance. You should get out of this room, out of this town, out of my world."

She couldn't help it when her head fell back against him and her eyes slid shut. He still held her arms, but they'd both stopped shadow boxing, and now his hands stroked up and down her sensitive skin, his hips pressed against her ass, his breath and lips on her neck.

"Is that what you want?" she whispered.

"I want you to be safe," he said, one finger tracing along her shoulder, then down over her collar bone, into her cleavage. "I want you to be happy." His tongue flicked her earlobe. "But I also just want you."

"I never saw you coming," she rasped as she arched her back and moaned softly under his onslaught. "I never saw any of this coming."

"I know," he answered, and there was anguish in it, a brush of despair.

"I know I need to leave, but for tonight, can we just do this?" she asked, pulling away so she could look him in the eye. "For tonight, can we pretend you're not you and I'm not me and this is all there is?"

He gently pushed her hair back out of her face, his eyes blue pools of mystery and danger.

"If that's what makes you happy, then yes."

She nodded, and he took in a shaky breath before lowering his lips to hers. It started tentative, tasting, exploring, but then turned hungry, tongues twisting, lips sliding, skin on skin, breath hot and heavy. He pulled away, and his eyes glittered. Her skin was heated, sensitive, wanting.

He took her hand and led her down the hall to his bedroom with its big bed and luxurious sheets. In the silence and the darkness, he peeled her tank top down, leaving her arms trapped by the straps as he traced her small breasts with his index finger before lowering his head and taking one firm nipple in his mouth. He sucked once, and she gasped, the sensations so intense, her knees nearly buckled.

His breath was harsh as his stubble scraped against the skin over her breastbone. When his mouth reached her jaw, he cupped one side in his big hand while his lips explored the other.

She cried out quietly, arching her neck and melting into his touch.

"You're so beautiful," he whispered, taking a hank of her hair and running it through his fingers before his lips came down over hers again, seeking, devouring, worshiping.

Lila's head swam, and her heart expanded, pressing painfully against her rib cage. This wasn't supposed to happen, but she felt entirely unable to stop it. As he slid her tank top and yoga pants over her hips and down her legs, following their path with his lips, she knew more than just her throat was going to hurt like hell tomorrow. Because she did need to go, and even if she didn't, there was no future for her and this man. Only tonight.

Yes, Lila thought as she pushed the waist of his sweatpants down and felt all the hard smoothness of him, tomorrow she was going to take the chance she was being given to finally leave her father's legacy far behind. Maybe she'd see if she could bring her mother with her—give them both a fresh start without the man who'd turned them into people they never intended to be.

And as Cian pressed Lila back into his deep, rich bedding, and filled the darkest, sweetest places in her, she knew she'd never be the same again. Her world had changed forever, and at the center of that change was this man, this perfect, beautiful, frightening man. While Lila's nails dug into the wings that graced his back like those of an angel and her raw throat shredded with her cries, she knew the real mistake hadn't been working for a mobster. It had been falling in love with one.

**

The sun had barely risen when Danny was shown into Robbie's office. The old man was sitting behind his desk, a cup of Irish coffee next to him, the newspaper spread out over his computer keyboard.

"You find Connor yet?" Robbie asked gruffly as he folded up the paper.

"No, sir. But we're pursuing every avenue possible. We'll find him eventually."

Robbie harrumphed. "Better be sooner than later," he growled.

Danny agreed silently, because sometimes it was best not to use too many words with Robbie.

"You have anything else for me? Any more pictures?"

Danny pulled out an envelope from his inside jacket pocket and handed it over. While Robbie opened the clasp and slid the photos out, Danny explained.

"Cian got a call from the girl at Rogue two nights ago. We went to the office Rogue uses as a front, and turns out she'd offed the nerd boss."

Robbie looked at the photos of Xavier's body, then at Danny, silently questioning.

"They argued, I don't know what about, and he attacked her. She fought him off, but in the scuffle, he hit his head, and that's all she wrote."

Robbie examined the rest of the photos for a moment. "What did Cian do about it?"

"Had Finn clean it up, then took the girl to his place. She's been there ever since."

Robbie's slow smile was as cold as ice.

"Did he now?" Robbie focused on Danny. "Pretty girl, isn't she? And he doesn't want anyone to find out she killed her boss. Where's the body?"

Danny told him what had been done with the corpse.

"Good. It'll be safe there for now, but I want you to check every few days, make sure Finn hasn't had it moved." Robbie's lips turned up in a smile. "And then I want to know what his relationship is to this girl. I want her watched all the time. Let me know where she pisses, who she talks to, what her favorite thing to eat is."

"Sure thing, boss," Danny said before standing and moving to the door.

"There's a little bonus for you on the table in the hallway as you leave," Robbie directed.

Danny grinned. This was why he liked working for Mr. MacFarlane. He always made sure to express his thanks in the most generous way possible.

As the door closed behind Danny, Robbie swiveled his chair to look out the window at the garden.

Insurance. He was going to have a new policy, and her name was Lila Rodriguez. Because Robbie knew his oldest son, and Cian was soft. Especially for pretty brunettes who needed rescuing.

But now Lila was a murderer and Cian was an accomplice, and Robbie had one hell of an insurance policy. He was going to use it to get his youngest son back where he belonged, and then he was going to use it to make sure his oldest never betrayed him this way again.

Robbie MacFarlane was out for blood.

THE END

About the Author

Selena is an award-winning and USA TODAY best-selling author who writes romantic suspense as Selena Laurence, and paranormal romance as Eden Laine. She loves mocha lattes, the mountains in Colorado where she lives, and her goldendoodle. Her favorite city is London, her favorite color is purple, and her favorite shoes are Converse, but really anything that will get her feet from point A to point B works.

Selena's award-winning Powerplay series was called "a superb mix of sexual and political tension" by Publisher's Weekly, and her debut indie romance won the Reader's Crown award for best contemporary romance of 2014. Since then, Selena has gone on to publish more than twenty books, both as an indie author and with traditional publishers. She also coaches writers through her blog and workshops on turning #Passion2Profession.

Selena likes to make it as easy to read her books as possible, which is why they're in ebook, paperback, and audio formats, in four languages, on the Radish Fiction app, online, on bookstore shelves, and at your local library.